M000032826

Behind the Bid

A NOVEL

Li-En Chong

ISBN 978-1-9701-0954-2
eISBN 978-1-9701-0955-9

Copyright © 2021 by Li-En Chong

All rights reserved, including the right of reproduction in any form, or by any mechanical or electronic means including photocopying or recording, or by any information storage or retrieval system, in whole or in part in any form, and in any case not without the written permission of the author and publisher.

This is a work of fiction. Names, characters, places, and incidents either are the product of the author's imagination or are used fictitiously. Any resemblance to actual events or locales or persons, living or dead, is entirely coincidental.

Published June 2021

ANEWPRESS

"Two of the world's oldest professions
conduct their business in a house –
prostitutes and auctioneers."
– Anonymous

Chapter 1

A WHOLE NEW WORLD

———————‖   ‖———————

Enid, formerly known as Yi Nin, appraised herself in the elevator's mirror. Her freshly permed and dyed auburn hair looked sophisticated whilst her three-inch platform heels gave her petite frame an authoritative boost. She was on top of the world – it was her first day in the internship program at the international auction house Rothesay's.

The elevator arrived on the 20th floor, and Enid's new red-soled shoes squeaked loudly as she strode across the white marble lobby. Although she introduced herself in her very best American sitcom accent, the receptionist barely gave her a cursory glance before motioning toward the conference room on her right. Enid felt slightly disappointed at this lack of fanfare, but the lukewarm reception barely dampened her excitement. *I am here! I have made it out of Zhabei![1] I am part of this world of art and glamor.*

Enid looked around at the other graduate interns. They looked so plain — nothing like what she imagined people who worked at Rothesay's would look like. She felt a shiver of awkwardness as they whispered and smiled familiarly at each other. *But I am different. Exceptional. Unique. I possess "je ne sais quoi."* After all, she had been the only one in her year from Guangzhou University

---

1 A small outer ring road suburb on the outskirts of Shanghai.

to win the coveted one-year scholarship to Université Sorbonne. Plus, she was fully prepared, having extensively and exhaustively studied everything about Rothesay's. She was adamantly sure that Rothesay's was her one-way ticket onwards and upwards.

The Human Resources Director, Julia, asked everyone around the table to introduce themselves and Enid snapped to attention. It was important to size up the competition. She would be jockeying against these other men and women for a prized permanent position in the graduate internship program. Naturally, Enid would rise to the top. In Zhabei and Guangzhou, she had always been the star — the most popular, prettiest, and smartest girl. Even today, former high school classmates avidly followed her on Instagram.

Julia allotted each intern to a department where they would spend the next few months before rotating through other specialist departments. Enid was pleased to hear that she had been assigned to jewelry. It was at this point that her day rapidly started going downhill. Julia handed each intern a sizeable employee handbook. She instructed everyone to take it away to read at their leisure before pausing and pointedly looking at Enid. "You may find the dress code section on page 13 to be of interest. No hair dyed an unnatural color. No excessive make-up and nail polish. No brightly colored clothes. Minimal jewelry that does not attract attention or make noise." Enid flushed and felt a trickle of sweat pooling in her armpits, spreading like an inkblot across her turquoise satin shirt. Everyone was looking at her. And not in the way that she had fantasized they would. Tears smarted her eyes, so she stared fixedly at her acrylic bedazzled fingernails.

After what seemed like an eternity, the briefing was over, and it was time for the interns to head to their assigned departments. Enid tottered as fast as her heels could carry her to the bathroom. She gulped in big breaths of air to calm herself down and unclasped her Return to Tiffany & Co. charm bracelet (originating from 5th Alley Shenzhen rather than 5th Avenue New York), then scrubbed off her fashionable tangerine lipstick with a paper towel and swept up her barrel curls into a tight ponytail. *God. I reek of perspiration and hair product. My cheeks are burning, I feel like I am wearing my small-town Miss Zhabei Teen Beauty sash.* The same detailed strategic planning had gone into her job application as her outfit. On the day that she had submitted her resumé, she had folded dog-ear after dog-ear on the pages of *InStyle* and *Tatler* magazines and scrutinized everyone from the ladies who lunch at Café Landmark to the office workers sitting on the Central MTR.[2]

Enid glared at herself in the mirror. Beneath layers of drugstore makeup, delicate tofu skin glowed and alluring almond eyes blazed with ambition. The sweetness of a stereotypical Chinese beauty. *You can do it. Enid Ma. Do*

---

2 Mass Transit Railway, Hong Kong's answer to the subway.

you want to be Ma Yi Nin forever? You are going to become a Coffee Bitch[3] and not work in some miserable Mainland Chinese import-export business bringing a cold baozi[4] lunch to work.

Enid straightened her spine, pulled back her shoulders, and held her head high as she strode with bravado down the long grey corridor toward the Jewelry Department. Her student work experience at Chow Tai Fook[5] and, more importantly, her semi-fluency in French would definitely equip her to catalog all those exquisite French maison

3 'Coffee bitch' is a term used on Weibo and other social media to describe high-end office ladies who speak in a mixture of heavily accented English and Chinese, follow the very latest fashion trends, take selfies of themselves in fancy restaurants and exotic destinations to the envy of other 'coffee bitches'.

4 Chinese steamed bun, sometimes with meat or vegetable fillings, typical cost is less than USD 1 per bun.

5 China's biggest group of jewelry chain stores. Considered by the auction world to be commercial and regarded as catering to the mass-market.

pieces. Cartier, Chaumet, and Van Cleef & Arpels were her favorite brands. She calmed herself; there was no apparent reason to be so apprehensive. After all, it was better that she had been assigned to jewelry, rather than watches or works of art, which she barely knew anything about.

The office was simple and clean, orderly rows of grey cubicles with dividers. Enid saw her future teammates hard at work. There was a peaceful hush in the office, punctuated by the clicking of keyboards and the sweeping movement of velvet jewelry trays being shifted around. Enid immediately fell in love with how refined it all was. She longed to belong here — to speak in muted voices about shimmering sapphires and glittering baubles. This was a far cry from the rough and ready goldsmith shops with noisy bargaining housewives and oily salesmen that she was used to.

Enid was put straight to work arranging catalogs by season and sale venue. It was mind-numbingly boring, but it gave her more of an opportunity to observe her surroundings. The Head of Department, the formidable Vera Li, was ensconced in her glass-walled throne room surveying her dutiful retinue. Like a dynastic empress, Vera preferred to surround herself with trusted relatives. Every employee in the department was a Li in some shape or form, with the exception of Bahasa Indonesia-speaking Christine. She was indispensable as she gave Vera an inroad into the extremely lucrative Southeast Asian market.

Christine was a kindly matron and the only one in the department that granted Enid more than a passing glance or deprecating sniff. She charitably rescued Enid from a lonesome foraging trip in Central by inviting her for a welcome lunch. After ordering the daily special at Cova, Christine warmly asked Enid about her background and interest in precious stones. By the time the appetizers had been served, Christine was dishing the meatiest main course.

"You know everyone is scared of Vera, but I am not. I have been working with her for over three decades. Her trademark black turtleneck sweater is calculated so that she doesn't overshadow the *tai-tai*[6], *sam-tai*[7], or new money clients. Everything Vera does has a purpose. I knew her when she was a lowly office administrator, but she steadily worked her way up. No one can do what Vera does, like that time when Chan *sei-tai*'s[8] pigeon blood ruby fell off its ring setting when she was doing number two in the toilet. Chan *sei-tai* called up screaming that all of her maids

6 Cantonese colloquial term for a wealthy married lady who devotes her free time to charities, lunches, shopping, gossip, and, of course, scolding her domestic helpers.

7 Third wife.

8 The number four wife i.e., pretty low down in the pecking order.

were refusing to pick it out of the toilet and that she would never, ever bid with Rothesay's again. Vera immediately offered to go to the house to do the dirty deed herself. This appeased Chan *sei-tai* and today, she is still one of our top clients."

Christine paused to swirl the pasta around her fork, "But of course, Vera didn't need to do it in the end. A number four wife is still a number four wife, Chan *sei-tai* could not risk that ruby being accidentally flushed away and she had already fished it out herself with her bare hands. Anyway, the moral of the story is that Vera will literally do ANY SHIT to get to the top. If you want to be a boss one day, you will need to be like that to survive in the auction world."

Enid queasily swallowed her mouthful of pasta. *This is not what I imagined Rothesay's would be like. It is literally down and dirty. So unglamorous. I thought it would be more spa than sewage.*

For the rest of the week when she was sorting out the catalogs with Vera staring imperiously down at her, she smugly imagined her on her knees before Chan *sei-tai*'s porcelain throne, panning for precious stones. That image was to help her through some of her most difficult times in the Jewelry department, where she was either completely ignored or ordered around like an indentured servant.

As time passed, Enid soaked in information like a sponge. Preparations were underway for the Spring auction — she learned how to organize client appraisal appointments, evaluate the Rapaport[9], and work on the copy-paste books necessary to keep track of auction record prices by carat and colored stone classification. No detail was too small, and a flippant command by one of the team could turn out to be of vital consequence. At first,

---

9 An industry in-depth weekly report that lists diamond prices according to the 4Cs — carat, cut, clarity, and color. Some see it as a handy reference guide, but others may argue that it is industry price fixing.

Enid dismissed her teammates as pedantic, but she soon learned that their nitpicking was not without reason. Enid thought that the administrator, Eileen, was being overly particular about her choice of typing font until Christine patiently explained that the bold text in the catalog was guaranteed and the only part of the description that could result in a canceled sale.

Enid was so appreciative of Christine, who was the sole person that took the time to explain the reasons behind the requests and consequences of her actions. Even something as insignificant as keeping dustbin lids closed at all times was finally explained — a tired colleague had accidentally swept an imperial green jade earring into an open dustbin, which ensued in the whole team (Vera included!) trooping down to rubbish disposal in the basement and sieving through the discards of every tenant in the building until the earring was miraculously found.

Subconsciously, Enid's appearance changed. She was too tired from the long hours to bother with smoky eye shadow and pancake foundation, her hair dye faded, and she naturally began to adopt the fresh-faced look of her other colleagues. Once upon a time she had delighted in accessorizing like a Christmas tree with earrings, bracelets, necklaces, and rings. It was a blessing that she no longer had the time to co-ordinate her outfits, and she no longer stood out like a sore thumb. Despite a less fussy ensemble, she still failed to completely blend in.

I don't think anybody tries to remember my name. Enid was in a funk as she moved around the office completing her tasks. Beyond work-related conversation, no one stopped to chat or made an effort to get to know her. It was pretty lonely, but Enid tried her best not to feel offended. Department members were part of an extended family, but they were so aloof with each other. As invisible as Enid felt, she knew that she had passed the test by being allowed to remain. The stories of what happened to those that failed to make the cut were the stuff of urban legend.

A frequently whispered tale was told of the one and only time that the Head of Asia, Jean-Pierre, had insisted on Vera taking in a trainee of his choice: Caroline Brown-Aberystywyth-Gore. Vera loathed her. Firstly, Vera did not like to speak English and, secondly, Vera suspected that Caroline was a spy for Jean-Pierre.

Vera made Caroline's life a misery, setting her menial office tasks like sorting out all the stationary so that the pen nibs faced in the same direction and removing lint from the jewelry trays by hand. She deliberately insisted on calling her Cacca, despite Caroline repeatedly telling her that it meant feces in French, Italian, and German. "So what? It doesn't mean shit in Hong Kong and you are in Hong Kong now. Caroline is a difficult name to pronounce. The name Cacca suits you better and you look like Cacca to me."

Needless to say, Caroline did not last longer than a month before pleading for a transfer back to the London office.

Enid made a few friends, but they were all administrators and clerical staff, and she did not need to leave Zhabei to make friends like these. They were lunch buddies, no more. Instead, Enid tried desperately to break into the circle of graduate interns and young specialists. They were friendly, but it turned out that she had nothing in common with them; their conversations about getting an Hermes bag in this season's new color, table service late nights out at Dragon-i, weekend getaways to Samui, which dermo had the best microdermabrasion, which restaurant had the best molecular tasting menu...it was all so benign — and the list was endless. When she spoke to them in the pantry whilst they were eating their salads and seared toro rolls, she couldn't escape the fear that she had *kailan*[10]

10 Common leafy green vegetable that typically accompanies rice or noodle dishes.

stuck in her teeth and herbal soup splatters on her dress.

June was an intern too, but not part of the program — June was a prime specimen of Rothesay's Second Generation[11] who sat a couple of desks away from her. She was eventually going to join the family business in ground shipping (to put it with blunt honesty, goods trucks plying the highways from sweatshop factories in Guangdong to Hong Kong distribution centers). The internship was "for fun" so that she could learn more about her family's extensive collection and to ensure that her mother did not bid beyond market value. She was constantly braying down the phone to Groton chums, tottering around in Louboutins, and drinking endless skinny lattes from Mandarin Oriental's

11 *Fu er dai* in Mandarin, the offspring of wealthy parents. The Second Generation are *noveau riche* offspring born with silver chopsticks (well, more like gold-plated and gem-encrusted) in their mouths. The Asian media is obsessed with tracking their achievements and, more often than not, their debauched antics.

Café Causette. She wasn't confrontationally bitchy, she was just extremely self-centered and utterly bored by anyone that was not her.

Nevertheless, she was pleasant enough to Enid as long as nothing affected her pedigreed pampered existence.

One day, June came bouncing up to Enid, pouting, "Boohoo, I have a super-hot date tonight and I can't stay late because I really need a blowout. But I need to finish entering the New York consignments into the system." Pout. Pout. "Be a babe and fill in for me, yah, and I will bring you along to the Lane Crawford preview sale because you definitely need a proper handbag."

Enid was shocked. Firstly, this was the most that June had ever spoken to her. *It was practically a conversation! Perhaps we can be friends!* And, secondly, she loved her Coach handbag; she had bought it with over two years of *hongbao*[12] savings. She was so shocked that she immediately dared to question June's opinion. *Coach was an imported fashion brand! Wang Leehom*[13] *was its ambassador!*

"Well, it's so logo-ed, it is snowing alphabet Cs — it's practically a blizzard! Plus, it's the wrong kind of C," June waved airily in the direction of her Chanel handbag with its barren double Cs. "You do know it's a *faux pas* to carry a bag like that, right? Wait a second, do you know what a *faux pas* is?"

Enid did not know whether to feel flattered that June was taking such an interest in her or to be insulted that June could not tell that she, Enid Ma, was as cosmopolitan as her.

12 Red packets filled with money given to young adults and children during Chinese New Year for good luck. A seasoned recipient can estimate the generosity of the giver by feeling the size of the billfold through the envelope. The contents show the giver's affection and/ or desire to impress.

13 Taiwanese movie star and heart throb of screaming tweens and fainting housewives.

After all, she had international exposure too — she had strolled along the banks of the Seine! And repeatedly too... because there was not much else for her to do in Paris on a strict scholarship stipend. Enid set the record straight, careful to enunciate each accented letter, "*J'ai étudié un an à Paris.*" She could see that June was taken aback, impressed even, until she shrugged and walked away with a nonchalant parting, "Cool."

The next day, Enid was exhausted. No amount of concealer could hide the dark rings underneath her eyes. They were of the same violet-black as June's, except June's was accompanied by a blissful cat-that-got-the-cream smile. It had clearly been a good date, and this was confirmed by her numerous phone conversations and the symphony of WhatsApp alerts as she updated her many friends. At least June had smiled and winked at her this morning.

Then it happened. One of the worst fears of any auction house employee, whether newbie or old hand. The strongest espressos failed to keep her eyes open and fingers nimble enough to tag each consignment with its contract number, and a 30-carat Colombian sugarloaf emerald ring slipped between her fingers, bounced off her lap, and rolled underneath the desk.

Chapter 2

BLING BLING

———————— ‖   ‖————————

Enid stifled a yelp and swiftly got on her hands and knees, searching for the precious stone. The catalog description ran through her mind.

A highly important platinum, emerald, and diamond ring. The Asscher-cut emerald weighing 30.36 carats, flanked by two triangle-shaped diamonds weighing approximately 5.00 carats total, size 5 ¾ with French workshop marks. Estimate USD 1,200,000 – 1,600,000.

Even if I trade body organs, I will still not be able to pay for half of the LOW end of the estimated value of that ring. What would they do to me? Her mind raced to her spartan four-digit bank account and the dismal sixth-floor walk-up *tong lau*[14] that she lived in. *I will never, ever be able to pay back the cost of the ring!* After fumbling around, she finally found the ring wedged in a cranny between the drawers and cubicle divider. She trembled with anxiety and her hair was standing on end. As she clambered out from beneath the table, ring in her clenched sweaty fist, she saw a pair of feet. *Please God, let it not be Vera. I swear that if no one finds out, I will pray to Buddha and not eat beef for the rest of my life.*

Christine whispered, "I saw that. You are in big, big trouble. You had better hope there is no damage to the stone. Emeralds are the

---

14 The direct translation for *tong lau* is Chinese building. These are old tenement buildings from the 1850s - 1960s which house partitioned sublet rooms. A bunk bed and wardrobe can be squeezed into each room; bathrooms and kitchens are communal to the whole floor.

softest of the Big Three[15], why couldn't you drop a diamond instead?"

As if I had a choice Enid scowled.

They quickly took the stone over to the binocular microscope. Not that any intensive magnification was needed, the white light was sufficient to see a hairline fracture inside the top right corner of the stone. Christine shrugged, "I don't know what you can do. I am so sorry. You have no choice. You have to tell Vera."

Enid closed her eyes for a good minute. *I should have taken that job as a trainee premier banker at HSBC.* Her simple and unexposed mother had steadily nagged and dismissed this job as a salesgirl selling second-hand cast-offs. At that time, Enid had dismissed her as ignorant but now she fervently wished that she had listened to her advice. Christine emphatically walked back to her desk and motioned toward Vera's office

---

15 Ruby, sapphire, and emerald. Other stones are merely semi-precious.

with a pointed nod. If Enid could, she would have made a run for it. *There is no escape; even the windows do not open in this place. I am trapped like a pig to the slaughter.*

Vera barely glanced away from her papers when Enid entered her room. And for the rest of the entire conversation, at no point did she bother to make eye contact with Enid. She barely flinched when Enid revealed the whole sorry tale. "Adjust the condition report, and YOU are going to make sure it sells for at least mid-estimate."

No threats or dramatic reaction. Enid was so relieved — and surprised. She wanted to dance the conga down the corridor. She marveled at Vera's composure and vowed to herself that she would be like that one day — so pulled together, so steely and, of course, so feared. *Imagine having the power to dispense judgment like Vera Li and King Solomon!*

Over the next few weeks, it wasn't completely bad. The catalog was nearly finished, and Enid worked later than everyone else in the office, entering proofreading corrections into the computer system. She had even been brought along to some client appraisal appointments, hovering in the background ready to serve refreshments or whizz away the jewelry as soon as the consignment was confirmed. Perhaps it was because she was pulling her weight, or the dreadful incident had humanized the team toward her.

Enid witnessed first-hand the unique medley of talents required of auction specialists with their alternating Dr. Jekyll-Mr. Hyde personas. Clients were alternately bullied and cajoled into parting with valuable jewels for reserve prices way below market value. Attractive estimates were the only way to attract buyers to bid at auctions, despite the considerable 20% premiums.

Competition was tough, not just internally amongst specialists who were possessive of their clients, but amongst the other auction houses — from the established Western ones to the new kids on the block, recently founded on the whim of some newly minted Chinese billionaire.

A patchwork of different personalities and diverse individuals from all walks of life streamed steadily through the consignment rooms. Although the catalog featured elegant phrases describing the 'Property of a Gentleman' or 'Private Collection of a Lady,' Rothesay's hunted and sourced aggressively. A key source was from attorneys disbursing bankruptcy and death estates. Vera pitched alongside two other houses to auction off the Hung estate after the patriarch's death. Each of the four heirs present at the valuation had their own legal and accounting counsel. It was a highly publicized airing of the family's squabbles with the so-called consultants principally benefitting. It was one of the most detailed 'pitch projects' that Enid worked on.

One of the collections that generated the most interest during the season was the twenty emerald, ruby, and colored sapphire suites consigned by a Middle Eastern Emir.

They were absolutely gorgeous and looked like Christmas decorations with ornate designs and flamboyant settings. Each stone was over 10-carats, so it was a shame that every single one of them had been heat-treated.

The wow factor was there, but sadly, it did not appeal to any truly discerning jewelry connoisseur. It was consigned in Hong Kong with the target audience of all-flash, all-cash, newly minted millionaires. The Emir claimed that he loved to spoil his wives with the very best, but (the fit of the rings, necklaces, and bracelets was huge, too loose for his svelte female entourage) internally it was whispered that the suites had been made for the personal adornment of the Emir himself.

Unlike some of the other houses, Rothesay's did not work with pawnshops — a business decision that was being rapidly reconsidered after a newspaper exposé featured a Graff 16-carat yellow diamond used as collateral at Yao On pawnshop in

Tsuen Wan. Consignments were typically sourced from the 4Ds – Dealers, Debtors, Divorcees, and Death. Clients ranged from wily Indian dealers, strolling in off the street with sparkling rubies in their pockets to former *tai-tais* dressed in dated designer gear, shakily pulling out a previous marriage's worth of jewelry from crocodile Birkins.

"How the mighty have fallen, to think of how Ngan-*tai* used to boss me around — hold the mirror higher, I can't see my reflection... you are standing in my light, you are making the alexandrite look like the color of phlegm... can you move faster, my driver is waiting downstairs," Rita, one of the specialists, muttered to Enid. "Let Jennifer Ngan be a lesson to us; it is better to divorce well than to marry well." Rita inspected a ring.

Enid did not know how to respond to Rita's venomous and yet-oh-so-practical statement.

Sure, if I ran in the same circles as Rita or Jennifer Ngan, that advice would be helpful, but I have zero social life and have met zero eligible bachelors. So much for Apple's[16] *auction house stories.*

Department members consulted, commiserated, and applauded one another as the sale gained momentum, steadily growing in lot size and value. Enid had a small role to play too, helping to organize traveling previews to New York, London, Singapore, Taiwan, Guangzhou, Beijing, and Shanghai, where the auction highlights were to be exhibited. She was beginning to feel accepted, especially when Christine told her that she would be joining the China leg of the tour. Nevertheless, the invitation came with the admonition that Vera had included

---

16 Hong Kong's tabloid answer to Heat, People, and OK! magazine. Apple reports on the comings and goings of celebrities, the rich and famous. A source of gossip and core reference for wannabes as well as the people featured on the pages.

Enid so that she could push the emerald to a Mainland Chinese client.

Enid felt so exhausted and run down. When she looked in the mirror, she looked like she had aged five years in four months. Korean beauty masks and daily herbal tonics from the Oneness World Chinese health food shop in the MTR were stopgap solutions. They certainly did not have the effect of the collagen injections and laser facials that the luminous-skinned brat pack debated on daily, but at least it psychologically balanced the late-night greasy rice box takeaways and carcinogenic Calbee potato chips.

Enid sighed, blowing on the surface of her fragrant pig lung and almond soup. It seemed endless. Another Monday evening — it should have been a fresh start to the week, but she had been working non-stop for nearly a month. The days and nights were a blur of repetitive tasks and solitude. Social media was her social life, and no amount of likes to her carefully orchestrated posts could overcome the crushing loneliness. Leaving for previews next week would be a welcome departure from takeaway meals for one, the chipboard furniture of her rented room, and the bulk carton of cup noodles that she used as a dressing table. She was so reluctant to leave the office that she took her time packing up the jewelry for Malca-Amit logistics and making everything in the office spic and span for Rupert Bosewell's visit.

Rupert Bosewell was a majority shareholder of Rothesay's, and he regarded himself as the epitome of a perfect English gentleman. Although over a hundred years too late, he was firmly implanted in the mindset of a colonialist *sahib*[17]. It was revealing of his character that he was a famous collector of Victorian first edition books and referred to

---

[17] A polite term of address in British colonial India. The root source of the word is Arabic, meaning directly 'master or owner'. Nowadays it is used sarcastically for condescending expatriates who assume a superior attitude toward the locals.

Hong Kong in true Orientalist fashion as the Far East. Nevertheless, it was not without reason that Mr. Bosewell was respected to the point of worship. The exacting decorum and professional precision with which he conducted himself was correspondingly expected of his employees.

Mr. Bosewell detested seeing badly dressed employees. The penchant of office workers to slip off their high-heeled Louboutins or bespoke patina Berlutis for flat shoes or canvas slip-ons was anathema to him. He was frequently heard exclaiming that proper shoes and clothes were not meant to be comfortable. There was a legendary tale of how after work one day, he had personally moved from desk to desk with a black garbage bag, throwing away personal shoe collections. Enid giggled at the thought of elegant Mr. Bosewell fishing underneath a desk for a cataloger's gym-fresh sweaty Nikes.

"What in God's name is that revolting smell? I bloody hate the smell of hot food;

it has no place in my office. What carrion do you people eat?"

Enid could hear shouts echoing down the corridor. She swiftly swept the discarded catalog proofs into her dustbin, squashing down the mountain of polystyrene soup containers, half-used packets of chili oil sauce, and fish ball satay sticks. Christine next to her chuckled, "HR really should arrange for the office to be fumigated before Mr. Bosewell arrives. Everywhere he goes, it's the same issue every time. He's more bark than bite if you know how to handle him. Everyone is so scared since he fired that administrator for eating a kebab in the Bids Office. His last secretary was let go because she doused herself in perfume. Not Chanel No. 5, mind you — apparently she had the nerve to wear Designer Imposters perfume!"

Christine's words hit too close to home and Enid flushed thinking of the acrylic perfume flagon on top of her makeshift dressing table. *So what if I have to shake it around now and*

then when it gets murky, it still smells good.
She rolled her eyes. *If Mr. Bosewell did not like smell-alike perfumes, he should have paid his secretary more! Everyone here is so detached from reality. They will never be able to comprehend what a treat it is for me to have an egg for breakfast or to buy the latest copy of Apple. They live in their own shiny world and have zero empathy for us unfortunates.*

She petulantly questioned herself if all this was really worth it — *all these long hours at work, and we are not even allowed to have a hot meal at our desks!* —all the while knowing deep down that she was thoroughly hooked. Rothesay's was turning out to be everything that she had ever dreamt about and aspired to, but she hated suffering from the persistent self-reproach that she was not good enough. Worse still, that she would never make it. The depth of Enid's ambitions was beyond question, but she remained awkwardly wedged between two worlds, too insecure about her working-class parents and scornful of her second-tier city origins but not sufficiently confident or experienced to have Rita's cunning or Vera's killer instincts.

With the pressure of faking a glamorous life, Enid snapped photographs of the floral arrangement at the office reception and pretended they were from eager admirers. She even captured a picture of June's lunch and wrote a subtly jaded caption: "Toro rolls from Zuma again, yawn." The façade made her feel that she was more than an expendable paper pusher toiling away, constantly trying to keep up.

Mr. Bosewell stalked into the office. A tall statuesque man, he exuded the confidence of a man who had never heard the word no. Enid also watched as Vera smiled. For that sight, it typically required the total net worth of people standing in the room to amount to over a billion — USD obviously, not Renminbi. It made Enid shudder to see her smile — the skeleton grin breaking over yellow tea-stained teeth in that bony mask. Vera broke her reverie hissing, "Why are you standing there, catching flies with your mouth open? Go now and get whatever top lots that aren't with Malca to show Mr. Bosewell!"

Enid nervously placed the tray in front of Mr. Bosewell and deferentially stood to one side. Although not a jewelry specialist, Mr. Bosewell appreciatively fingered each precious stone, weighing up the fluid link of each piece in his hand, closely magnifying them under a loupe before taking a second evaluative glance from afar. He took his time to scrutinize every single piece placed before him and asked detailed questions about their provenance, market potential, the rarity of the gems, and design. It was a revelation; Enid had wrongly expected Mr. Bosewell to be entitled and shallow. Now she understood why he was so highly respected in the art world despite his notorious child-like temper tantrums.

The short encounter with Rupert Bosewell made Enid realize how much she needed to learn on a personal level, and how judgmental she was becoming. Her knee-jerk reaction to the way people dismissed her was causing her to look past their strengths. It was extremely immature, but she could not help the sour grapes. She so desperately wanted to soak in that easy poise, sophisticated charm, and strategic savvy. Regardless of how they treated her, their professional demeanor and depth of knowledge were inspirational. Whatever personal foibles and agendas each person had, they were united in a shared love of beauty, luxury, and the adrenalin of the auction business.

Enid was addicted to the splendor of the auction house, she could not begin to put into words the thrill that ran down her spine when she clasped an ornate art deco bracelet studded with Burmese pigeon blood rubies and diamonds on her wrist, or how it took her breath away when she coiled the spectacular

Bulgari Serpenti emerald necklace around her neck. Even the most serious of specialists could not resist trying on the precious glittering ornaments or holding up the faceted gemstones to refract the light.

Enid's understanding of gemology advanced as she learned to appreciate not just the wow factor of a carat count, but also the design of a setting and the quality of a stone — a subtle shade's difference meant a diamond could be classified as fancy vivid pink-brown or the less desirable fancy dark brownish pink. Rita condescendingly sniffed that "bigger stones equals younger mistress, older wife, or newer money." Enid finally understood this allusion when private viewings began.

Self-made and more established clients did not need the affirmation of "bling-bling." Instead, they would seek out understated nuances such as delicate filigree work or signature styles like the Van Cleef & Arpels mystery setting.

On a professional level, the auction house was an unbeatable learning experience. But this did not stop Enid from feeling rudderless, set off course by surface tensions and small slights. She was hit rock-hard by the slow but sure realization that the success she desperately craved for was not going to happen overnight. Her fantasy scenarios were wide-ranging and varied — retirement for her father from the factory, driving around in a shiny convertible, dutiful workmates hanging on her every word, her face on the front page of Apple, the list was endless. She felt embarrassed by her naivety; she had not given a semblance of thought to her game plan beyond getting an internship at Rothesay's.

The harsh reality check that none of it was going to happen anytime soon was crippling. Every night as she went to bed, Enid choked back tears of misery and remind herself of Lao Tzu's teaching, "The journey of a thousand miles must begin with a single step."

Enid vowed to turn every setback into an opportunity; the emerald was going to be her chance to prove herself. After all, it was through sheer willpower that she had transformed from Ma Yi Nin into Enid Ma. There was no reason why she could not make it to the top, particularly as she did not care how she got there — whether it was standing up on the auctioneer's rostrum or sitting front row with a bidding paddle and an ancient tycoon by her side.

Chapter 3

BACK HOME IN STYLE

———————— ‖   ‖ ————————

The previews were run with military precision, with schedules precisely set in place to the hour. Higher value lots were sent ahead by professional logistics companies whilst the rest were discreetly hand-carried by the specialists in inconspicuous trolley bags with secure locks, no name, and no identifiers. This precious cargo was codenamed 'The Baby'. It was thrilling for Enid that despite her lowly trainee status, she would be responsible for USD 3 million in her nondescript canvas Muji bag. She was given strict instructions not to fall asleep or leave her seat on the plane without informing her colleagues or the two burly security guards accompanying them. The Jadeite Senior Specialist, Edward, told her the horror story of a jetlagged colleague who checked in 'The Baby'. Needless to say, that colleague's career at Rothesay's did not last beyond her flight duration.

Enid warmed up to Edward and realized that she had mistaken his self-effacing shyness for aloofness. With his awe-inspiring reputation as a rainmaker and uber elegant addiction to Savile Row, she had kept a worshipful distance. Usually suavely dressed to the nines, he was dressed like a Mongkok[18] stall vendor with a bulging fanny pack on the flight. He winked and whispered, "Chinese Works of Art's Imperial Qianlong snuff bottle, sold last sale for USD 3.3 million, I am helping my VVIP client to bring it home to Beijing. I'm not taking this loathsome fanny

---

18 One of the most congested shopping and residential areas in Kowloon, Hong Kong. Famous for the Ladies Market and its open-air stalls selling cheap trinkets, souvenirs, knock-off Rolek watches, and Guzzi bags.

pack off my body, even if I am sitting next to Anna Wintour!"

Enid could see why the clients adored Edward. Once the initial reserve had broken down, he chatted away nineteen to the dozen. "Don't be nervous. If someone comes to rob you at gunpoint, push the trolley bag toward him or her and run away in the other direction. Don't be a hero and try to show off any kung fu skills. They have zero interest in you, they want the Baby! It's all insured at the low end of the estimate anyway, so Vera won't bite your head off. Hmmm, maybe just one of your non-essential limbs that you don't need for work."

They stayed at the plushest hotel in every city — St. Regis or the Four Seasons. *I wish I could cut out a piece of the thick carpet to take home. Maybe under the bed, no one would notice if there was a hole there...* There were marble bathrooms, gold taps, and wallpaper everywhere — even free cable television and Internet! It was the first time she had ever had a hotel room to herself, let alone a 5-star one. Originally, she was meant to share a room with Rita. Of course, Enid did not mind at all, but Rita had kicked up a big fuss. Employees were allocated room categories based on their seniority, and it was not unheard of for male and female colleagues to share rooms. Sometimes, support or junior staff were relegated to a nearby 3-star hotel. Where, what floor, and what room you stayed in was an indication of your place in the pecking order. The club floor was the Holy Grail.

Pampered with the privacy of her very own room, Enid was incentivized to work harder. After thoroughly scoping out her room and sniffing the bathroom amenities, she uploaded an Instagram photo with the tagline, "Checked-in and on the move." She was sure to tag the location. After all, it was one of the very few posts taken from her real life, and she had zero qualms about curating her perfect Instagram world. Being a Rothesay's employee brought her one step closer to the life she wanted to project. Her daily reality was the polar opposite, but Enid did not realize the irony and bore little resentment. She worked diligently and without any resentment at low-level tasks — setting up the showcases, cleaning sticky fingerprints from the glass, and sorting out the jewelry stands.

No task was too small for Enid, and she was eager to help in any way. One of the more interesting responsibilities was helping Vera, Edward, Christine, and Rita to display the lots beautifully. Each case was carefully curated to attract the bidder's interest, with lots grouped by appearance and value. Security cameras were linked to each display case, and itemized lists were made so that the condition of each lot was noted four times a day. There was only a very remote possibility of any piece of jewelry disappearing or getting damaged under Rothesay's Big Brother efficiency.

Enid was so happy to be back home despite all her years of believing (and behaving) like she was better than everyone else. Her heart soared with yearning to see her parents, despite their bewilderment over her latent ambition to leave their simple world behind. She arranged to meet them for supper far away from the hotel. It was not solely because she was ashamed of them; she felt deeply protective of them and their simple ways. The plush environment of the Four Seasons would impress but definitely overwhelm them. Enid did not want them to realize how tormented she was every single day at work, but, most of all, she did not want anyone staring down their noses at her loving parents. It would break her heart if any of these condescending snobs scornfully gave her parents the once-over.

As usual, her father was gruff and well-meaning but did not speak much. It was as if the permanent toothpick dangling from his lips levered his mouth shut. It touched Enid that he made the effort to wear his Sunday polo shirt, with its carefully ironed creases in the sleeves. Enid's mother was on top form, as usual, a source of endless information about the neighbor's lottery winnings, the price of chicken at the market, how Enid was getting too skinny and needed a man to take care of her — her mother went on and on. In the past, Enid would have rolled her eyes and snapped at her mother but now she embraced the warmth of so much unconditional affection. Enid's mother had the vitality of an Energizer Bunny, chatting ceaselessly as she simultaneously peeled *xiaolongxia*[19] for her husband and Enid, popping meat into her own mouth, and motioning the waitress to refill teacups.

The emerald and Rothesay's weighed on her mind, but it was impossible to explain to her parents what she was going through. She could see how proud they were of her. In their entire lives, they had left China just once, on a package trip to Singapore. How could they

19 Spicy crawfish cooked in aromatic flower wine, ginger, chillies, and peppercorns.

even begin to understand how complicated life was beyond their day-to-day routine in Zhabei? It was at the tip of her tongue to tell them how desperately homesick and lonely she was, but she took a gulp of Tsingtao beer and willed herself to stay calm. She reminded herself of their sacrifices and her father's late hours at the tire factory. They had never enjoyed the kind of opportunities that they had given her. And unlike many of her friend's parents, they did not constantly harp on about it and try to make her feel guilty/obligated. It was foolish to whine. She had to succeed. She had to. She was their only child and retirement plan.

Thankfully, over the rest of the trip, Enid had no time to brood. All sorts of clients came to attend the preview, from the awestruck and curious to the checkbook-ready bidders. The preview was held in the hotel's grand ballroom and it was a marvelous sight to see, with every department presenting their auction highlights together. There were exquisite colors and forms everywhere like Aladdin's Cave — paintings that rightfully belonged in a museum, unique edition wristwatches, and one-of-a-kind ancient Chinese artifacts. The intense snobbery and dog-eat-dog office environment slipped beneath the surface as Rothesay's staff turned acquiescent overnight, willing and able to attend to every request. Enid grew to realize that her fluency in Shanghainese and Mandarin was of far greater importance than her conversational French. After all, China minted a couple of new billionaires every week.

Standing on her feet all day, smiling at every single client, and maintaining the perfect balance between being of service and a source of expertise was not an easy role. Observing Edward and the Beijing Representative, Angela, she learned hat if you were too eager to please, you would be treated like a service lackey, but on the flip side, if you were too much of a know-it-all, you could come off as annoyingly arrogant.

There was so much foot traffic that Enid had to allocate her time wisely. First and foremost, she was on a mission to sell the emerald. Unfortunately, she had made little headway, it was not easy to determine if the client was a country bumpkin fertilizer farmer or the world's largest textile producer. Some of the clients were so casually dressed that Enid realized that the important lesson that the more unassuming the client was, the deeper his pockets could be. The only tell-tale marker was observing whom Vera and the formidable Head of Rothesay's China, Liu-jie[20], went to great lengths to devote personal attention to and fawn attentively over.

During a quiet lull in the early evening, after the departure of the post-high tea ladies and the arrival of the pre-dinner crowd, Edward stood next to her and whispered *sotto voce*,

---

20 Respectful term for 'older sister' in Mandarin. It should imply familiarity but here, not so much…

"Do you know how to spot the *shui yu*[21] yet? Don't look at the men who are all dressed up as if coming to this preview is an occasion! Especially those who walk like their feet hurt because they usually wear slippers and they had to borrow someone else's shoes," he sniffed scornfully. "The wealthiest and most successful men have no time and no need to consider how they look, plus no one will dare to judge them. In Watches, they look at the client's wrist or even his shoes to judge his potential!"

Edward paused and sighed appreciatively as he polished his top lot — a pair of stunning translucent lavender jade bangles. "Here in Jewelry, we are lucky. Firstly, career women are easy to spot and even easier to sell to. They are the most decisive and don't need to get anyone's permission to buy whatever they

---

21 Meaning 'water fish', a fish that is easily caught. It implies someone who is gullible and spends money like water. In other words, a good catch and a Rothesay's dream client.

---

want. The next two categories that have the most potential are the wives and girlfriends. But don't waste your time focusing on the garden-variety first wives or the latest trophy girlfriends. The prize money lies with the girlfriends who act and dress like they are already wives. Those are the ones in the most favor, with the largest budgets and the biggest insecurities. Whether they made their money two months or two generations ago, ladies always know how to deck themselves out in style." Edward clapped his hands in reverence and Enid giggled in response.

To her dismay, it was at this point that Liu-*jie* and Vera passed by. In curt Shanghainese dialect, Liu-*jie* barked at Enid to stop playing and remember that she had one sole purpose — to work. Enid felt a tremor of fear. After all, Liu-*jie* was legendary. She was a walking phone book of anyone with high net worth in China, and popularly nicknamed the Golden Pages. Not a single one of the specialists dared to antagonize or offend her. And she was very, very temperamental. The clients adored her and trusted her implicitly, which was what mattered. No one in management cared an ounce about colleague camaraderie or employee respect. Liu-*jie* rose above office politics because she simply didn't need to play it. In playground speak, she was a bully. At last season's wine auction alone, her client Mr. Wang had purchased the Liquid Gold Chateau d'Yquem lot, fifty bottles of vertical tasting for the astronomical sum of USD 2 million. The client had yet to settle his bill but still! Clients of that level were a level beyond *shui yu*, they were the proverbial golden goose.

One of the catalog photographers Francesco summed it up, "Do you know why Golden Pages always wears those silk trousers? To conceal the fact that she has more power and bigger cojones than anyone in this office, including Rupert Bosewell. Liu-*jie* has zero specialist knowledge, and the principal highlight of her career prior to

Rothesay's was her ascension to the apex of an herbal supplement multi-million-dollar pyramid marketing scheme. And so darling, this is proof that it is not what you know, it's who you know." Enid missed Francesco. He was warm, funny, and extremely flamboyant. It was a shame that he came to the Hong Kong office for only two months a year to photograph the watch and jewelry lots.

Despite his aristocratic Italian lineage, he was humble and down-to-earth, preferring to explore the grimy *dai pai dongs*[22] for supper and shop for all kinds of counterfeit branded merchandise in Shenzhen. Louis Vuitton dustbin? Fendi sweatbands? Yves Saint Laurent sleep masks? "Special, special edition, darling. You can't get this logo-fied anywhere else in the world." Francesco

---

22 Literally, 'restaurant with a big license plate', these are casual open air cooked food stalls. Although this *al fresco* dining option may involve sitting next to a drain or an over-friendly rat, many people frequent *dai pai dong* and see them as purveyors of authentic Hong Kong cuisine.

---

always left Hong Kong two suitcases over his airplane luggage limit. Unlike the majority of Rothesay's employees, Francesco was no corporate slave. He was so talented at his product shoots, bringing lots to life on the pages of the auction catalogs that the department heads were willing to turn a blind eye toward his boisterous cheekiness and flamboyant appearance,

Thankfully, Enid had little interaction with Liu-*jie*, but she made fast friends with Angela. Angela was so sympathetic and genuine. Throughout the fortnight's preview tour in China, they became close, and Angela introduced her to many clients. One of whom was Mr. Bai — a very prominent princeling who was, of course, phenomenally wealthy. His upcoming third marriage to a recently retired soft porn starlet presented Enid with the ripe opportunity for a bid on the emerald. With the crackdown on corruption, Mr. Bai could not be seen shopping around for precious gems, so he discreetly came to the preview after it had been officially closed for the day. He seemed genuinely interested and filled out a bidding form. Enid enjoyed meeting Mr. Bai — he was so chatty and approachable — teasing the two girls that by knowing too much about expensive things, they were scaring away future marriage prospects.

When they shook hands to say goodbye, Mr. Bai's third finger lingered, softly and persistently stroking the warmth of Enid's palm. It was definitely not her imagination, and Enid blushed furiously. She felt queasy but flattered — Mr. Bai was rich, prominent, and charming, the kind of man she imagined being swept off her feet by (but minus three wives). Later, Angela brushed it off, "A pretty girl like you and it's your first time experiencing The Wriggle? It's not a big deal. These *hamsup*[23] clients just want to dip their toe in the water and see if you are interested.

23 In Cantonese, literally meaning *ham* = salty, *sup* = wet. A *hamsup lo* is a perverted guy.

You can shove him in the friendzone later, but make sure it is AFTER the auction!"

Enid was shocked at Angela's nonchalant attitude and embarrassed by her own wide-eyed innocence. Angela elaborated further, "If you want to get ahead and sit in Vera or Liu-*jie's* chair one day, you need to play the game with whatever cards you have. Of course, you shouldn't sleep with the clients, but a little bit of flirtation isn't going to harm anyone."

Enid was not so sure. Angela was upfront with her in so many ways, but she received so many phone calls from clients at all hours of the night. *They couldn't all be about work, could they?* Angela appeared so confident and self-assured, but Enid was worried for her. Not solely because she was a true friend, one of the few that Enid had made since moving to Hong Kong, but because Enid could see so many similarities between them. They shared a desire to better themselves despite their family background and the awkward way that Angela would forget to roll her Rs and drop her pseudo-American accent when she was distracted. Whilst everyone else bonded over country clubs, ski slopes, and old school ties, Enid and Angela had no pretensions with one another. They could not stop giggling when the zipper on Angela's bag burst open at the seams to expose the mother lode of hotel amenities swiped throughout the preview. Enid felt that Angela really looked out for her whether it was introducing her to clients or teaching her how to tip housekeeping so that they would close their eyes to the disappearing towels that Enid squirreled home.

When the whole team arrived back in Hong Kong and the Babies were safely snuggled up in the office safe, Enid took the long tram journey home that evening. She was exhausted, but taxis were a luxury she could not afford, and she needed time to reflect after the whirlwind fortnight. It had been immensely comforting to see her parents. And of course, they had not forgotten to nag her about getting married. She was still young — only 25 — although she was conscious that this was considered a ripe age to settle down by Chinese standards. Enid was determined to make her mark on a personal and professional level before she committed herself to anyone.

The hum of the tram on its tracks, the fresh night breeze, and the twinkle of the city lights made her feel so alive. Alive but inconspicuous. She was a small speck amongst the throng of people in Hong Kong. It was a heady feeling that everything she had dreamt about since her teenage years was within the realm of possibility. *I am glad that I bit my tongue and did not confess to Pa and Ma about my loneliness and ineptitude. On the flip side, being alone had its advantages, there would be no one around to bear witness or give empty commiserations if I fail.*

Chapter 4

VIP

Once the traveling previews were concluded, bidding forms came flooding in fast. Asia was riding the wave of a bull market, so people were eager to spend and be seen spending. It was thrilling to watch as each lot was spoken for in the auctioneer's book. Behind the scenes, it was a revelation for Enid to see which clients' interests materialized into a signed bidding form or remained a passing utterance of fancy. It taught her a lot about reading people from their body language and facial expressions — the forehead wrinkle as a client calculated if he really had the liquidity to place the next bid up. Or the stealthy wink on a client's face indicating that she would be back later to bid against her best friend.

So much of the bidding traffic was drummed up by the importance that people placed in having face. Many clients attended the preview in the company of their friends and relatives, placing generous bids, only to quietly call back later and withdraw or lower the amounts. It was not uncommon. Well, better bidder than buyer's remorse. Enid thoroughly understood why previews were conducted with so much pizzazz and showmanship — every client who walked in was made to feel like he or she was the star of the show. After all, no one wanted to disappoint if they were the focus of so much attention.

Internet bidding revolutionized the workings of the house. A job like Francesco's was increasingly crucial as a client from thousands of miles away could drop a million dollars on a lot without having ever touched or seen the lot in person. However, this also unleashed a new variety of excuses and an increase in the number of regretful claimants. "I honestly didn't click the Bid button, my mouse got stuck... My Wi-Fi signal dropped, and I heard the previous increment... Someone hacked into my account..."

Every department aimed to have a White Glove[24] auction. It was the administrator's duty to let the specialists know which lots were not spoken for that needed an extra push. Rothesay's was run with great precision and it was very rare that any auction would be left to flounder. Bidding history from the in-house system tracked and identified client interest from genres as specific as Georgian memorial brooches in black enamel to 3-carat padparadscha sapphires. It was an often-repeated mantra that there was no such thing as a weak lot that could not be sold, merely a weak estimate that did not appeal to clients.

---

24 An auction with 100% sold lots. Not an easy task, whether in a bull or bear market.

There was an incredibly diverse assortment of jewelry. When the entire consignment was laid out in the office in preparation for catalog layout, it looked more junk shop than pirate's treasure trove. During the layout meetings, it was Edward with his refined sense of style that made the key decisions. He made the analogy that each page was an ensemble that one of their clients would happily be seen in. Edward elaborated, "Mix-and-match is for pajama sets, NOT jewelry. Grouping a Panthère bracelet, Edwardian seed pearl sautoir, and basic 5-carat diamond ring is an unforgivable dishonor to Louis Cartier. Style, stone type, aesthetics, and value have to seamlessly gel together. And of course, the price has to be right. Cheap as chips in the front to get the ball rolling."

Despite the general public's impression that auctions were reserved for the very wealthy, there was a lot for every pocket. The auction was split into day and evening sales, with the lower value lots hammering earlier.

No reserve ones that typically commanded a flurry of bidding were interspersed by less popular lots with higher estimates. The auction finale belonged to the most valuable pieces, which were given auspicious lot numbers, whole page photo shoots, and mini-essays. It would not do to have a lull in the auction with scant paddle raises or a continuous row of unsold buy-in lots. A dire situation like that could leave the auctioneer sweating on the podium, reaching for his natty silk pocket square to mop a drenched brow. Nothing was left to chance to ensure the attractiveness of each lot and the overall success of the entire sale.

To Enid's immense relief, the emerald was now covered with multiple bids — Mr. Bai on the telephone, an absentee bid from an aunt of a junior specialist from Chinese Paintings, and Christine's client, a corrupt Thai politician's wife infamous for bidding without restraint. The telephones rang nonstop. One day, when Vera was surprisingly away from her desk, Enid picked up her extension to hear the famous stutter of Warren Lee, one of Hong Kong's biggest tycoons. "Vera ah, as usual, make sure you send me my wives' bidding forms. I pay enough commission to you people and don't want them to bid against each other."

Enid quickly transferred the line to the highly unpopular Business Manager, Patty. It turned out that as a long-standing and valued client of Rothesay's, the house was only too glad to acquiesce to Mr. Lee's juggling act. Each of his three wives would send their individual bidding forms to Rothesay's and although unconfirmed but suspected by them, Rothesay's would then send these back to Mr. Lee for his final veto. They shared the same husband and the same taste in jewelry. Each season, their bids would overlap, and this was a subtle way for Mr. Lee to reward or discipline.

It was crunch time now, but Vera had not appeared in the office for the past two days.

There were whispers in the department and ludicrous rumors floating around the rest of the office. Vera was having a face-lift. Vera has defected to the competition Thompson's. Even the completely random rumor that Vera has disavowed material goods and become a Buddhist nun. A week later, she showed up in the office, wan and shrunken in her usual cat burglar black turtleneck.

Her husband was having an affair. It was an immense blow to Vera; she had sacrificed so much to be the breadwinner of the family. She had found out because her husband was stupid enough to pay for his hotel trysts using his supplementary credit card. Once a former chauffeur, her ungrateful husband failed to appreciate that he could now drive his own Mercedes instead of someone else's. Their only son was another disappointment, an idle layabout who drifted in and out of the best Swiss boarding schools.

Enid expected ice queen Vera to throw tantrums and vent her hurt on everyone around her, but it was quite the opposite. She was broken. Humbled. She moved around the office like a marionette with broken strings. Everyone, even Patty, was quietly sympathetic, and it was tacitly agreed that there would be no gossip. Despite Vera being a relative of nearly everyone in the department, the compassionate solidarity was not strong enough for anyone to make an overt gesture of support toward Vera. She was far too intimidating.

It was now the week before the auction, a lull before the storm, with the hectic preview travels completed and catalogs in the clients' manicured hands. As usual, everyone was working steadily at his or her desk. Vera had scarcely left her room since her return. First in and last out to leave the office. What was once her throne room now seemed like a glass-walled observation tank. She paused at the door and cleared her throat. Her reedy voice was hesitant but sure, "I don't want anyone in this department working past 7 pm anymore.

It doesn't matter if the auction is tomorrow or next week. There will always be another auction and another day to work. Family life is as important, if not more important, than your career."

Everyone paused, loupes and pens suspended. Vera did not wait for a response before sweeping out of the room. Once the sound of her footsteps faded away, everyone began to whisper. There was a palpable shift in the dynamic. Previously, they had been awestruck by her unwavering ambition but now she commanded fierce loyalty. The department was touched by her instinctive care for them, despite her own troubles. They had always been made to feel like dispensable cogs in a smoothly oiled machine, but now they appreciated that she had let down her guard.

One by one, the team silently packed up and left for the day. Unsurprisingly, Patty was the one exception — she defiantly shifted the tortoiseshell glasses perched on her greasy hair to the tip of her nose and furiously pounded away at her keyboard. It was no secret that Patty and Vera did not get along. Then again, Patty did not get along with anyone; she had recently been reassigned from the Paintings Department after a spectacular episode of politicking. Nevertheless, she had still managed to survive after rubbing so many people the wrong way, hence her nickname the Cockroach. She could survive any nuclear fallout.

Cockroach belonged to a layer of business managers that Rupert Bosewell had put in place to crack the whip and drive the specialists after a recommendation from McKinsey consultants. The relationship between the business managers and specialists was rather tenuous. The former held the keys to the once-upon-a-time generous expense accounts. They were also resented for dictating auction goals with little exposure and interest in the lots that were being auctioned or the clients that were

buying them. It was far from an easy role —
babysitting, cajoling, and nagging people
who were so confident (and some might say,
borderline arrogant) in their personal charm
and specialized knowledge. Of course, there
were also some highly revered business
managers who graduated to this role after
specialist training, and they earned the
sincere respect of their charges.

Cockroach did not fall into the latter
category. In an industry where connections
mattered, she had garnered more enemies
than influential friends. With three decades
under her belt, she knew the auction
business like the back of her hand and every
single dirty office politics tactic there was
to know. She should have been a director or
sitting on the management board by now,
but she had to compensate for three grievous
handicaps — being the daughter of a second
wife in a middle-class family, the spouse of
an unsuccessful expatriate, and, the last but
most damaging, an employee who needed

her monthly salary. Cockroach was barely civil to Enid because she evaluated her on the same terms that everyone else evaluated her. Nevertheless, Enid did not allow herself to feel hurt. She was not green enough to need the esteem of someone who did not command much respect herself.

At the China previews, Enid had proven her worth as a diligent employee that could be entrusted with clients. Her work responsibilities increased to include minor client interactions such as confirming viewing appointments and mailing addresses. The fleeting moments of self-doubt persisted, as she wondered if she possessed the ruthless resolve evident in colleagues that did not have the safety net of a trust fund or the foundation of a famous family. With too much time on her hands and not much of a life outside the office, she spent too much time imagining "I should have's" and "what if's?" Angela and Christine, her only friends, chided her for being paranoid each time she went running to them, the answers to her many questions were painfully obvious, but her confidence had taken such a beating from the daily slights and humiliations. *I hate that I have become such a needy wreck, but it is easy for them to say, they don't need this job as much as I do. Who wouldn't want the cozy security of a pearl leash and Hermes cashmere blanket?*

At the end of every busy workday, Enid went home alone and prepared a simple meal of boiled vegetables and noodles in the communal kitchen of the *tong lau*. Even though she downloaded dating apps like Tinder and Momo on her phone, she lacked the urge to take flattering Meitu[25] photos. She shirked at the thought of taking one of those misty photographs that would make her eyes Bambi-like, lengthen her legs, or deepen the

25 Dating app hopefuls beware. Meitu is one of the most popular image enhancing apps. Considered as pain-free plastic surgery for a more voluptuous body, blemish-free skin, and bigger eyes. The possibilities are endless.

V shadow of her cleavage. Living vicariously through Instagram was her sole social life. Work was more than enough to occupy her at the moment, but she promised herself to make more of an effort to make genuine friends, maybe even date a little once her future became stable.

The only male attention she received were daily messages from Mr. Bai. Sometimes the messages were so flowery and feminine that Enid was very sure that his personal assistant had written it or that it had been forwarded from one of his countless girlfriends. Enid was curious but not enough to pursue matters further. *What's the point? I don't want to be used and thrown away like a good time girl! I'm looking for rings or THE ring on my finger!* Nevertheless, it was definitely flattering that he had not forgotten her.

To think, just five months ago when I began my internship, I vowed to myself that I would do anything to get to the top. How naïve I was, not knowing what that "anything" could constitute. Ewww, gross, the thought of being with one of the balding, flabby men with their leftover strands of hair combed over like a barcode. Letting them "wriggle" their sweaty digits in my hand is as far as I am willing to go. Enid sent screenshots of Mr. Bai's conversations to Angela and they played at being worldly women with cynical discussions on wealthy playboys and their playthings. Angela swore that she would chaperone and not leave Enid alone with Mr. Bai if he came to Hong Kong.

Enid enjoyed working on the exclusive VIP events used to cultivate clients. They were usually held in conjunction with a charity for that feel-good factor. Money could not buy happiness, but it most certainly could alleviate guilt. Rothesay's did not really care which charity benefitted, as long as it was the charity *du jour*. Save the Children was the current favorite. Enid learned a lot about table manners, how to plan a good table seating arrangement, and how to flatter clients. Knowledge of basic etiquette came second nature to June, but to Enid, it was a revelation. She devoured *Tiffany's Table Manners for Teenagers* like it was the Little Red Book.

The list was restricted to clients who had purchased at least HKD 10 million in the season before. No SYBUNTs (Some Years But Unfortunately Not This) or LYBUNTs (Last Year But Unfortunately Not This). Vera had the final say on the list, and each specialist pleaded with her to include their client.

"Aiyah, not her! She doesn't buy anything," Vera scowled. "She wants to see and be seen, get free catalogs. Everyone knows she doesn't work, and her in-laws don't give her any money." And on the opposite end of the invitation spectrum, "Christine, you need to get Wanda Lui in, I know she hates these kinds of social events but she will MAKE the event." Enid's heart raced with excitement; Wanda shared pole position with Lipstick Brother in Enid's browser traffic. Enid spent hours analyzing and memorizing their facial expressions and gestures as if she could absorb their savvy and success.

Wanda Lui was the darling of all the gossip magazines and idol of many ambitious millennials. The self-made CEO of a multi-national telecommunications company, she was known for her sharp wit and even sharper deal-making skills. One of her companies was headed for NASDAQ listing this quarter, so she was in every issue of the business periodicals and gossip magazines. Wanda loved colored diamonds —the rarer, the better. What made Wanda such a desirable client was her legendary decisiveness. All her money was her own and she was not beholden to anybody. If she wanted something, she did not hesitate to pull out all the stops to seize the object of her desire. Cases in point were her two beautiful children, borne by Olympian surrogates, the product of Wanda's eggs and Ivy League-catwalk-model sperm donors.

The event was a terrific success. Not solely because Wanda dropped by for twenty minutes and placed a telephone with insurance bid on the 3-carat fancy intense blue diamond. For once, publicity was unparalleled. There was more column space than the usual banal one-inch "Goings On About Town" listing because of the Chao cousins. At the luncheon, the poised and image-conscious duo reached for the same pair of JAR ear clips. Desired for their uniqueness and creativity, the coveted earrings were spheres reverse-set with aquamarines and diamonds.

However, it was not the HKD 200,000 – 280,000 estimate that sparked their wrath. Each clutched a single earring and refused to hand it over. The elder audibly hissed, "You are such a brat, you think you can always get your way. Give me the earring NOW! You insist on wearing Dice Kayek Haute Couture at amfAR when you know that Ayse is in the middle of designing something especially for me. You constantly want to be the center of attention and steal the show! I am older so I should get first choice." In immediate response, the beringed hand of the younger cousin reached over and seized hold of her adversary's glossy mane of keratin-ed hair.

Everyone paused, entranced by the scene. Frenemies who had passionately air-kissed the pair earlier now strongly resisted the urge to record the altercation. Enid could see restless fingers tapping on clutch bags and surreptitiously searching in pockets. A single camera flash could set off pandemonium and all hell would break loose. For once, Vera was speechless and she gaped, motionless in shock. You could almost see her brain cogs whirring away as she calculated her next move. She was damned if she did and damned if she did not. The Chao cousins would take offense if she interfered but if she did not, her cherished event could rapidly descend into a vicious society girl-on-girl wrestling match. The older Chao had already started twisting the arm of her relative. Strong from months of Krav Maga personal training and years of battling for inheritance, this promised to be far more than any run-of-the-mill bitch fight.

It took Edward's deliberate campy facetiousness to diffuse the situation, "Now, now. Ladies, ladies, that is not the only JAR lot from Ellen Barkin's collection! Give me both earrings, they will look far better on me than either of you." He rested his soft manicured hands on both their shoulders like an animal whisperer. Mental calculations ran through their minds like thoroughbreds racing at Hong Kong Jockey Club. Should long-standing feelings of rivalry and jealousy outweigh the desire for face? There was clearly no love lost between the two despite their professions of ardent affection on social media.

A split-second of indecision followed Edward's verbal counter-missile. Neither wanted their allowance cut off by enraged parents. Reality hit, and it appeared that Edward had saved the situation and earned his bonus for the season. Shame-faced and sullen, both ladies silently handed over the earrings, which Edward pocketed with a flourish. Patting his pockets and announcing, "All for me!" with a wink, Edward was every inch the debonair and consummate showman. After the older Chao stormed off in a huff, Edward ignored the empty seat and perched on the corner of the remaining cousin's seat, lightening up the whole table with witty one-liners and sweet-talking introverted guests. Clients continued to place bids and the conversation seamlessly flowed as if nothing untoward had happened. *Now, this is class.*

Everyone would have forgotten about it and moved on as if it were last season's runway show if the press had not got wind of the incident. "An inside source" breathlessly sensationalized the Chao cousins almost coming to blows over the exquisite JAR earrings at Rothesay's upcoming auction. Unsurprisingly, no mention was made of the haute couture competition; this would not have helped the "inside source" in any way. The skirmish was undoubtedly re-invented by Rothesay's genius marketing team, so it became a most fortuitous incident. A great deal of additional interest was generated in the earrings as well as other lots in the auction. Even catalog sales increased as people were eager to know what all the hype was about. Since the Chao cousins were consistently on Asia's best-dressed lists and from one of the wealthiest families, the assumption was made that the earrings must really have been worth fighting for.

Chapter 5

UNDER THE GAVEL

E nid gazed up in awe at the towering structure of glass and steel. Signature royal blue banners with the Rothesay's auction gavel insignia adorned the Hong Kong Convention Centre (HKCC). It was a glamorous spectacle. As an employee, she was impressed, and if she were standing in the buttery Italian leather shoes of a client, she would be convinced that the 20% buyer's premium was worth every dollar. Rupert Bosewell was back in Hong Kong for auction week, but, this time, the collective aspirations and nervous energy of the office were not focused on him. Everyone was fully revved up for the auctions. It was time to earn their keep and prove their value. The oft-broadcasted chant rang true: *You are only as good as your next auction.* No one — junior cataloger or international director — could afford to stand on the merits of past auction results.

New haircuts, the very latest outfits, but the same tried and tested fake smiles. Everyone looked even better groomed than usual. A young ceramics specialist reapplying lip-gloss in the bathroom advised Enid, "Applying just the right amount of make-up is a token of respect to the clients! Not wearing anything shows that you can't be bothered. I don't have the gravitas yet to wear Mao collar suits and appear scholarly like my boss, but I want to be taken seriously."

This was not the first time that Enid heard this echo of Angela's well-meaning advice about the importance of appearances and taking full advantage of her youthful beauty. Auctions were a cut-throat business and as the next generation of specialists, they needed to arm themselves with any weapons in their arsenal to get ahead.

Competition between the specialists for the clients' attention was a Darwinian battle — colleagues from the various offices, as well as clients, had flown in from around the world. Country representatives exhaustively wooed and entertained their wards, no request was too ridiculous to keep a *shui yu* happy. It was payback time for some of the snobby specialists who looked down their noses at anyone that they had not shared a ski lesson with. The more insecure *shui yi* knew that the people nicest to them were the ones being paid, so they took full advantage of the my-rocks-are-bigger-than-yours situation. Specialists like Rita that needed taking down a peg found themselves slurping noodles in grimy dai pai dongs or trying not to grimace when their clients shrieked a smidgen too loudly in the exclusive Club Lusitano. With spouses who ignored them, Second Generation children who scoffed at them, and so-called friends, the auction season was balm for many a *shui yu*'s soul.

Socio-fiscal hierarchies aside, it was a wonder to walk around the preview listening to exactly the same saccharine-sweet compliments and sales lines being pitched in an Ivy League or Franglais accent, lilting Thai, or strident Swiss German. Enid adored the contrived façade and the underlying tension — everyone was fighting for that valuable scrap of attention with primal instinct. Enid loved it. *The perfume of privilege is so intoxicating, a rush to the head like breathing in pure oxygen. Mmmmm, that smell of bespoke calf leather, new bank notes, dry-cleaning solvent, and custom-made shampoo all rolled into one.*

Temporary display cases and mini department offices were set up at the HKCC within forty-eight hours. Logistics staff took photographs of workspaces to ensure that computers moved down to the sale site would be reinstated exactly as they were previously in their cubicles. Everything was to fall back in place exactly as it was the day following the auctions, regardless of whether it was an excessive decoration of motivational stickers, photographs of a family holiday from too long ago, or cutesy desktop mascots. Enid did not understand why people put so much clutter on their desks. To her, they were anything but morale builders, more like sad reminders of a life missed out on, stuck in the office.

The Hong Kong auction came second in the calendar after Geneva, and it was followed closely on its heels by the London and New York auctions. Rothesay's, like its contenders, was a global business. Although there was some rivalry between each saleroom to attain the best results, top lots from the other auctions were brought in for viewing. These overseas lots were carefully chosen and deliberated upon to ensure that they would not compete head-to-head against the local lots. God forbid that a lower price per carat or better quality of stone resulted in a withdrawn bid.

Each individual saleroom's characteristics were apparent in the catalog but this was reinforced when viewed in real life — Geneva and London offered more vintage pieces typically from historical European collections whilst New York concentrated on coveted heritage houses like Cartier and Van Cleef & Arpels. Tiffany & Co., which was desired in the West, was not as popular in the East. Hong Kong jewelry auctions typically featured jadeite and laid emphasis on the quality of the gems themselves rather than the overall design of the jewelry piece.

For the most part, the international jewelry team worked well together and was cautious not to step on each other's toes. Most of the regular and every single one of the VIP clients had their preferred specialist, so there was not much risk of outright poaching. By now, with three days to go before D-Day, 85% of the book was covered. Although it was more than likely that in-room bidding would cover the remainder, Rothesay's inherent driving force for success maintained that it was better to provide for all eventualities. The specialists worked aggressively to cover the remaining lots by subtly hinting to clients that they ought to try their luck for certain lots at the low end of the estimate, tactfully skirting the supposedly transparent but secretive premise of the auction market.

Of the lots, there was a multi-colored sapphire bangle which was proving to quite be a challenge. It was part of a large London consignment, and the consignor was adamant about selling it in Hong Kong despite Kevin, the specialist, advising that it was the wrong fit and style for the Asian market. Kevin repeatedly cajoled the Hong Kong team until they started avoiding him like last season's Gucci belt. The bangle was simply not bling enough to blind bidders into forgetting its utter hideousness. There were just a couple of casual prospects — a dealer who debated melting the bangle down and a portly lady from the prominent Ani family less known for her jewels and better known for her collection of complimentary catalog subscriptions.

On her second visit to the preview, over-enthusiastic Kevin lapsed into barrow boy speak when attempting a hard sell, "You will regret it if you don't buy it. You can't get better than this." Mrs. Ani barely blinked an eyelid before emitting a stream of chastisement about the extensiveness of her jewelry collection and how rudely Kevin was talking down to her.

Like The Princess and the Pea, Mrs. Ani believed over-sensitivity was proof of high birth. Poor gormless Kevin. Too much of an Essex chav, less of a Chelsea rah, and on his second trip to Asia, he failed to realize that Asia was more of a stratified society than England. He had been lulled into a false sense of confidence by confrontation-adverse Asia, where expatriates and bratty locals could get away with obnoxious and excessive behavior without anyone batting an eyelid. Mrs. Ani's reaction was unwarranted, but even agreeable Christine was annoyed. Everyone was too busy to placate her, but she was one of the most verbose doyens of Sindhi society.

Such culturally wincing incidents were far too common. Prior to the jewelry auction, Jean-Pierre thought it wise to host a VIP dinner for brand new clients featuring truffles on the menu. The specialists faced a tough time convincing the less sophisticated clients to attend. After all, how could this French "fungus" compare to the Chinese *ling zhi* "mushroom of immortality?"

The majority of top management belonged to the very best European families and had attended the most prestigious boarding schools, but they remained blissfully unaware and willfully dismissive of the minefield of Asian social niceties. Six feet tall Jean-Pierre bowed at a 90-degree angle to a Japanese tycoon in a wheelchair but then later, on the same day, offended a major Taiwanese client by absentmindedly flipping and drumming his chopsticks on the table. The well-meaning American Head of Chinese Works of Art, Victoria, went around *nihao*[26]-ing anyone with a head of black hair until she was firmly admonished that not all Asians were Mandarin-speaking Chinese.

The morning of the auction, the team held their final interest meeting. These war room gatherings had been held regularly throughout the previews, sifting through the entire catalog lot by lot to find the ones that needed the extra push. At this late juncture, reserve adjustments were being made. Enid and Eileen worked tirelessly to ensure that consignors signed contracts with new terms. Vera then sat down with the auctioneer

---

26 Meaning hello in Mandarin Chinese; a basic phrase that does not fool anyone that you are fluent in Mandarin. Asians are extremely insulted when their nationalities are wrongly guessed. Woe betide the person who asks a Malaysian if they are Singaporean or a Cambodian if they are Thai.

Rajah to note down when he could expect telephone or room bids, so that he could eke out a bidding war or smooth over a stagnant and silent auction room.

During telephone bid training for newbies, Enid learned that the auctioneer was the main actor, the staff were the supporting cast, and the bidders were there to enjoy the spectacle. It was important to look lively, back Rajah up on the rostrum, and be conscious of the room's mood. A world record high bid warranted enthusiastic applause and hopefully an ensuing encore. Throughout the preview, Enid carefully adhered to the Rothesay's dress code. She finally stepped up her wardrobe game and stood out in the right way, not quite yet the Pretty Woman on Rodeo Drive metamorphosis but enough to not stick out like a sore thumb. On the day of the auction, she followed the less is more adage of Rothesay's strict guidelines, appearing in a nondescript black shift Zara dress with a pop of color from a pastel pink shawl.

The shawl was a concession to Vera and Rajah's superstitions. If they had to slaughter a chicken and howl three times at the moon, they would have done so. Wearing something pink was far easier and every single one of the team was required to do so. Rajah, despite his serious demeanor, wore shocking pink socks. He had a clipped, cut-glass English accent particular to people from former British colonies. Extremely charming and good-looking, his sole fault was a tendency to say it and spray it. Those sitting on the front row of the auction room were showered with every carefully enunciated consonant, "Seh-Ven Mih-Liohn Doh-lars." It was never a good idea to wear suede to the jewelry auction.

The auction went at a steady momentum, at the standard speed of fifty to sixty lots per hour. Seated up on the telephone bank terrace, Enid spotted Mr. Bai making a brief appearance at the back of the room, before heading upstairs to bid discreetly from the skybox. She smiled at the familiar clients and dealers. *Even if I am just one of the supporting cast, I need to show how at ease I am so that everyone thinks I know what I am doing. I feel like a star with everyone looking at us.* As a rookie, she had been given five low-value telephone bids to handle. Enid was delighted to sit next to Edward, exchanging gossipy notes more savage than Project Runway as they poked fun at the clients. There was plenty of material to go on — a show-off in an ermine fur stole in humid April as well as a couple of *nouveau riche* ladies wearing the same head-to-toe Bottega Veneta outfits, no doubt directly inspired by the boutique's window display.

They allotted each other points for spotting the clichéd arm-tugging and subsequent snuggle when a lucky lady managed to convince the object of her affections to win a lot for her. With a 300-lot auction and a fully staffed telephone bank, the bids were evenly distributed so neither of them was particularly busy. The emerald came and went without a hitch, selling at the high end of the estimate to the Thai collector. Enid was beyond relieved, although it was a bit of an anti-climax after all those gut-wrenching months. Mr. Bai had played a role in bidding it up the high estimate. It was such a relief that he did not win the lot, so she would not have to fawn over him excessively at dinner later.

The market was buoyant, but the truly thrilling moment was when the hammer came down on the star lot — a USD 12,000,000 ruby and diamond necklace belonging to the Hung Estate. Liu-*jie* steamrolled the bid against the entire room and telephone bidders, holding the paddle outstretched like a pledge of allegiance. Enid was confused to see Liu-*jie* on her mobile phone, but she guessed that she probably had to save the recorded landline for the following lot. Liu-*jie* and Dewi, the Indonesian country representative, were the busiest telephone bidders. They were each assigned two recorded landlines from which they were fielding multiple clients. It was a jaw-dropping world record high for a ruby necklace and every single person in the room clapped resoundingly for Liu-*jie* and her anonymous client.

Enid was on top of the world. In a rare display of affection, the team hugged each other after yet another successful auction. The tension disappeared, like wrinkles after Botox. Enid knew that she would make it to the next stage of the internship. She was proud to have played a small role in the department's success and, more importantly, she was recognized for it. Mr. Bai was the underbidder for the emerald ring, so all her efforts to cultivate his support had worked. This was the first time he had ever bid so aggressively, and, with his father's ascension within the politburo, Mr. Bai was widely acknowledged as a big juicy *shui yu* waiting to be caught.

Mr. Bai, Angela, and Enid were too exhausted to venture further afield, so they celebrated next door at Grand Hyatt's Grissini. With both of them, Enid had no airs and she cheerfully asked them to explain the Italian menu and why people preferred the chewiness of *al dente* pasta. It was her first time in such a stylish and sophisticated restaurant. It was a far cry from her usual cup noodles dinner. Enid took many photographs to upload to Instagram later; it was an enchanting and elegant scene straight out of a Korean romcom. *So, this is how the 1% of the 1% live.* Mr. Bai enjoyed their undivided attention. The awkwardness evaporated and Enid took a cue from street-smart Angela to treat Bai-*gege*[27] like a wise older brother. Dessert was about to be cleared and Bai-*gege* was trying to convince them that the fiery tasting grappa would not get them drunk when Angela and Enid's mobile phones rang in quick succession. It was Christine urging Enid to rush back to the HKCC office. Angela shrugged and

---

27 Respectful term for older brother in Mandarin. It is common in Asia to 'adopt' someone of the opposite sex as a sibling if the romantic interest is one-sided. It is a gentle (and face-saving) way of putting the brakes on feelings developing further.

---

rolled her eyes, announcing that Jean-Pierre's assistant had similarly summoned her.

The girls were relieved to escape without being too drunk, knowing full well that a party-loving princeling like Bai-*gege* with his legendary carousing could drink turpentine or Tignanello with no side effects. They strolled back and were shocked to see Jean-Pierre himself, his assistant, Vera, Christine, and Rajah seated in the office with grim faces. It was dire. Liu-*jie* had sold the star lot to last season's Liquid Gold buyer. Mr. Wang had been unequivocally banned from bidding because he had yet to settle the outstanding USD 2,000,000 and now, he owed an additional USD 14,000,000 including premium for the ruby necklace.

If he was unable to cough up a paltry couple of million, it was unlikely that he would settle seven times that amount for a piece of jewelry. The chance of collection was next to none and Liu-*jie* had flouted the rules by allowing him to bid. Fully cognizant that Mr. Wang was persona non grata, she had deliberately opened an unregistered paddle and used an unrecorded mobile phone to call him. There was no legal recourse for Rothesay's to make the client honor his bid. Mr. Wang was a tiny man with an enormous ego, and the chances of him ponying up the dough were unlikely. All he wanted was to hear the cheers of a record-breaking bid.

Liu-*jie*'s unapologetic retort that the house did not understand China tycoons, and that by refusing her clients their right to bid, Rothesay's was not giving them the face they deserved. Every sentence she uttered in her own defense was a nail in her coffin. She harangued Rothesay's shortsightedness in maintaining the relationships that she devoted herself to developing. Enraged at Liu-*jie*'s audacious auctions and insolent behavior, Jean-Pierre swiftly fired her on the spot. Liu-*jie* was now at Grand Hyatt unrepentantly packing her bags.

As Liu-*jie*'s second-in-command, Angela was closely questioned if she knew of her supervisor's intentions and if she had access to Mr. Wang. Luckily for Angela, Liu-*jie* had protectively and disparagingly excluded her from any contact with the top band of VIP clients. Enid was stunned. She thought of Golden Pages as indispensable and vital to the business. To be unceremoniously executed halfway through auction week in such an expeditious manner showed the management's iron-fisted nature. There were either two choices — toe the line or be thrown overboard.

Enid stood flabbergasted, and Christine interrupted her reverie by physically leading her toward the computer. Everyone in the Bids Office and Eileen had left for the day, so it was up to Enid to search through the book to dig out the underbidders and their contact details. There was no time to be lost. It was too late to call anyone in Asia, but management needed to decisively outline a strategy without seeming too desperate.

Once the administrative rigmarole was completed, Enid was summarily dismissed. *Well, the generals don't let foot soldiers see what the battle tactics are. That stress vein on Vera's forehead is going to need more than sclerotherapy and Rajah is the color of his socks! I really wish I could do more.*

By late morning, the news spread like wildfire. The other departments were more annoyed than affronted for Liu-*jie*. Throughout her illustrious career, she had truly managed to offend everyone. The winds of change were swift, colleagues that bowed and scraped to her yesterday, now openly relished her downfall. The general reaction was an unsympathetic grumble that Jean-Pierre should have milked Golden Pages to the maximum for all her contacts and that she should have been fired only after the entire auction season was over. Nevertheless, they were somewhat consoled that only the Jewelry Department had been directly encumbered.

Vera, Rajah, and Jean-Pierre did not betray a hint of anxiety when they spoke to the underbidders, citing Internet bidding issues as the reason. It was imperative to have a firm offer before news of this debacle leaked out.

In the end, the necklace was palmed off to one of the most famous Bukharan Jewish dealers based in London. The husband-and-wife team would undoubtedly find a Middle Eastern royal willing to pay a hefty price tag. Absorbing the 12% cut in buyer's premium was a bitter pill for Rothesay's to swallow. To everyone's relief, the Hung family were none the wiser, and their Chinese painting collection slated to be in the Autumn auctions was not jeopardized.

In spite of everything, the overall results were as impressive as ever – USD 116 million for the first auction of the year. Enid expected a post-sale lull and a moment to catch her breath, but it was a hive of non-stop activity before, during, and after the auction. The lots were carefully packed up and taken back to the office in Central, where clients came in round-the-clock to pay and collect their lots. The glitz was scrubbed off, and it was all about efficiency and administration.

As a result of a strict Confucian education, Enid settled nicely into the methodical routine of signing out lots, checking payment details, and confirming proof of release documentation. The fluid ease that June showed during the preview when handling clients disappeared; she misplaced release forms and even handed over the wrong GIA[28] certificate. Eileen and the warehouse boys were frustrated with her, but Enid was secretly pleased. Although June was not an internship program competitor, Enid was conscious of being compared to her. *Finally, they can see that I am the workhorse they need. Not some thoroughbred show pony.*

During what should have been a simple client collection, June ran to Enid in a fluster. She made the mistake of showing a client

---

28 Gemological Institute of America

his lot before processing payment, and he claimed that the setting of his earrings was missing some tiny pavé diamonds. They had been warned several times about this — some clients who experienced buyer's remorse would try to discharge themselves from their bids or bargain for a lower premium. Mr. Tai was disproportionately irate and demanded to see Vera.

It was lunchtime, and none of the specialists were anywhere to be found. No doubt having a celebratory pat on the back massage. Eileen came to the rescue without batting an eyelid, she did not even bother to leave her desk to meet Mr. Tai. "Aiyah, I told Vera that you girls are too junior to release lots! Always make sure they pay BEFORE they see their lot. Remind them that everything is sold 'As Is.' For sure this *mo liu ma fan*[29] guy will try to get out of the bid. Small money anyway!

---

29 *Mo liu* is Cantonese slang for nonsense or empty-headed and *ma fan* is troublesome or annoying. A combination of the two shows a speaker's extreme irritation.

Tell him we will repair it at the *sifu*[30]. He was stupid enough to pay HKD 60,000 for heated tourmaline earrings — and now he is even stupider to ask to see Vera, she has no time for a small-fry like him!"

After kicking up such a fuss, it was surprising how rapidly Mr. Tai lost his bluster. For small-time clients like Mr. Tai, defaulting on bids tarnished their reputation and landed them in court cases they could not afford to fight. With hundreds of years of history, Rothesay's would never do something as crude as their American competitor, Thompson's, who publicly shamed defaulters by publishing names in their hometown police stations. Tycoons like Mr. Wang did not bat an eyelid; it was water off the golden goose's back. They were untouchable. Naturally, Rothesay's

---

30 Literally meaning teacher or person of skill. Auction houses have *sifu* budgets for repair and alteration work. Immensely talented, they can do everything from repair a bracelet clasp to reset an emerald ring. Access to a *sifu* is an insider's secret; the best jewelry *sifu* in Hong Kong does work for Rothesay's, Cartier, and Bulgari.

picked their battles carefully. Once again it was underlined to Enid how the entitled were given additional latitude when they already had so much.

Releasing the jewelry to happy buyers was one of the most fulfilling aspects of the auction. *I long for the day when I can be one of these lucky winners. It is true that the biggest presents came in the smallest box. A 10-carat diamond ring that can be slipped into your pocket was a much better present than any household appliance.* What fascinated her during the lots release was observing how the style of jewelry went with the personality of a client — design-centric pieces usually went to the more confident and established clients. Edward had been right about "bigger stone, more mistress." It took a certain kind of lady to carry off a jewel the size of a Christmas bauble on her finger. The kind of lady who knew exactly what she wanted, how she was going to get it, and how she was going to show it off.

One late afternoon as the appointments were winding down, Enid spotted a lady planted firmly on the reception couch. Dressed in ripped stonewashed jeans and an over-worn under-washed singlet that looked like Pa's undershirt, everyone was ignoring her. Mindful of how others judged her, Enid whispered to the receptionist who reverberatingly responded, "I think she is someone's helper. Must be meeting her boss here." The lady's eyes glowed in anger and her tanned face turned puce, but before she could retort, the lift doors opened, and a stocky bodyguard appeared. He deferentially handed the lady the latest Goyard bag with the personalized initials FDLS and stood aside. They stood gobsmacked as Enid took in the disheveled ensemble. *Uh, she isn't even wearing a proper bra, I can see nipples, looks like she's smuggling Tic Tacs!*

Their misapprehensions were confirmed when Edward rushed in, "Darling, you snuck here to Hong Kong? I was going to bring your sapphires on our next Tubbataha diving trip."

Edward, dive? In the hot sun? And spoil his La Mer perfect porcelain complexion? She must be a foie gras goose he is fattening up.

Air kiss, air kiss, air kiss, muah, muah, muah. Enid watched, fascinated.

"Daddy's new wife has me on such a limited allowance, I am dirt poor, I am practically a middle-class De Los Santos!" Edward laughed as she faux-pouted. "Did you hear that I am not allowed to fly PJ[31] anymore and had to hitch a ride with a friend?"

June magically appeared and gushed softly, "OMG I can't breathe, that's my style idol, Flora De Los Santos, heiress to the instant noodle empire. I looooove her outfit, so original, so outrageous."

Enid and the receptionist locked twinkling eyes and stifled their laughter. *Only here in this warped Rothesay's world is being middle*

---

31 Sigh, need I explain? Private jet of course, darling, not pajamas!

class an insult and an old singlet is high-fashion just because it's worn by so and so. These people are the Emperor's New Clothes come to life.

Not all of the auction lots fared so well. The Emir's suites had hammered with dismal results. Jean-Pierre had convinced him to place achingly low reserves of USD 20,000 and, in the end, most of the lots sold for below USD 50,000. Instead of concern that the Emir made a huge loss on his jewelry, Jean-Pierre was overwrought that the Emir's magnificent collection of Impressionist landscapes was slipping out of consignment reach. The jewelry was a test run for the Emir; he was definitely more of a buyer than a seller. Letting go of his personal possessions at bargain prices was a markedly different experience from adding to his collection to his advantage. His Eminence was absolutely furious. When Jean-Pierre tried to placate the Emir by flying immediately to the Middle East to explain face-to-face about the workings of the auction house, he was simply told, "If you come here, you will not leave." Even Jean-Pierre, the most determined of wheeler-dealers knew when to seek for cover and admit defeat.

It was now officially the end of the season, and the interns received confirmation of whether they were staying or leaving. It was done with little fanfare, just a plain white piece of paper thanking the unsuccessful for their efforts. After all, Rothesay's had done them a favor by permitting them to slave away for long hours for a stipend. Enid genuinely thought that she made a positive impression, so all day long she waited for someone to yell "Surprise!" and sing "For she's a jolly good fellow". *Well, it looks like I won't be having a leaving party. They could at least have added my name in icing on June's farewell cake. She doesn't even eat sugar anyway! She thinks adding croutons to her salad is a cheat eat. They probably can't expense the cake since I am not a client's daughter.* She expected her colleagues to be sad that she was changing departments, but as she packed up her coffee mug, stationary, loupe, and takeaway packets of soya sauce, no one paid any attention.

Her next season was in the Watch Department, and she felt nervous as she recalled overhearing Vera and the team's derogatory remarks about them. Jewelry and Watches were supposed to complement each other, but they were rivals. As Enid walked out with her paper carton of possessions, she was somewhat mollified as she earned a few smiles and "see you around's". Even Vera nodded at her! Enid was not one to remain downbeat, and she quickly cheered up. *They probably didn't throw me a leaving party because I am moving down the corridor to Watches.* She smiled in recollection of how foolish and juvenile she had been when she first walked through the door six months ago. *I've made it through the first round!*

Chapter 6

TICK TOCK

—‖   ‖—

It was mid-morning and Enid was perplexed. *Is today a holiday?* The Watch Department was completely empty, and even the ubiquitous glow from the rows of computer screens was absent. She put down her carton box of belongings and walked around the room. It looked like a messy college dorm. There were funny team photographs and caricatures pinned up haphazardly, a mountain of snacks and junk food in the corner, a dart board with a picture of a cockroach pinned to it, and a strange assortment of trophies with slam book categories like "Most fake smile," "Most annoying laugh" and "Best imagination."

Enid was thrilled; it was somewhat childish but at least the people in Watches shared more than a sales target.

It was nearly noon before the Head of Department, Tom, and senior specialist, Penny, casually strolled in with wet hair and casual clothes. "Urgh, it's impossible to do anything in this heat. All the clients and consignors are away for the holidays anyway, so why don't you get acquainted by reading some catalogs, and we will go for happy hour later." The Watch Department was notoriously easy-going, and Enid looked forward to a breather after the tense atmosphere of the Jewelry team.

Enid and her liver were not ready for the onslaught of happy hours and outings that prevailed for the duration of the slow period. Drinks, hikes, beach barbecues, tuneless karaoke sessions, and spicy hotpots — Enid felt like she was finally making some real friends, and she began to let her guard down. She was so comfortable that she let Alison, one of the specialists, spend the night at her hole-in-the-wall *tong lau* after a fifteen-shot challenge at Geronimo's.

Enid's need to constantly watch over her shoulder disappeared. Everything was open and transparent. With the notable exception of the departmental secret that Tom was leaving his domineering American wife for Penny. The rest of the office and the clients were left wildly speculating. It was tricky when the Cockroach cornered Enid in the pantry to ask if there was any substance to the rumors. Enid had been duly warned about the Cockroach's transparent attempts at subterfuge, so she evaded the inquisition.

What made it complicated was that this was not Tom's first entanglement in the office. There was justified reason why his nickname was Tom Cat. His soon-to-be ex-wife Blake had been his boss in the New York office. And she had given up her career with the proviso that Tom replaced her in the office. Blake was a bottle blonde from North

Carolina who understandably could not let go since she had given up so much to advance her reprobate husband's career. She popped into the office with sniveling kids in tow, sending Penny hiding in the bathroom or on a fake coffee run. Blake clung wretchedly on to the shreds of her dignity like the tattered First-Class Priority airport check-in tag on her toddler's stroller, trying to show some semblance of elevated status.

When Blake showed up at the office one day with a recently rhinoplasty-ed button nose that looked a little too much like Penny's, Enid's feelings changed. *Shame on me for being so judgmental, I know exactly how it feels to obsess about other people's opinions. It's a vortex that sucks you in... A pity party that nobody wants to attend! Treat others as you would like to be treated. I am going to be nicer to Blake, even if she asks me to research Seminyak villas as if I am her personal assistant.*

Regardless of how much Enid liked Penny and Tom, the relationship created difficulties as the sourcing itineraries were being planned. The couple was slotted on the roster to travel everywhere together, giving none of the other junior specialists the opportunity to meet overseas clients. Penny was head over heels in love with Tom and eager for any honeymoon opportunities. Fortunately, she eased the situation by apologizing profusely and repeatedly telling the other specialists that they could claim credit for the consignments that she brought in.

As the remaining specialists, Lara and Alison, were grounded in Hong Kong, they split the workload of local and walk-in clients. Enid mastered so much more than she had in the Jewelry Department, she was encouraged to study the horological periodicals and given tutorials on mechanisms. As her learning curve accelerated, the administrative drudgery grew bearable. She no longer hovered in the background like a Wimbledon ball girl, she was given a seat at the grown-up's table examining watches with the clients. Watch clients are true geeks and passionate beyond reason, so Enid was happy to absorb their knowledge like a sponge and take her cues from the clients. It was impossible to surpass their specific and random horology knowledge, ranging from the difference between PVD and DLC coating to the advantages of Silinvar mechanism components.

Beyond the camaraderie of the team, Enid enjoyed how down-to-earth the majority of the watch clients were. Appreciators of technical precision, there was little need for flattery and pomp. There was little procrastination when it came to making decisions about whether to bid or consign. Enid's favorite client was the billionaire owner of China's largest tractor manufacturer. When Mr. Li consigned his collection of Rolex SARUs[32], they looked like

---

32 Nicknamed the SARU for its Sapphire and Ruby settings, these Rolex watches are gem-set versions of the original 1950s blue and red bakelite bezels.

they had been run over by one of his tractors. When Enid asked why some stones were missing and cases were heavily dented, he grinned toothily, "Aiyah, I am a simple man, I bought Rolex because I am a fan of Li Na[33] — we are from the same hometown. I thought I need watches to show that I am a success. They are beautiful but so uncomfortable to wear! Heavy when I test drive tractors and take apart engines. Casio is better, got light and alarm." Enid grinned back; this was one aspect of the job that she really enjoyed. She liked how some well-established and self-assured clients treated auction employees as equals because they respected their specialist expertise.

The majority of watch clients were men, but most of the people working in the auction house were women. This was not because of any chauvinism; it naturally gravitated toward this gender bias because a certain

---

33 Li Na, China's top tennis player and the first Asian-born spokesperson for Rolex.

---

personality type was needed to provide the exacting level of client service required. In this predominantly alpha male market, Tom played the boy next door whilst the rest of the team used charm and affability to woo clients. There was nothing as crass as a hard sell and the client was rarely disagreed with, corrected, or refused.

Tom got along like a house on fire with clients of all genders, sometimes a little too well. On one of their sourcing trips, Penny was banned from accompanying him on a valuation to the infamous Maria Chua's home. Maria strictly dealt with male specialists only — and no one dared say no to her. She had whole rooms devoted to each of her collections. Specially designed salons with customized display cases for watches, jewelry, handbags, and makeup. Maria prided herself on being unsentimental, so, with the introduction of each new tycoon beau, she would rid herself of all the gifts and memories of the previous incumbent.

The entire household was stripped bare, monetized by Rothesay's, and a clean slate provided for the candidate with the good fortune to be Maria's latest love.

With back-to-back appraisal appointments, the team was rarely in the office at the same time. Specialists popped in and out of the office as consignments trickled in, the season was building up into full swing. Colleagues from Geneva and New York came to Asia for sourcing trips. The Head of Geneva Watches, Florian, was in town, so, out of politeness and the department's 'leave no man behind' maxim, he was reluctantly but cordially invited to join a dinner hosted by Mr. Lee — a long-standing and well-liked client. *I hope that Florian won't ruin the jolly atmosphere. He is the typecast European Bond villain, with his Lego helmet slicked back hair and absent humor because it has been permanently deposited in a secret Swiss bank account. He is so rude, that nasty condescending sniff just because dinner is at the Shanghainese*

Association restaurant. I mean come on, when else is he going to have the chance to drink wartime Lafite!

Every inch the consummate host, Mr. Lee generously ordered the first hairy crabs of the season and the finest Chinese delicacies. As the Lafite and *huadiao jiu*[34] flowed, Florian discovered that the very humble Mr. Lee owned as many luxury hotels as exquisite A. Lange & Söhne watches in his portfolio. Suddenly eager to please, Florian was only too keen to show his newfound appreciation for Chinese cuisine when the braised abalone and sea cucumber dish arrived. He spiritedly lifted up the entire sea cucumber using his chopsticks, swinging it around flaccidly like an uninhibited pensioner on a nudist beach. As Florian craned his neck forwards to take a bite, the phallic delicacy slipped through his chopsticks, rolled down the front of his

---

34 Fermented rice wine, 18% alcohol content. It tastes fragrant and sweet, so the drinker is in danger of forgetting its potency.

bespoke suit, and came to rest forlornly between his Zimmerli sock and polished Church's shoe.

Everyone except the kindly Mr. Lee and scarlet-faced Florian burst out laughing. Florian hurriedly excused himself and rushed out of the room. Obviously, Florian could not stomach being laughed at — he wanted to be the center of attention on his own terms. The dinner rapidly lost its convivial atmosphere and drew to a close. The next morning, Florian, accompanied by his evil sidekick, Cockroach, stalked into Tom's room. Voices were raised but nothing was audible through the thick glass.

It was more than a stained suit... Florian had spotted Tom and Penny playing footsie under the table when he bent down to retrieve the errant sea cucumber. In the auction world where everyone was poised to maximum effect and conditioned to charm, flirtations were commonplace. It barely warranted gossip, let alone disciplinary action. It was so matter-of-fact that during a lull at the last preview, Carl, one of the visiting specialists from New York, asked Tom for an extended lunch break to take an "afternoon nap" with a Chinese Works of Art colleague.

Whether it was Rothesay's, Thompson's, or China Prestige, artifice and entanglements abounded everywhere. It went with the territory. For now, there were none of the heightened sensitivity and over-the-top political correctness prevalent in industries like banking. After all, if you were repeatedly being told to lose weight and look presentable, it was ridiculous to make claims about fostering a workplace free of gender and sexual discrimination.

The true crux of the matter was that Florian believed Tom was not exploiting the Asian market to its true potential as the department's auction value ran neck-and-neck with its competitor, Thompson's. He felt that Tom spent more time running after women than running the Asian business.

Florian did not care an ounce for Penny, Blake, or anyone else; he aggressively wanted to get his tentacles on every market. Florian itched to get his hands on Asia, where billionaires sprouted like mushrooms. Switzerland was stable but it lacked the adrenalin of the newly minted Asian economies. It was never going to work anyway, two international co-heads with such diametrically opposed personalities.

Never one for level-headed behavior, Tom resigned on the spot. He said it was based on principle. Whilst that was admirable, nobody knew exactly what principle it was. And just like that, he was gone. It happened so swiftly that even his precious golf clubs were left behind. To their credit, Florian and the Cockroach still bothered to buttress up their case against Tom. Both held one-on-one clinics asking awkward questions that were repetitive and annoying — "Did you consume alcohol during office hours? Did you go out by yourself with Tom? Did he make you feel ill at ease? Do you feel your work was affected by your relationship with Tom? Do you feel objectified?" #MeToo had finally dawned at Rothesay's and Tom was cast as an abusive and intimidating misogynist who used his position of power to take advantage of junior female staff.

Enid knew she had to pander to the new sheriff in town, but she was irritated and did not have time for these empty gestures. Tom had not been the easiest of bosses because he was hardly around and put his personal life first, but a conscientious employee like Enid appreciated the breathing room to grow. If the bosses had truly been concerned, they could and should have stepped in earlier. There was still an auction round the corner, with sourcing trips to be re-scheduled and cataloging in its infancy. She also had to cover for Penny, who was devastated and barely functioning. The department was in chaos and there were mutters from other departments that watches would bring down the overall auction season results. The unthinkable could happen — Thompson's beating Rothesay's in the total sales results round-up.

Morale was at an all-time low, but the show had to go on. Those late-night Ebenezer kebabs had been surprisingly camaraderie building. They knew each other as individuals, friends even, away from the brutal dog-eat-dog office environment. For that moment at least, the team that plays together stays together. Lara and Alison broke down the numbers — it was a blessing that nearly all the star lots were already in place and they amounted to approximately USD 8 million. Florian was bringing in unique vintage pieces in an attempt to smooth over the chaos he had stirred up. They calculated that around 250 more lots, at an average value of USD 30,000 each, were needed. Although these so-called bread and butter lots brought in half of the total auction value, they were the most labor-intensive as each individual watch had to be sourced, cataloged, and then photographed.

Dealers and collectors in the know were like rats jumping off a sinking ship. "Maybe next season" and "You don't have a *lou sai* — who's going to supervise you girls?" As next in seniority to Penny, and a super alpha female, Lara was particularly incensed by the last refrain. Lara took it as a personal insult that these narrow-minded clients thought Tom was needed for a successful auction; the juniors were always the ones to do the work anyway. Lara was brilliant and aggressive. The naysayers made her even more determined to succeed.

"So, Enid, spill the tea," Edward giggled and leaned over the workspace partition. Feeling a sense of loyalty toward her new friends, Enid reluctantly relayed the bare facts to which Edward shrugged. "Yawn. So boring, old news. If you had told me something juicy, I would have let you tag along to eat roti canai and see Mokhtar Hussain's 150 watches."

Unperturbed, Enid waved him away and continued her cataloging, she was used to his teasing. It was only later when she was looking for Lara to help open some stubborn pocket watch cases that she found out that Lara had taken a flight to Kuala Lumpur that same afternoon.

Edward was extremely upset, particularly as Lara offered a trifling 3% Seller's Premium to the Hussain family. Now it was going to affect his bottom line if he had to offer the same for jewelry consignments or risk upsetting the client. Edward was the Hussain family's designated contact (D.C.). According to auction house rules, no one was supposed to contact a client without going through the D.C. first. Part of your worth in the auction house was weighed by who and how much your D.C.'s were worth. Lara had deliberately flouted those rules and worse of all, she did not care or pretend to care. Cockroach publicly admonished Lara, but privately patted her on the back.

"Me, me, me, me." Lara did not pause to take a breath as Cockroach reassigned Tom's client contacts. No one else had the energy to volunteer themselves for the additional responsibilities at the post morTom meeting. Enid's admiration grew as Lara wrote her initials in bold red beside nearly every name on the client list. *Lara's work ethic and ambition are the real deal. I need to grow up and stop acting like I am in the running for a high school popularity contest. I have become such an insecure scaredy-cat. Look at how Lara is working the system and poised to seize control.* Usually, if you were not a family member or personal friend of a client, you had to wait your turn. A *shui yu* would never fall into your lap. Those automatically went to the most senior staff members, regardless of whether or not they actually worked at maintaining the relationships. To be the gateway to an important client was power. You were only as good as your next sale, and you were only as good as your client lists.

No one at the top level of the house reached where they were by being a shrinking violet in the scramble to be appointed D.C.

As much as the team harbored resentment toward the Cockroach and Florian, they recognized the efficiency of their oily machinations. There was no room for feelings and festivity in the New World Order, but the department was now run as efficiently as Jewelry's. After Penny, the person most affected was Francesco. His work required a certain creativity that prevented a 500-lot watch catalog from becoming too monotonous as well as an exacting attention to detail that showcased each timepiece's technical specifications. Unfortunately, the Cockroach brought bean-counting to a new level. She put Francesco's productivity on a data chart measuring productivity against cost and demanded a schedule of forty pieces a day. This sounded like a low number, but it was time-consuming work.

The graph did not take into consideration that special shots were needed for star lots. A photograph of one watch was a multiple-image compilation — hands, dial, subdial, case, and strap were shot separately and then merged using software. Whether it was a metal bracelet or rose gold case, jewel-set bezel, or high complication moon phase subdial, all involved specific lighting and technical set-ups. Francesco was miserable. He wailed "Cockroach and Vera are Death Eaters, worse than Voldemort! I'm losing my soul. I don't even have any energy to swipe, let alone wink at anyone on Gaydar." Everyone had so much affection for Francesco, so they tried their best to cheer him up with White Rabbit candy and visits to his darkroom between cataloging breaks. It was for his sanity as much as theirs.

Cockroach fostered a culture of unwarranted persecution, fearful that the team was telling Tom about the upcoming auction and threatened that they would resign at a crucial moment. This was baseless and pure paranoia. Everyone was fully committed to an auction that they had devoted time and effort to. No one was looking back misty-eyed, except for Penny, of course. Plus, Tom was on a beach in Danang Bay, enjoying the sunshine as much as his year of paid gardening leave. Work continued to progress without a hitch; the catalog was soon at the printer's, and they began work on press releases. Less than half of the auction was sold on the book. If it was Jewelry, there would be a mad panic, but the Watches team remained unperturbed. The estimates were good, and it was going to be the biggest watch auction in Hong Kong ever, USD 20 million total value. Two decades of work at Rothesay's and with a snap of the fingers, Tom's abrupt departure was celebrated and Florian was vindicated. With approximately 490 lots, the auction was the ultimate Christmas stocking-filler for all budgets and wrists. Santa did not care who was naughty or nice.

Chapter 7

WATCHED OUT

―――――――― || || ――――――――

Before the days of the infamous Brother Watch[35], it was widely acknowledged and quietly whispered that watches are the "currency of bribery." Enid witnessed the smooth cycle of a client inquiring about a particular lot, a follow-up bid by his acquaintance, and then the consignment of the watch a few seasons later. A fluid and low-key transaction. Watches were a convenient medium of exchange because even a layman could spot a fake. The so-called Grade AAA

---

35 In 2012, Netizens spotted Yan Dacai, a provincial head from Shaanxi smirking at a tragic scene. Public rage ensued in a 'human flesh search' that uncovered Yan's expensive watch collection funded by corruption.

Shenzhen special editions were unable to attain the smooth polishing of a Swiss-made watchcase, let alone distinctive features like hand-cut gears or perlage finishing. With jewelry, a trained eye was required to tell the difference between cubic zirconia, synthetic, and natural diamonds. Certificates offered little assurance, which is why GIA diamonds were micro-laser inscribed.

With less than a year of experience under her belt, Enid found it incredibly difficult to remember the details of the many kinds of complicated mechanisms. Lara rolled her eyes in exasperation when explaining for the umpteenth time what a chronometre and a suspended tourbillon were. With little technical aptitude, Enid's strength lay in spotting if a case had a post-manufacture polish or if the bezel was set with after-market stones. Her saving grace was a knack for identifying after-market craftsmanship, which voided the watchmaker's warranty and deflated the watch's value.

The previews were crowded. This was not unexpected, with such a wide range of appealing estimates from No Reserve to million-dollar pieces. It was a challenge to keep up with the VIP collectors as well as curious casual clients, but Enid could not get over how friendly the watch clients were. Once she got the hang of how to work the mechanisms and memorized the terminology, watches became more fun than jewelry. Watches were tactile and functional. Enid enjoyed activating the slide of a minute repeater to hear the chime of the hours, quarters, and minutes, and or watching the rattrapante hand of a chronograph make two separate measurements.

Unlike jewelry, watches introduced Enid to approachable people in her age group. She even made a couple of new friends at the preview, Ping and his wife Jill. They were so friendly that they invited her to their home for Christmas Eve dinner. Enid knew her place in the client food chain, she took care of newbie tadpoles like Ping and Jill, as well as slimy ancient frogs like Gareth Birch, who never placed a bid, demanded a great deal of attention, and made a huge fuss that none of the watch straps could fasten around his thick furry wrist. Seasoned veterans Lara and Alison studiously froze out these "time-waster" clients. Well-trained by Edward, Enid fawned over Gareth by praising his strong manly wrist. In the auction house, no client was ever too fat to fit a watch or piece of jewelry. Instead, they were flattered with compliments that they were powerfully built or "*yau fook.*[36]"

Jean-Pierre's elegant wife and teenage son dropped by the preview; Emile had his eye on a basic time-only IWC watch for his 18th birthday. Enid and Penny could barely keep a

---

36 A literal translation of this sugar-coating phrase is to "have prosperity." Usually uttered by sycophants or sales ladies hoping to sell an unflatteringly tight item of clothing. However, it is far more pleasant than telling someone that they really need to go on a diet or, horror of horrors, size-up.

straight face when his mother hissed at him, "Darling, these premiums are crazy, let's get Papa to buy you a brand-new watch at one of those Kowloon retailers. I am sure he will get a good discount." So much for the claim that auction houses needed to raise their buyer's premium to 25% to remain competitive. Thankfully, the rising premiums did not seem to dampen the enthusiasm of others further removed from the razzmatazz of the auction world.

With cameras trained on every case and an army of temporary exhibition helpers to assist, Enid, Lara, Alison, and Penny felt confident enough to serve multiple clients at once. *I love having someone answering to me, even if it is a part-time student on a school holiday. This is what power feels like to Cockroach, deciding when someone can take a bathroom break and forbidding them from chewing gum.* Clients came in steadily throughout the day, and they served more than one person at a time, cautious to count the number of watches brought out on trays and making full use of the unmotivated viewing assistants. Half her time was spent making sure that the timepieces were not overwound or flung around by an over-enthusiastic client.

On one of the busiest afternoons when Enid was pretending to know what she was talking about, they were interrupted by a loud commotion. The Head of Security, Gregory, spotted a young man swapping watches around. Smarter than the usual trickster, he had taken the trouble to study the catalog and swapped the genuine article for a Grade AAA knock-off. Lara was extremely flustered as it happened right under her nose. She had been about to place the counterfeit copy back in the display case before Gregory had swooped down.

Even to Florian, such a mistake was understandable; he knew the strain of non-stop preview traffic. Lara's eyes welled up with angry tears as Cockroach jumped on her high horse and launched into a tirade of criticism. *What a bitch. It was ridiculous, getting a telling-off from someone who doesn't know what it is like to work the preview floor. Honestly, Cockroach has no leadership qualities. She could have taken the opportunity to motivate rather than crush Lara. Telling her that the thief targeted her because she looks weak and lacks poise. What have looks got to do with it?*

Even the policeman that came to arrest the would-be thief was taken aback at Cockroach's acrimonious attack. *Anyway, aren't all these watches covered by insurance?* Enid was becoming immune to the stream of digits on the auction valuations. *So what if it's worth a hundred thousand or a million, it's not in my bank account and it is pocket change for the client who buys it.* Slowly but surely, Enid's mindset was changing. *I don't know how Lara stomached that tongue-lashing without standing up for herself. No job should be worth that kind of personal humiliation.*

At the end of each long viewing day, a tally of the latest bids and client interests were noted. Enid was exhausted, and her body was so sore that she slept with her calves propped up on a pillow. Her toes had lost all feeling from being stuffed into high-heeled shoes all day. She longed to wear flip-flops but, of course, this was tantamount to showing up to work with a fluorescent pink Mohawk or nose piercing. The team's feeling of relief was palpable when the last evening of viewing drew to a close.

All pretenses were off; Alison dabbed tissues to a moist armpit, and Lara pressed an oil blotter to her shiny nose. From now on, bidders would only be able to handle the watches if they paid in full for their lots. Enid could feel the adrenalin building up in her. The auction was a whole day affair tomorrow, starting at nine in the morning. It was hard to believe that six months of work would come to fruition in a few hours.

And now it was time to prep herself. At the all-staff meeting, Jean-Pierre reminded them that the bidders were a paying audience with a very short attention span. The auctioneer was on stage, and they were there to assist his performance. It was essential to portray the very best side of Rothesay's, "no chewing gum, eye-rolling, snacking, examining nails, or split ends." As performers, they were all on show and primed to perfection. Naturally, cheers and claps were encouraged for world record high bids. They were not to emit sighs of disappointment for any unsold lots.

Back home, Enid carefully sponged down and steamed her lone black suit from Shanghai. It was not as fancy as many of her colleagues' tweed Chanel or embellished Dries Van Noten jackets, but it looked good. The asymmetrical cutting made her look confident and a bit edgy. *So what if it is a copy of last season's Roland Mouret that I saw June wearing and that she probably gave away.* Enid stood in front of the bathroom mirror rubbing in the last treasured drops of snail collagen mask on to her neck, skirting her hairline, which was slicked back with a hot oil hair treatment. She giggled to herself, *Florian must be doing the same thing in the privacy of his fancy-schmancy hotel suite because now my hair looks exactly like his. Gordon Gekko wannabe. I have never seen him with a hair out of place or a hangnail. He is as inexpressive as he is impressive.*

The only body language Florian permitted himself was the studied removal of an imaginary speck of dust from his custom-tailored suit. This gesture gave him a moment to collect his thoughts, and Enid noticed that he did it whenever he was assessing the situation and plotting his next move. Heaven forbid that it was anything that could be construed as a signal of insecurity or nervousness. It was a very elegant gesture that drew attention to the fine cloth weave of his suit. Enid was very careful to stay far away from him. It was childish, but she was actually a bit scared of him. She stood in front of the bathroom mirror posing and trying to look authoritative, but her babyface big eyes, button nose, and small chin just would not cut it.

Countdown to fifteen more minutes before she could rinse off when she heard her phone ringing repeatedly in quick succession. *Urgh, it could be Pak Budi placing a bid on that Graff Fascination, and there is only one bidder on it at the moment.* Enid raced back to her room and saw five missed calls from Lara. She rolled her eyes; Lara was probably having another stress/ panic attack. *She will be the boss of the department one day, but she really needs to get a life.* The dial tone barely gave a single ring before Lara shrieked into the phone "Turn on the news now, there's been a terrorist attack on the Exchange, our auction is screwed!"

Enid watched in horror. Multiple car bombers had simultaneously targeted the European Stock Exchange building. Its historic foundations had not been able to withstand the blasts, and half the building had collapsed. Newscasters were almost speechless with shock, and footage showed disheveled and bleeding people. The news ticker read that emergency services were unable to enter the precarious structure, so the death toll could not be fully accounted for. With such a limited circle of friends and family abroad, Enid was certain that she would not be personally affected, but she was devastated by the tragic and senseless loss of life.

It was too late to call her parents, but Enid ached to hear an affectionate voice. After tossing and turning for an hour, she went to spend the night at Angela's hotel. She could not bear to be in her spartan room that looked like a low-budget capsule hotel. *I am thankful that I have a true friend who understands what priorities ought to be in life. How ridiculous Lara is to place a silly watch auction first and foremost! How superficial!* Enid and Angela vowed to each other to build lasting connections and meaningful relationships. Not to become bitter and lonely "Rothesay's Spinsters." Enid shuddered with the realization that she was on the brink of becoming so wrapped up in the auction world that she could have shared Lara's inhuman reaction.

They barely slept a wink before it was time to head to the HKCC. The exhibition hall was eerily silent. Everyone had somber faces, and some of the overseas colleagues had puffy eyes and tear-stained cheeks. The European Stock Exchange could not open today, and markets everywhere around the world observed a moment of silence to pay their respects to the victims and their families. You could cut the tension in the Watch Department's room with a knife. Internet bids were being pulled as bidders took stock of their priorities. Everyone expected the international markets to crash the moment they opened. Enid and Penny did their best to avoid sitting next to Lara. Lara was as flustered as Cockroach, and both of them were short-fused with everybody.

Edward, who had now openly declared himself as Lara's mortal enemy, circulated rumors of Lara's overly generous guarantee to the Hussain family. Unsurprisingly, Lara had pulled out all the stops and was promised a big fat bonus and promotion if the sale went well. And if it did not... Someone's head would roll.

Edward sniffed, "I believe in karma, and that sneaky upstart is going to be served a big slice of humble pie. She deserves what is coming to her." He gave another affronted sniff, "So unrefined, the way that she went behind my back. Now she is going to learn the hard way that it's worth it to play nice — especially with me!"

Enid could not help smiling as Edward pretended to sharpen his talons and have a hissy fit. *Sure, it's funny now but mental note to self — avoid being on the receiving end of that! You can fall out of favor in this industry quicker than the time it takes to squeeze on a pair of jeggings.*

The auction room held less than a dozen people; it was so quiet you could hear a pin drop. The last time it had been this still was Black Monday in 1987. Despite having one of the house's most experienced auctioneers on the rostrum, Charles could barely elicit a response. Chandelier bids[37] and gestures toward the Internet bidding cameras failed to generate any action. Charles tried his best to eek the bids up to reach the reserve, but the few wily dealers in the room were far too experienced to be taken in by such ruses. They held back, and Charles had no choice but to sell below the reserve or announce

---

37 Bidding toward an unseen bidder in the back of the room, a tactic to generate interest where there is none. After all, if someone wants to buy it, it must be a deal worth considering.

"Same as before. Same as before." Subtle code for unsold bought-in lots.

Great beads of sweat lined Charles's forehead. His jaunty polka-dot pocket-handkerchief was sopping wet. Across the telephone bidding bank, Enid could see Florian fidgeting away at his suit like a monkey picking lice. Specialists from the other departments were ruthless. They had better things to do. There was little solidarity at this point when they realized Watches was a lost cause, and there were possible repercussions on their own sale. One by one, they shrugged, silently shuffled their papers together, vacated their seats at the telephone bank, and went to work their own previews. A previously grand show of thirty country representatives and specialists working the telephones dwindled to ten miserable Watch department staff. Enid copied Alison, who had her finger on the switch hook, mouthing into the receiver, pretending to avidly speak to a client.

It was an unmitigated disaster. 56% sold by lot and 47% by value. The department barely covered its keep. They had been too aggressive with their seller's commission offers, averaging 4% instead of the usual 15% because of the single-owner collection. The 20% buyer's commission and charges formed the bulk of their revenue. It was clear that heads would roll. Enid knew that Florian and the Cockroach were grand masters of *tai chi*[38], there was no way that they would take the fall. Lara, Alison, and Penny remained quietly confident. As it was, the department was a bare-bones operation, and it was not like watch specialists grew on trees.

Whether an auction had good or bad results, the amount of work remained the same, it was so demoralizing. The checklist of things to do was longer than a waitlist

---

38 A 3,000-year-old meditative Taoist martial art, know for its health benefits. Slang usage for the art of re-delegating work, pushing responsibility or blaming someone else in a fluid movement.

---

for a limited edition Patek Philippe. Seller reports, after-sale offers, release forms, and shipping logistics. Even though more than half the lots had been sold to approximately a hundred clients, it seemed like the client handovers ran on endlessly. Enid counted her blessings that this was not like the New York or Geneva salerooms, where a single lot ended up with an individual client. Asian clients were notorious for spree bidding on multiple lots, and this considerably lessened the client-facing workload.

By now, it took a lot more to faze Enid. The chip on her shoulder was many carats lighter, the proof of that was she stopped equating the value of one lot with the cost of her entire education or her parent's home. Even Gregory was nonplussed when an unassuming Macanese client refused the offer of a security escort. A horology fanatic, the client purchased eleven extremely high-value lots, totaling USD 1.5 million in value. He casually dropped by without an appointment, armed with his own precision tool kit. In ten minutes, he swiftly adjusted the bracelets, strapped them on both his arms, and rolled down the long sleeves of his thin cotton Giordano shirt. "Aiiiii why do I need a security guard, if I show off then everyone will want to rob me! I am going to take the TurboJet[39] at Sheungwan. Why do you think I have money to buy expensive watches?" He grinned toothily, "It's because I don't waste money on helicopters and Ubers pffff." Clients like these were Enid's special favorites. *They are so honest and humble. If my parents were billionaires, I hope that they would be like this. That they would still prefer to eat scallion pancakes over salty caviar and blinis.*

---

39 Although it sounds impressive, the TurboJet is a stomach churning, low cost, and low-key Jetfoil sea journey that takes fifty-five minutes from Hong Kong to Macau. It is not the usual option for high rollers, who take the fifteen-minute Sky Shuttle helicopter service at 10 times the price.

Every auction season was not without its stories of client behavior. The highlight for the whole department was the release of one of their most expensive modern Patek Philippe timepieces, still in its vacuum-sealed packaging. Florian's jaw dropped when the Burmese general snatched the watch out of his officiously clad gloved hands[40] and ripped open the manufacture seal with his teeth.

Enid and no-nonsense Lara could barely stifle their laughter when the General took it one step further by asking them to throw away the presentation box and certificate, as he did not want any evidence of his purchase. The box alone on Amazon fetched thousands of dollars! Florian's mouth continued to hang agape when the General flip-flopped the watch around to wave away Florian's offer of a quick tutorial on how to work the watch.

---

40 Although a watch is meant to be held and worn on the wrist, it increases the snobbery and hype for clients when specialists wear pristine white gloves to handle the watches so there is no taint of fingerprints or a sweaty palm.

It was a shame that the watch did not fly out of his hand; that would have been slapstick comedy at its finest. The icing on the cake was when the General wound the watch backward to set it to the correct time.

With his starched demeanor and rigid behavior, it was tough for Florian to build rapport with Asian clients. He tried his best to project a superior air of expertise but unfortunately came across as an officious butler at a Las Vegas high roller's suite. VIPs deliberately asked not to sit next to him at client dinners, and, as a result, Florian surrounded himself with dodgy European dealers and starter-level clients who were debating buying their first Breitling.

For all his faults, Tom fit in better with Asian high-net-worth clients because of his devil-may-care attitude. On business sourcing trips, Tom was most concerned with fitting in as many rounds of golf as possible, whilst Florian was most obsessed with fitting in with name-drop-worthy people. Faced with the Burmese General, Tom would have laughed it off and asked if the plastic was tasty. General ignored Florian's outstretched hand as the latter sycophantically walked him to the lift, bowing and scraping effusively.

Chapter 8

Every Story is a Love Story in Italy

——————|| ||——————

Ping and Jill's apartment was one of the most tasteful homes Enid had ever been in. It was a rambling old walk-up apartment on the South side with a sweeping view of Stanley Harbor. She liked that it was not the typical cookie-cutter Philippe Starck designer pads that she visited on client calls. She had a phobia of modern design after failing to find the concealed voice-activated toilet flush on one such visit. It was mortifying and ever since then, she refused to eat anything overly spicy before client visits.

Ping and Jill's place was intimate and full of character. Bric-a-brac from various travels was scattered throughout their home — a hand-stitched leather pouf from Morocco, a vintage crystal decanter from Madrid's El Rastro, vivid batik throws from Terengganu, and candid photographs everywhere. The high ceilings, black-and-white mosaic tile floors, and tarnished brass fixtures lent their place a rustic old-world charm. Despite meeting them less than a handful of times at the preview, Enid felt immediately at ease. Ping brushed aside Enid's profuse apologies at his unsuccessful bid on a vintage Omega Speedmaster.

Friends floated in and out of the apartment, creative types from Ping and Jill's circle. They were a perfectly matched Hong Kong hipster couple — Jill with her artisan cafe/design gallery and Ping's animation studio. For the first time since she arrived in Hong Kong, Enid felt the best dressed. Jill, the hostess, was wearing a simple white t-shirt and ripped skinny jeans, although skinny was not the right description. Jill was actually one of the chubbiest Hong Kong women that Enid had ever met. She could clearly see Jill's muffin top bulging above the waistband of her jeans, but it did not stop Jill from reaching for yet another fried spring roll from the party platter. *Clearly, she is not on a keto diet... Geez, WTF is wrong with me. Stop it, Yi Nin, before you turn into one of those green-eyed catty girls. Don't be a hater just because you are envious of how contented Jill is.*

Enid was blown away by how thoroughly confident Jill was. *I don't even know her; I almost want to hate her, and I want to be her best friend.* Jill was endearingly vivacious with dramatic gestures and a broad smile leading into deep dimples. Everyone was drawn to her magnetic personality. The party was in full swing with non-stop laughter and fluid conversation. Enid shyly hung on the fringes, but random strangers made a sincere effort to include her in their conversations.

In a clichéd scene from a movie, Enid was standing on the balcony admiring the twinkling harbor lights when Luca came to introduce himself. Gangly, geeky, and wearing fashionable tortoise shell spectacles, Luca looked like one of the many trendy young FILTH[41] expatriates from Lan Kwai Fong. What initially passed for shyness turned out to be quiet self-assurance. As he brushed his mop of curly brown hair away from his eyes, Enid was struck by how good-looking he was. He had beautiful long eyelashes and cobalt blue eyes. Luca was so easy to chat to, and although they were from different cultures, they rapidly found that they shared a quick-witted sense of humor and many interests.

Enid did not feel shy around Luca because he was so relaxed. Tired from the stratified auction world, Enid was drawn to Luca's disarming charm and how little he cared about what others thought of him. He briefly mentioned working at one of the

41 Failed In London Try Hong Kong

international banking behemoths but did not delve further. Enid gathered that he did some unfulfilling back-office work, and he had only taken the job because it offered a visa and a posting to Asia. Luca was definitely not the moneybags type that the old ambitious Enid had fantasized about. Indeed, the closest that Luca could ever come to Rothesay's was if he worked in their I.T. Department. *He is definitely not client material.*

It was refreshing to be with Luca, and he reminded Enid so much of Francesco, with a fun and easygoing nature. Thankfully, Luca was not a stereotypical superficial orientalist with yellow fever. Luca openly embraced and was genuinely interested in everything Chinese from TVB drama series to the proper way to eat *xiao long bao*. One of the couple's favorite discussions involved comparing Italian and Chinese culture with their shared values of food and family. They loved to debate whether there were more Chinese or Italian restaurants in the world, arguing if adding dubious establishments that served Hawaiian pineapple pizza and General Tso's Chicken was data manipulation.

Luca reminded Enid of the reasons she had fallen in love with the auction world — because of her love of beauty, history, and curiosity about different cultures. They grew closer as they explored Hong Kong and shared experiences together. Long hikes on Dragon's Back, off-the-beaten-track places such as the Sam Tung Uk Museum, day trips to Cheung Chau. When they were together, they did not have to seek out the elaborate or extravagant because they were so content with each other's company. It seemed almost too good to be true.

One of Luca's sexiest traits was his fluency in Italian, French, and Spanish. Luca and Enid roamed the streets of Hong Kong and Kowloon speaking their "secret language" — a random pidgin of French, Mandarin, and badly accented Cantonese. It came in handy for diverse situations — from when they needed to leave a boring party early to when they had to move away from a deodorant-deficient commuter during rush hour. At ease with Luca, Enid stopped being so wound-up and obsessed with jostling for career pole position.

Before, she felt like she was tiptoeing on eggshells, constantly stressed about saying the wrong thing or making the wrong move. She learned to take a step away from the precarious tightrope act. He teased her about her lack of perspective and the way that she acted as if every day at work was a life-or-death situation. "How many hearts or watches stopped ticking today? Was anyone executed today for forgetting the client's name?" Luca's perspective made Enid realize that power and success in the auction house were fleeting. Tom Cat's dramatic departure or the fall of Liu-*jie* paled in comparison to the horrible and tragic stock exchange bombing.

Of course, it was not a complete bed of roses. There were many things about Luca that drove Enid crazy. He climbed into bed with dirty street clothes and shoes on after a long day in the office. And most frustrating of all, he seriously lacked ambition; he was content to be a white-collared salary earner living in a tiny studio in Kennedy Town. He rarely mentioned his work, did not network with clients or colleagues, and worked the shortest possible hours. He went to the office after her and always returned home before she did.

Enid could not understand how someone who graduated from the best universities in Europe and was so proficiently multilingual could be so averse to earning more money. Luca dismissed her queries and teased Enid about her obsession with success. "Cara mia, money can't buy happiness. And my iPhone tells the time better than one of the fancy watches you sell at work. Why should I work myself to the bone to buy things I don't need or want?" *Urgh*. Enid had to bite her tongue to stop herself from scolding him like a washerwoman. *He will never be able to understand how different the streets of Rome are from the alleys of Zhabei. What it takes to get ahead. He is lecturing me from the top of an ivory tower.*

Enid remained close to Angela and the rest of the Watches team, but their friendships remained constrained by the cutthroat auction "me first" environment. Everyone was occupied with saving his or her own skin. In the end, Angela actually benefitted from Liu-*jie's* departure. As acting head of the Beijing office, she was finally getting the recognition she deserved. It was left to Angela to pull the China clients and colleagues together. Now that she was given free rein without Liu-*jie* breathing down her neck, Angela showed her flair for building strong and lasting relationships. There were fewer client complaints, and the revolving door of junior employees slowed down to a standstill. Enid took Angela as proof that good things could happen to good people.

Only gentle Luca, so blasé about his own career prospects, had time to get drawn into hours and hours of discussion about Enid's future. It was drawing to the end of the season but according to Enid and Luca's extended analysis of Cockroach's commands, "Next Shanghai preview, you should take the 5 am flight so you don't waste an extra night of hotel" to the more subtle "I want you to start cataloging 30 watches a day," Enid's time in the Watch department would be extended. While this was some comfort after not having made the cut in Jewelry, Enid remained frustrated that she was not a permanent Rothesay's fixture. With no Head of Department in place and no headcount, Cockroach claimed that they were unable to confirm Enid as an administrator or trainee specialist even though they were desperately short-staffed.

It sounded like an excuse to her, and she wondered if it was due to Cockroach's dislike of her. She tried her best to push it to the back of her mind and shrug it off. *At least I made it to the next season. Maybe they can tell that I am not passionate about watches and the technical details bore me. I miss working with jewelry but more importantly, I want to plan ahead so I can budget and move out of that depressing tong lau. Granted, I don't spend much time there but whenever I go back for a fresh change of clothes to pick something up, that sour smell of chicken-flavored Doll noodles, bathroom bleach, and desperation trails after me like cheap air freshener.*

Luca asked her to move in with him. A mere couple of months had passed since they started dating, but they saw each other every day. Her reluctance was now an unspoken weight in the air, "Why are you making such a big deal about living together? We can save on rent and it would be a much nicer place for you. I have always lived with my girlfriends." Enid did not understand how he could be so cavalier about such an important commitment. It was a cultural gulf between them, and she used her parents as a flimsy excuse even though they never visited. *I don't want people thinking I am a cheap SPG*[42]. *Like one of those girls who act so whitewashed, especially the pretentious sort who hyphenate their last names after marriage and pretend that they prefer risotto over rice.* She blushed to think of her heavy pseudo-American accent on her first day at Rothesay's, when the closest she had ever been to the U.S. was watching every season of *Friends* and *Sex and the City*.

There was plenty of time to think about the state of her personal life now that the season was at an official close. Results including aftersales were tabulated and most importantly, bonuses were announced. The team received a measly token sum, but they

---

42 Sarong Party Girl. The subject of numerous jokes and sociology studies, the SPG seduces and entices the hapless Western man for money and a passport. In return, the man gets flattered by his fantasy of a docile exotic beauty. See Puccini's "Madame Butterfly."

were glad to hold onto their jobs. Florian and Cockroach had faces as black as thunder. This was supposed to be their big bang after ridding themselves of Tom Cat, but the celebratory fireworks turned out to be damp squibs. Management meetings were run like struggle sessions, and the dynamic duo was mercilessly grilled as to why they had no backup plan. All this was routine posturing by the higher-ups, there was no excuse and no exit route.

Enid shook her head in exasperation. *It is definitely normal to gear an auction towards the economic climate, but how could a human tragedy like this have been anticipated? It seems the more senior you are, the less likely you are to shoulder the blame.* Finally, management conceded to barrel over the shortfall in revenue to the next year. It was going to be an even tougher season ahead for the team. Enid was not looking forward to having her nose to the grindstone again.

One by one, the white letters were sent out. A mere 25% of the faces that surrounded her on the first day were all that remained. Enid did not miss the other graduate trainees; they had never been very inclusive of her with their old school network and bottle service bonding sessions. By now, Enid began to understand the method to the madness. By driving the interns to the bone and seeing their response to pressure cooker situations, they were separating the wheat from the chaff. The ones who were left behind were serious and driven about their work at the auction house. With each round of layoffs, Enid grew in confidence that she had what it took to get to the top, but it was definitely taking longer than expected!

Sigh, if I had taken up that HSBC training program, I would at least be a Premier Bank officer. I don't know why I am so enthralled by all this. My bank account is as depressing as my wardrobe. Enid struggled to make ends meet and had to borrow money from Luca to refill her travel card. She felt split between two separate worlds — the heady glamour and glitz of the auction world during the day and her miserable *tong lau* existence at night. It was a senseless addiction to the heady adrenalin rush of closing a consignment deal and the elevation she felt when an aloof VIP client personally consulted her on a bid. During those few moments, she basked in the glory of Rothesay's as if it were her own.

Of course, Enid was aware that she was not going to appear on the Who's Who list anytime soon, but it was so gratifying when her childhood friends or university mates asked about her work. Her jobs sounded so much more exciting and fulfilling than theirs. At least when she had to get coffee for someone it was for an eccentric tech billionaire or a fabulous style icon with over a million followers on Weibo, not some frumpy middle-aged office manager on a factory floor.

The yearly review was a rare delight; she had to hold herself back from skipping around the office. Even Florian complimented her on being a valued team worker! He said that he wished that he could offer her a permanent position. That was fine praise indeed. Enid felt like she was back in primary school with pigtails and a shiny gold star on her report card. There was no point dwelling on the fact that she was still a lackey without her own business card. *Surely when the department hits its target next season, a headcount will open up. Some of the colleagues from the other departments are starting to smile or nod at me when I pass them in the corridor.* It sounded trivial and much ado about nothing to Luca, but the recognition meant a great deal to Enid.

Enid's state of mind was reaching a gradual equilibrium despite the occasional crisis of confidence. Rothesay's office was closed for a whole fortnight, and over the Christmas break, Luca's mother was coming to Hong Kong for a month. Enid looked forward to this opportunity to get to know Luca's family better. As close as Enid and Luca were, she felt a barrier remained between them. He did not easily disclose vulnerability and, when prodded, he shrugged that he had no issues whatsoever. It sounded like he had the most idyllic childhood aside from the tragic death of his father when he was a teenager. Enid still did not know the full details of what had happened. She did not pursue it and contented herself with appreciating his positive and easy-go-lucky nature. Luca was a breath of fresh air — a world apart from her friends and colleagues who strategically deliberated on how to get ahead in every aspect of life.

It was not to say that Enid's relationship with Luca was making her lose sight of her objectives; just that it was no longer her sole focus. In her mind's eye, she still pictured herself as a lauded auctioneer on the podium or a world-record-breaking bidder nonchalantly raising her paddle. But with more time spent out of the office and more time wearing Converse than high heels, it appeared that Enid's resolve had shifted. The current focus of her fireball energy shifted toward charming Luca's mother, Marchesa. It was banal, but Enid believed that the way to cement her relationship with Luca was through his mother. Her very name connoted old world class and allure.

Enid took it as a good sign that Marchesa had the same name as one of her most coveted fashion brands. One of her many mental markers of success was to possess one of these beautifully embellished tulle Marchesa creations. Her dream was to get married in the same wedding gown that Blake Lively had in the Martha Stewart Weddings magazine. Luca laughed until he was out of breath and tomato-red in the face when Enid pronounced her name as "mah-cheese-ah" like a dairy product. It was perplexing that he was not as enthusiastic as Enid about the upcoming visit; he had not seen her since last Christmas and rarely mentioned her. He did not even want to pick her up from the airport! To Enid, that was the most basic show of care, and it struck her as out-of-character that Luca could not be bothered to make this minimal effort.

Enid finally managed to obtain Marchesa's full name and flight details because she was using the Rothesay's corporate discount to book a room at the Mandarin Oriental. She was pulling out all the stops. If she managed to gain Marchesa's approval, then... *Who knows what it could lead to!* (As usual, Enid was getting ahead of herself and full speed ahead on a flight of fancy.) She hummed to herself while matching gift-wrapping to the ribbons. She had pondered long and hard about what to get Marchesa for Christmas and finally decided on a Shanghai Tang shawl and an Aesop mandarin skincare set. It was not easy buying presents for someone she hardly knew, but she was happy with her final choice — the perfect combination of Western luxury and Chinese aesthetics.

To be honest, the question of what to get was not that difficult compared to her reservations about buying everything at full-priced retail! If she had known earlier that Marchesa was coming for Christmas, she would have bought the presents in the Summer Blowout Sale at Sogo. Enid smiled to herself, Luca was going to love his Nespresso machine. At 30% off, it was such a good deal, and it was going to stop him from frittering away his hard-earned dollars at Starbucks.

Chapter 9

APRON STRINGS

———————|| ||———————

"This is why I don't date foreigners; you are an unpaid 24-hour tour guide." Alison shook her head as Enid cradled the phone to her shoulder whilst frantically googling Michelin star restaurants in Hong Kong. Alison continued to chastise, "I wouldn't have made the effort to come out and meet you if I knew that all you were going to do was moan and whine about your boyfriend's mother. She isn't even your *lai lai*[43]. It don't mean a thing if you ain't got the ring, ya know. Why make such a big fuss?"

---

43 Cantonese for mother-in-law

Enid sighed. Even Luca had told her to not bother, but Enid could not shake her Confucian upbringing of respect and mindfulness to elders. She tried to come up with excuses for Marchesa Vittoria's rude and eccentric behavior, but there was simply no justification.

From the very first day that Vittoria arrived, Enid fervently wished that she had escaped home to Zhabei for the holidays. To start with, Marchesa was her TITLE! And Enid had been freely mispronouncing it like a supermarket Kraft product. *Luca could have warned me! But now I understand why he avoids any mention of her. He is such a kid, hoping that if he ignores the issues, they will disappear. Who has titles nowadays anyway? Didn't that go out with Marie Antoinette and the French revolution?* Fortunately, Enid brushed this over with the excuse that she was calling Marchesa by her title to be polite. Marchesa Vittoria made Enid feel coarse and common. If Vera made her feel miserable, it was nothing compared to Vittoria's snide and disparaging remarks. Now she finally understood why Luca was not fazed by the bitchiness and rivalry at Rothesay's, he had faced this kind of mean and belittling treatment on a daily basis since birth. Vittoria constantly compared him to his older brother, Michele, who lived in Paris and had a prestigious (hence, acceptable) career in the diplomatic corps. She mocked his job, "Working in a bank is crass enough, but you aren't even a penny-counting banker, you are a pencil pusher in an Asian back office."

Enid witnessed how non-confrontational Luca was and how desperately he tried to avoid any discord. Whilst she admired his equanimity, it made her cringe inside when he evaded Vittoria's barbs. *I, of all people, understand what it is like to grin and bear it, but he seriously needs to stand up to his mother and grow a backbone.* When Luca tried to describe all the cultural activities that Hong Kong had to offer, she curtly dismissed his efforts. "You aren't an intellectual, don't even try to pretend. What engaging activity can there possibly be in this post-colonial backwater?" Enid was completely dumbstruck by the level of acidic condescension. By comparison, Rupert Bosewell was an endearing teddy bear.

Every mealtime was a trial. It proved impossible to find a restaurant suited to Vittoria's dietary requirements, let alone for a special occasion like Christmas Eve. Enid thought the macrobiotic diet was pure insanity — she had never heard of it, despite Vittoria's claims that it balanced yin-yang and the elements of the body. It was strange that Vittoria would strictly follow a diet with its roots in Asian philosophy when she was so contemptuous of "The Orient," as if Mountbatten were still ruling India.

Her comments were venomous, "The barbaric way that THEY serve animals with their heads on. The eating habits of these

Chinese people sicken me, all that slurping and bone-crunching. Peasants. Communists."

Enid longed for the holidays to be over so she did not have to spend a minute longer than necessary with such a nasty and acrimonious woman. Luca tried to explain that Vittoria was not racist, "She hates everyone; you shouldn't feel like she is singling you out. She acts like a bigot to goad you into a reaction. Just ignore her. There is nothing she loves more than a melodramatic confrontation." This further infuriated Enid, and she lost her temper. "This is not a shruggie-type situation. Grow a pair! It's bad enough that I have to deal with prejudice at work, but nothing and no one is worse than your mother. Stop giving excuses for her! I deal with some very important clients, and they may be difficult but at least they have some respect for me. Your mother's antiquated hereditary title does not mean she is entitled to treat everyone like dog shit on her shoe."

Christmas was ruined. Vittoria sowed the seeds of discord wherever she went. With her around, there was no peace on earth or goodwill to men. The Christmas card scene of hugs and presents exchanged that Enid had naively envisioned was the moment that she finally snapped. Despite Enid's careful consideration and hard-earned dollars, Vittoria's reaction was, even for her, beyond belief.

"Anyone brought up properly would know that it is impolite to give a lady soap for a present," she pouted. "You should buy me something else." (Pause for effect, dramatic eye roll, and shake of the head.) "I shouldn't even bother to lecture you. What is the point? You simply don't have the right foundation. This is why it is called 'class structure' for a reason — you can't move upwards by association."

The sheer greed, utter rudeness, and viciousness were far more than Enid could endure. She could not bite her tongue and bluntly retorted, "In Chinese culture, which you love to disparage, we are polite — it is the thoughtfulness and the gesture of giving that matters. Oh, we certainly know our place, which is to be respectful to elders even if they do not deserve it!"

For once, Vittoria was at a loss for words. Enid immediately felt a pang of guilt for not controlling her temper. *But I can't stomach this reprehensible behavior. Why should I? I am not going to enable this bitchiness and I am not a wimp like Luca! Look at him — cowering in the corner — the Christmas tree has bigger balls!*

To his credit, Luca tried his ineffectual best to shield her, but Enid was conscious of her growing disdain. When he tried to comfort and hold her hand under the dinner table during yet another of Vittoria's vitriolic outbursts, she impatiently shook it away. *Holding his hand is like grasping a clammy rotten fish, limp in all senses of the word! His feeble lack of aggression is so revolting. Why did it take me so long to realize that I make all the decisions in the relationship? From what time he should leave for work to what brand of toilet paper we buy! Why am I the one busy making plans for the future and trying to come up with a savings scheme? I've always dated and needed an alpha male partner! A successful and dominant gentleman of course — not a stereotypical chauvinistic toothpick chewer like Pa. Luca is the antithesis of what I am looking for though. He's just so basic!*

What she had misinterpreted as a casual and non-committal attitude toward relationships boiled down to mommy issues. *I don't want to be anyone's knight in shining armor! It's supposed to be the other way round! How can I be with someone who is so defensive to the point that he can't be proactive about anything?* The sad truth was that Enid now knew deep down that the relationship could not last — *Imagine seeing Vittoria on a regular basis! Urgh, even if it was once a year at Christmas time. She would be grandmother to my children! Sure, they could inherit this pretentious fancy title, but I cannot bear to have children with the washed-out personality of Luca or the sociopath traits of his mother!*

New Year's Eve dinner was the final nail in the coffin. Enid painfully forfeited a deposit for the Italian restaurant at IFC, which was turned down with a haughty sneer. "Please, they probably serve ketchup on pasta! What sort of people eat at a restaurant in a shopping mall? The only Italian I would consider going to is Cipriani, and only if Arrigo is in town." Luca shrugged in response and sat back like a neutered puppy. Naturally, it was Vittoria's reciprocal membership that landed them a last-minute table at the hoity-toity Hong Kong Club.

Embarrassingly enough, Enid had nothing suitable to wear and spent an hour before dinner scrubbing away at the deodorant stains on her auction suit. She felt out of place in mourning colors, like a charity case or poor relative brought along to accompany the dowager on bathroom visits. The way that the waiters were especially courteous to her made her shackles rise, she could see the pity in their eyes. The scuff marks on her black shoes colored in with Sharpie pen must have been so obvious. Like a heat-seeking missile, Vittoria decided to make Enid even more uncomfortable. "Love this place. The only thing missing is the 'No Dogs or Chinese' rule from back in the days you could call a spade a spade, before all this nonsense about political correctness."

Without a word or backward glance, Enid got up and left the table. Running down the stairs, she blinked back hot tears of anger. Sadly, and as expected, she could not hear Luca running after her. She waited across in the park opposite for ten minutes to see if he would appear, checking her phone for messages but there was a complete and eloquent silence. For the rest of the night, Enid wandered around completely alone, finally reaching the harbor where extravagant countdown fireworks lit up the sky, and joyous revelers cheered in the start to a new year.

Luca's pathetic excuses that he could not leave his mother alone and that phone use was not allowed at the club failed to elicit any response from Enid. Her feelings for him were dead, past the point of resurrection.

Neither of them knew what to say to each other. There was no point in flogging a dead horse, but there was no way that this relationship could culminate in a swift and painless separation; they were bound together by the astronomical cost of Hong Kong real estate. Enid deeply regretted putting her name to the tenancy agreement; she could not afford to lose her deposit and she dreaded the prospect of another year in a cramped *tong lau* half the size of a *tai-tai's* closet.

On the very first workday back in January, Enid went in even earlier than usual. If you had told her half a year ago when she was still in the Jewelry Department that she would come to see the office as a sanctuary, she would have laughed out loud and dismissed you in complete disbelief. Now the office minefield provided respite for her clouded mind. Her distaste for Vittoria, her disenchantment with Luca, and her doubts over the direction of her personal life formed a tangled and confusing mess.

At work, it was clear where she stood — the bottom-most rung of the ladder, but at least every effort made resulted in some form of progress. *At least I have a permanent position in Watches! With Luca and his mother, I am fighting a losing battle with no reward in sight.* The problem with Enid was that she was an all-or-nothing person. It was not in her nature to hedge her bets or rest easy with any kind of uncertainty. Even all her daydreams, of which there were many, ended with the same focused outcome. *Wealth, security, and privilege. Is it too much to ask for?*

Enid popped open the Clorox wipes container and marveled at how much dust had accumulated on her desk after the long holiday. Housekeeping soothed her and put her thoughts in order. It was unbecomingly hasty, but she was no longer dwelling on Luca, she had already mentally moved on. Now, she was plotting and scheming her next move. She hummed as she used the wipes to clean each of the green leaves on the department's giant potted plant in the corner. It was muscle memory tasks like this that gave her satisfaction. Enid recalled the obvious pride on her mother's face whenever she tended to her orchid and money plants. *I guess I am my mother's daughter after all. But at least I am doing this in a fancy office and not on a tiny balcony of an affordable housing project.*

Enid was still bent over the pot wondering whether or not to run the wipes along the catalog bookshelves when someone tapped her on the shoulder. Enid turned to see a pair of the most beautiful heels, embellished with gold embroidery and small peacock feathers aloft a ridiculously high 5-inch platform. When she had admired them last week in the store window of Guiseppe Zanotti, she had wondered if anyone could carry them off, physically, and stylishly. "My desk next, please, I should be sitting there since it's the only one available."

The delicate manicured finger pointed in the direction of Florian's spartan room. Enid could not help but burst out laughing. *Oh dear, so this is the latest intern. This makes June look positively low maintenance. She thinks I am one of the maintenance staff.* Enid restrained the temptation to set her up in there, imagining Cockroach's reaction. Of course, it sort of made sense as Florian was scheduled to be in Geneva for the next couple of months. He would only be in Hong Kong during appraisal and sale time anyway.

But she did not have it in her to be a bully, she would leave it for Lara to put her in her place. "I am Enid, the graduate intern on rotation in Watches, are you the new intern?" At least Mimi had the courtesy to blush and grin, "Oopsie, my bad, now you know that I am not the sharpest tool in the shed." Enid took an immediate liking to Mimi's self-deprecating sense of humor and motioned with her head toward the table by the shelves. It was amusing to see the open dismay on Mimi's face, once she spied the roll-away table piled high with old proofs and the department's stash of snacks.

Now in her third season, Enid settled into the work of the auction house as cozily as a broken-in Tod's loafer. She patted herself on the back for the quick ease with which she settled into the routine of client appointments and Invitation to Consign marketing. Mimi tried her best to provide as much help as possible but behaved exactly as she described herself, slow on the uptake. Enid saw through the bimbo act though — Mimi was far too witty to be as thick as she claimed to be. Mimi was just lazy.

However, no one lost their temper with Mimi as she was extremely amiable and a good sport. She did not have the makings of a great, let alone a very mediocre, watch specialist. Horology 101 was one big yawn to her, and she had zero desire to comprehend why a sapphire jewel bearing was used. When Alison took an hour to explain how they were used to improve accuracy, movement longevity, reduce friction, and temperature instability, Mimi shrugged, and giggled, "Yeah, but I bet the manufacturers wouldn't bother if they didn't make the watch movements look so pretty."

It was a calculated vacuous air, cultivated by a lifetime of leisure and pampering since birth. Clients took an instant liking to her and it was not solely because her grandfather was the first importer of Swiss watches into Hong Kong. Mimi shared instant chemistry with everyone; she was an embodiment of the saying that "Men want to know her, and women want to be her."

She was utterly indifferent to her appeal and put it down to her ability to be able to chat to everyone about everything. It was such a pleasure to finally meet someone without airs from the upper echelons of the auction house world. Mimi treated everyone equally — case in point, her favorite lunch buddy was the security guard Ah Fai.

Enid, who was so insecure and careful about appearances could not help but admire Mimi. This mutual affection was helped by the knowledge that Mimi was not a contender in the race to win the graduate internship position. Mimi tried her best whenever she fancied making an effort and because she would have done anything for her friends, but it was obvious that she was there to pass the time and get a bit of work experience before she headed to manage the family's chain of retail and repair watch stores.

Interestingly, the direction of their auctions had now changed. Florian wanted to "educate" the Asian market. Even his loyal sidekick Cockroach could not conceal her irritation at his condescending attitude. It felt like he had read the same edition of *Dummies Guide To The Oriental* as Rupert Bosewell. Florian's aim was to have a higher value and more diverse sale, concentrating on vintage watches. As with jewelry auctions, watches were traditionally divided into vintage for Geneva, contemporary pieces for Hong Kong, with the New York saleroom straddling the two genres. The upcoming auction focused on vintage Rolex through the years, offering collectible timepieces from a classic World War I Officer's watch with hinged lugs to an extraordinary one-of-a-kind Daytona with diamond indices and a highly unusual beige-pink dial.

The two main consignors were from Italy, and neither had ever consigned with the Hong Kong saleroom. Their requests were out of the ordinary — it was not usual to have hotel room bookings and plane tickets dictated in a consignment contract. They even had a per diem spending allowance. For professional dealers selling millions of euros of watches, their nickel and dime calculations frustrated Cockroach to no end. Florian dedicated easy-going Mimi as their babysitter, who naturally spoke some conversational Italian after an Italian romance and a semester abroad in Florence studying art history.

It made Enid roll her eyes almost to the back of her head. Italians surrounded her everywhere, and all of them were unreasonably demanding. There was one week left before Vittoria's departure, and she was still avoiding Luca and his mother like the plague. *What is the point of investing myself further? He doesn't give me material or emotional support. No pasta, passion, or Prada! Total waste of time.*

Using the benchmarks of Cosmopolitan magazine surveys, she confirmed that the relationship was at breaking point — all the characteristics that she had originally thought of as endearing were now completely infuriating. Not even irritating — infuriating.

By now, Enid had talked the ear off Alison, so Mimi was subjected to the excruciating minutiae of Enid and Luca's relationship. Pre-Vittoria's arrival, during harmonious days, they had jointly signed a lease on a charming one-bedroom apartment with a roof terrace in Sai Ying Pun. Enid sighed; *I wish we could go back to when we were so positive about our future. Looking back, my worries then were ridiculous, if my breath smelt in the morning or I needed to hide my period pants. I didn't know what real relationship issues were until his mother came along!*

There were too many insurmountable hurdles. She avoided being alone with him, in case they were finally forced to discuss the enormous elephant(s) in the room. *I feel so trapped. If I had money, I could give him a hug, send him a break-up text, and unfollow him on Insta but I am stuck in this situation because I am poor, dirt poor. Vittoria would never treat me this way if I were a tycoon's daughter. Money gives options and opportunities, and I have neither.*

On the day of the move, Enid recruited Mimi to help so she did not have to be alone with Luca. Conversation was stilted and did not extend between a "Pass this," "Put that there," "Do you need help lifting that?" Mimi's immature way of supporting Enid was to egg on her passive-aggressive behavior. Not that Enid needed much encouragement; she rolled her eyes constantly and issued forth dramatic sighs when Luca consulted her on small household matters like where to put his socks or place the cutlery. She did not even bother to hide her expression of disdain while he moped around like a chastised puppy dog.

Admittedly, minor details sparked off feelings of regret, perhaps revealing that their relationship was not at a complete dead end. Tears smarted her eyes when she saw that the Christmas coffee machine had been given a place of pride on their tiny kitchen counter. In a moment of weakness, she thawed slightly, but when she hugged him and saw his immediate elation, she was even more put off than before. *Why can't he be a real man, stand up for himself and take what he wants? He is never going to get anywhere in life if he lets everyone walk all over him. Scared of everything and everyone — even me, Enid Ma Yi Nin, a nobody. I may be silly enough to be attracted to bad-boy types, but he seriously needs some personality!*

Enid began spending more and more time at work. At home it was cordial, but the comfortable happiness they had once enjoyed had completely vanished. Initially, it was so awkward to lie next to each other in bed, but after a while, it did not even matter when they accidentally brushed against each other or ended with a limb sprawled across each other in the middle of the night. They could even go for a meal together like casual acquaintances and chat about the mundane day-to-day, but there were no more plans to travel to Europe together, and their sex life was non-existent.

Work became a crutch to divert all Enid's attention. The business was changing. It was announced that premiums could face a further increase! Christine recalled once upon a time when the premiums had been a paltry 11%! Facing off against the low overheads of online dealing and even retail stores with their VIP loyalty discounts was already arduous. Not to mention the competition against other auction houses. *How is an inconsequential workhorse like me supposed to pitch it to the clients? The bosses are so removed from reality.* The auction houses were global behemoths bloated in their structure, costs, and assumptions. Everyone was cautious about the cross-exchange of information since the 2002 price-fixing fine, but the industry remained contained and incestuous — specialists, consignors, and clients went back and forth from one house to another in a game of musical chairs. Everyone knew everyone else's business and if you did not, you were out of touch and on your way out of the door.

The team worked hard to justify mounting seller's and the buyer's premium to watch clients, who argued that they could get better results selling online through Hodinkee, Weibo, or Chrono24. The strategic game plan of those high above was a multi-pronged approach — to increase the number of auctions per year from two to four, start specialized brick and mortar stores such as private sales jewelry boutiques or art galleries, as well as an online shop for clients seeking instant gratification.

Marketing became increasingly important as Rothesay's banked on its hundreds of years of trust and tradition. Grumbles ran like an undercurrent throughout the office. The ever-increasing workload was shouldered by the same number of hands-on staff. The watch department specialists were far worse off than others because of the increasingly absent Penny. Luckily for Alison and Lara, Enid and Mimi were there to help where they could. Penny was no longer as passionate and fulfilled by the watch world as she once was. She tried her best to avoid any meetings with management, even the crucial budget and interest pow-wows.

No one was jolted when Cockroach announced the impending arrival of a new team member. Everyone had been feeling for a while that the team was in need of stewardship since Florian split his time between Hong Kong and Geneva. Sadly, their first impressions of Little F (as he became known) were not positive. He shared the same initials as Florian but that was as far as the resemblance went. He was the diluted version of Florian, 100% Swiss-made through and through, but not at all in the best possible way. More Raymond Weil than Patek Philippe. Cocky but not confident, arrogant and assuming, Little F was as little as his nickname. He acted like a know-it-all, see-it-all overlord. If he had the usual good looks and charm of the typical auction house specialist, it might have saved him. Disastrously for him, Little F could not even command that kind of superficial respect. He was shorter than the average Asian, bow-legged, chubby, and balding with a pallid complexion. No custom-tailored suit could salvage his unimposing figure.

The final nail in his coffin was at his welcome dinner. Social situations were never the Cockroach's forte to start with, and she hosted an awkward dinner for the team and their partners. Conversation was even more stilted than the morning after Tom Cat's departure from Rothesay's. Enid had wisely declined to extend the invitation to Luca. It was the sequel of Steve Carrell's comedy *Dinner for Schmucks*. To her credit, the Cockroach tried her best to bolster the mood. Bottle after bottle of wine accompanied the oyster platters. Omnipresent concerns about budget and cost-cutting disappeared for the night.

Penny got blindingly drunk and divided her time between trying not to noticeably ugly-cry at the table and throwing up in the bathroom with helpful Alison holding back her hair. Naturally, Cockroach sat Mimi next to her, as she was constantly trying to curry favor with anyone from Hong Kong society. Just for laughs, Mimi ignored her point-blank and proceeded to flirt with Cockroach's husband. The rest of the team could not hide their feelings of schadenfreude as the poor weak-chinned, weak-willed man almost exploded with excitement from Mimi's exaggerated attention.

In the end, the dinner did achieve its purpose by magically building camaraderie in the department, but not in the way Cockroach intended. The dinner provided fodder for endless jokes in the trying weeks to come. The life and soul of the party was not Mimi, it was Little F's wife. Given his stand-offish behavior at work, everyone expected his wife to be cast from the same mold. In the office, he claimed to have met Som through a Swiss-Thai cultural exchange program. This sounded like too much of a made-up story and, unfortunately for Little F and his puffed-up dignity, he forgot to pre-brief Som on the exact details. She proceeded to enthrall the whole table with the salacious details of how they had met one night on Soi Cowboy[44.]

Everyone adored Som; she actually humanized Little F. They could have left dinner with newfound respect if he opened up and owned his past. Instead, he stewed away on the sidelines in equal measures of fury and dread as Som told anecdotes about her backpacking travels and how her life changed as she moved from Bangkok, Geneva, to Hong Kong. Som's imitations of Little F's family and objections to their marriage had the team crying with laughter. "They say

---

44 Patpong's most notorious street of strip bars.

don't marry lady boy; we are respected bur-
ghers family"..."They are *choie farang*[45], they
believe everybody from Thailand is lady boy
or drug dealer so at wedding, I ask all my
nóng[46] to wear seksi sequins, red lipstick, and
put talcum powder everywhere."

No one understood how someone as
vibrant and captivating as Som could have
fallen for Little F, but she soon cleared up the
unspoken question with refreshing honesty,
"Bangkok I is broke and difficult to live off of
a day salary as property agent," she guffawed,
"easy to wear high heels on cobble of Geneva
than pothole of Patpong, *chai*." Som was not
a classic use 'em and lose 'em gold digger, it
was apparent that she had genuine affection
for him She treated him like a pet, pausing
now and then to affectionately ruffle his few
strands of hair or throw a piece of bread at
him to get his attention.

---

45 Slang for outdated/old fashioned Europeans

46 Form of address in Thailand for a younger person,
brother, or sister.

Enid sighed heavily to herself. *Even a mismatched couple like Little F and Som can work out a relationship balance. They have a mutual understanding, and it is obvious that he stood up for her with his family. God, it is pathetic that Little F has more nerve than Luca.* Try as she might to evaporate any thoughts of Luca, now and then, her thoughts were triggered on the status of their relationship.

Chapter 10

BITTER SWEET

————————|| ||————————

The next day, everyone was extremely hungover but, somehow, they managed to summon enough strength to crawl into work. They could not afford to miss a day in the office, and everyone was looking forward to seeing Francesco. Catalog photography was starting, and it was encouraging to see the sale forming shape. They were counting on Francesco to lighten the mood and make everyone smile. In all honesty, as unbearable and uncharismatic as Florian was, he was an excellent manager. For once, the consignment deadline was strictly adhered to. There was no last-minute panic about meeting the target number or deadline for sourcing. Enid and the rest of the team were actually able to finish work by seven in the evening every day, earlier than the rest of the office, with Little F leaving even earlier at five on the dot

The department was definitely more stable and running like Swiss clockwork, but the old intimacy had disappeared. Enid suspected that Penny was interviewing elsewhere as she came in a few mornings attired in charcoal black, from head to toe, which was definitely not Penny's usual hippy in heels style. *None of my business — I'm staying out of it. I am learning so much this season, and it is going to be me, me, me first. I am not going to end up a sad and forgettable nobody like Luca!* Although Lara was not the most understanding of colleagues, she truly appreciated Enid's thirst for learning and reciprocated.

This season, Enid began cataloging watches and removing straps. She learned to appreciate the micro-engineering precision of watches, how they served a purpose in comparison to the pure frivolity of jewelry. One of her favorite pieces was the Patek Philippe gilt and cloisonné solar-powered dome clock; it combined history, beauty, and practicality. Introduced at the Basel Fair in 1953, the Pendulette Solaire harnessed light energy to power a mechanical manual winding movement. It was exquisite with polychrome enamel and gold leaf-fired at least half a dozen times at around 800 degrees Celsius to create rich jewel-like colors.

Enid felt so honored when the marketing department picked her to hold the watches in the press release. Work was so demanding that she had almost forgotten how to bat her eyelashes and showcase her dimpled smile. Once upon a time, her good looks had been her primary asset but now at Rothesay's, she was forced to rely on her brains and build up her emotional intelligence. Nearly everyone was good-looking anyway, so if you were hoping to get by solely on looks, you would surely be disappointed. Like beautiful hothouse flowers, people like that did not last beyond a season, as many of Enid's fellow graduate trainees dismally learned.

Media coverage this season was unparalleled, and it made Enid proud to see the company logo on trams and billboards around Central. The marketing team was enjoying its most generous budget ever because of Rothesay's newly appointed Managing Director's background. As the former Editor-in-Chief of Tatler, Ian was bringing the old-world prestige of the auction houses into the 21st century; they even had social media ambassadors now! However, not everyone was convinced about this radical direction.

Many of the old guard sniffed at him, "Please, those high society wannabes featured on the pages of a glossy magazine are not the real buyers. Everyone with any real auction house experience knows social butterflies are just that — butterflies. They don't have the staying or purchasing power. There is a difference between the kind of person who voluntarily poses for a magazine and one who gets reluctantly tailed by the paparazzi." Influenced by the nose-in-the-air attitude toward social media mavens, Enid gradually left off updating her fantasy Instagram life; it had dwindled in the warm glow of romance. The reasons were twofold. Anyone from this new stage of her life would immediately spot the fakery, and she simply no longer had the time to make any effort. She was fully immersed in her real life and did not need any substitutes.

It was not a complete bed of roses. As sidekick to the specialists, Enid was responsible for one of the most tedious jobs. Carnet preparation was a mind-numbing exercise but essential for the duty-free import of watches into preview countries. Watch carnets were more challenging than jewelry ones as the categories were more repetitive. Ladies' or men's watches, metal bracelet or leather strap, gold-plated or 18k, white, yellow or rose gold, chronograph or calendar, it seemed relatively easy at first, but with 100 interchangeable lots traveling to various cities, it was easy to make mistakes. Happily, with Mimi around, the entire task was not left to Enid. She was in charge of paperwork whilst Mimi had the simple task of tagging each piece with the carnet number and supervising the exchange of alligator or crocodile straps for calf leather so as to abide by CITES regulations.

It was a quiet day in the office, and everyone was working diligently at their desks when Cockroach suddenly shrieked out Francesco's name. Even vapid Little F was startled into showing a reaction. Usually, she treated Francesco with great respect as he had worked at Rothesay's for fifteen years — plus, with a noble title on the back burner, she knew to tread carefully with him. Anyway, Francesco's work was of such high quality that he could shoot for any department or any auction house. Francesco sashayed to her room, stopping to pirouette before Cockroach swiftly shut the glass door. Everyone stared transfixed as the Cockroach gesticulated wildly and Francesco turned deathly pale; for once he seemed lost for words. It was dreadful: one of their star lots in the press release, a Richard Mille Flyback Chronograph Black Phantom, was all over Instagram.

Not known outside the industry but a standard practice in auction catalog shoots is to reuse part of a multiple image compilation. An image of the same reference, a similar strap, hands, or dial could be reworked to save time and money. A stellar photographer like Francesco would use an image over and over again from his stockpile but he would be careful to Photoshop in individual and identifying characteristics like the patina on a dial or the colored stitching on a customized strap. In this particular case, Francesco had reused the bezel of another Richard Mille RM011. It was picked up by watch obsessives, magnified, and blown out of proportion. The same incriminating piece of lint was spotted on a couple of RM011s in previous seasons. Armchair experts were having a geek field day. Post after post criticized Rothesay's and their competitors for false advertising and intentionally misrepresenting watches to clients.

Cockroach adored drama. Nothing gave her greater joy than an excuse to bitch slap someone with an iron fist in Florian's absence. Of course, she had known all along about this photography process. Her dictatorial productivity chart demanded forty completed timepieces shot per day — there was no conceivable way that this could be achieved without using an image archive. Now, she barked and frothed away at the mouth like a rabid dog. Lara and Alison grumbled that it was an annoying distraction from the detailed cataloging that the rest of the team was trying to complete. Little F chimed in to report that the Geneva office has "higher standards and they would not stoop to using archive images." For this — tiny input from a tiny man — he earned death stares, even from Cockroach.

The pantomime was a farce, and it was nothing new to Francesco. He shrugged, "No problem, I wasn't the decision-maker in the first place anyway. I won't use archives, but just so you know, you need to add an extra fortnight of work onto my schedule. I would never say no to earning more money, clocking in more hours, and spending more time with my sister-wives! 'Baby when you tear me to pieces, that's money, honey'[47]" With that stinging ode to Lady Gaga, Francesco shimmied and snapped his fingers to the beat, as Cockroach scurried to her office to pummel away at her keyboard. Presumably to report to Geneva the latest shambles in the Watch department that she had put to rights.

---

[47] As with all fabulous people of taste, Francesco loves all of Lady Gaga's hits and saved the lyrics for the right moments such as these lines from *Money Honey*.

"Thank God she is a business manager and not client-facing, that woman is so devoid of charm," Francesco muttered in a stage whisper. There was enough to do anyway, without brewing a tempest in a teacup. The marketing honchos of Rothesay's did not even deign it necessary to issue an official response to this social media furor. They wisely saw that it was only a matter of time before a more sensational controversy would come along.

When the news first broke that Little F was joining the team, everyone nursed high expectations. Coming from Switzerland and handpicked by Florian, everyone expected a horology aficionado. To everyone's overwhelming disappointment, his knowledge was as much as Enid's! He could not even take off a watch strap, and he was so hesitant about his technical skills that he adamantly refused to open the simplest of snap-ons, let alone screwed-case backs. His cataloging was a bad joke and made a complete mockery of his Senior Specialist title. Every bit of information that he was unable to access was marked with a glaring "xxx", an obvious signaler which cataloging was (in)completed by him. All his offending entries were devoid of any important identifying information such as caliber case, and movement numbers.

A short glance at his cataloging was enough to make anyone's blood boil. He appeared arrogantly oblivious to the fact that he was not pulling his weight, and unashamedly left his inadequate work for one of the junior staff to complete. Lara, Alison, and Penny were furious. Little F did not even have clients and could not speak any Asian languages. No one understood what the justification was for him to occupy a crucial headcount on an expensive expatriate salary. The atmosphere in the office was glacial as the pressure of work mounted. The team did not even bother to speak English anymore, so Little F was not kept in the loop about anything, not even the airport pick-up time for the Singapore preview.

This mess was not kept within the department, and it spread like an inkblot; everyone knew what was going on, particularly after the Singapore preview. At the airport, Rita from Jewelry and the security escorts were left alone with the Watch Baby for over an hour as Little F arrived late and then sauntered off for a free glass of champagne in the lounge.

It was sadly not the first — and most certainly not the last — of a series of errors, which plagued the season. Enid and Lara were blissfully unaware of the trouble ahead as they headed to Taipei for the preview. Enid was really looking forward to it even though they were staying at the notoriously haunted Grand Hyatt. For her, it was the best part of the previews, staying in ultra-lavish 5-star hotels with carpet so plush that she could not see her toes when her feet sank in. The toiletries, the huge bathtubs, the service with a smile. She promised herself that when she made it one day, she would only stay in 5-star hotels and would not need to steal the towels because she would have better ones waiting at home.

Time without moping Luca, too, this was practically a vacation! The country representative, Faye, was bubbly and energetic, the youngest daughter of one of Taiwan's billionaire shipping tycoons. A notorious party girl, she promised to take Enid out to enjoy the best of Taipei's nightlife. It was Enid's first time in Taipei, so she was really looking forward to this preview. Getting a visa with her P.R.C.[48] passport had not been easy, and she could not wait to make the most of her trip there.

The wait at the airport was long and tedious. It was such a comfort that they had an efficient local logistics company to ease them through customs and carnet checks. Xander was a great help to them, as he had been in

48 People's Republic of China.

the logistics business for over a decade. He knew the strict protocol required — Taiwan customs was as squeaky clean as the pristine white shoes of their uniform. The officials called out the carnet numbers one-by-one, and Lara brought the watches to Xander. It was confusing as the carnet numbers ran in a different sequence from the lot numbers, and the watches had multiple tags on them. Their confidence in Mimi's administrative skills was sadly misplaced. They did not even get past the second timepiece before Enid saw Lara turn ashen-faced, and Xander began to stutter away in confusion to the officers. "Oh my God, that stupid bimbo, she tagged the watches with the China carnet numbers!" Lara was furious beyond belief. "She spent all her bloody time flirting with Ah Fai instead of doing her work."

There was blind panic. Enid's immediate thought was of all the invited clients, would their Taiwanese preview have to be called off? Lara hissed, "It's going to be much,

much worse than that. Taiwanese customs can embargo our whole shipment, in which case, our carnets for the other cities will be a complete mess. If they keep the watches long enough, we will lose a quarter of the value of our auction! How can this shit storm be happening to us? This whole season has been a complete clusterfuck!"

It took hours of Xander appealing for clemency as well as a prolonged lunch break before the officers were placated enough to accept a compromise. They were given the choice of retagging the watches immediately or leaving Taiwan with the watches and canceling the preview.

As much as Lara was a hard taskmaster and a complete pest when it came to getting what she wanted, Enid had to applaud her swift presence of mind. She always got the job done, no matter what. For the next five hours, Enid and Lara focused fully on retagging the watches with the correct carnet numbers and triple-checking that everything was right.

They did not even pause to let Cockroach or Florian know what had happened. VIP private viewings had to be canceled that day, but it was not as considerable a disaster as it could have been.

Clearly, Taiwanese customs had only accepted the corrected carnet shipment because of Xander's groveling pleas. In the two decades that Rothesay's had organized previews in Taiwan, this was the first time that such a simple but terrible blunder had been made. Enid cringed when she heard Lara shrieking down the phone at the hapless Mimi. *Ouch! Definitely not getting on the wrong side of Lara, another person to be wary of! Soooo unnecessary to call Mimi a worthless piece of shit. Lara may hate Cockroach, but she sounds exactly like her. I am so glad that Mimi isn't looking for a permanent position at Rothesay's...*

She deserves better than this, well, and so do I. I am glad Mimi has options. What a bed of roses it must be to be her. No struggle with paying the rent. No 'treating' myself to a taxi or a sandwich for lunch.

Enid's eyes stung from squinting at the small tags, and her shoulders hurt from tensing up at the desk. Traveling with Lara was no walk in the park. She could be so cold and abrasive but in a situation like this, Enid was extremely grateful to have such a sharp and capable leader by her side. By the time they arrived at the hotel and put the Baby in the safe, it was past midnight. Plans to go out with Faye were unquestionably shelved. Tomorrow would be another long and taxing day. Starting at sunrise, they needed to set up the display cases. It would not look well for Watches if Vera got wind of yet another fiasco and example of gross mismanagement. At Rothesay's, everyone was always looking for any opportunity to swallow up someone else's clients or business. Whatever feelings of apathy or distaste the Watches team had for each other, the team would always pull through together. This was Rothesay's after all; no individual would ever be bigger than the institution. Sister-wives, as Francesco had affectionately named them, bound together for better or worse.

Client after client sauntered in through the doors of the preview room. It was a resounding success with over two dozen absentee and telephone bids filed. Half the lots they brought were now spoken for, Enid was so glad that they had managed to override their customs trouble. She saw how important it was to have a country representative on the department's side. Faye enjoyed spending time with Enid, so she took any opportunity to visit the watch department's display and invariably bringing along her entourage of clients.

Although Faye was just in her mid-twenties, Enid could easily see how she had earned herself such a position of responsibility. She was utterly at ease with older clients of her parents and grandparents' generation, and she brought in a whole new set of hipster clients that eschewed the millennial rejection of material goods. Faye's set believed in the adage "less is more," but their interpretation was to possess only the very finest and highest quality. Bids were placed on limited edition timepieces like the Greubel Forsey Double Tourbillon and even vintage pocket watches that her friends stylishly wore around their necks as unique pendants.

What Enid liked best about Faye was how incredibly relaxed she was. She made the whole job seem effortless. And she did it all in hotel slippers. That morning, she had tottered in wearing the latest must-have Givenchy heeled sandals with the braided leather ankle strap. By lunchtime, she was shuffling around in hotel slippers several sizes too large for her. Only Faye could carry that look off with such aplomb — an Altuzzara Audrey belted and striped midi-dress channeling the 80s corporate look coupled with Grand Hyatt monogrammed terry cloth slippers. A stellar family background meant that she could get away with anything, but Enid realized it was not arrogance that bolstered Faye, it was a remarkable confidence in her own brains, charm, and looks. She played the cheeky innocent to the older clients and projected a nonchalant "It Girl" vibe to her peers.

On the last night, they went from club to club, table to table, Enid could not even keep track of where they were. She vaguely remembered that they started the night out at Omni and, somewhere in the middle, they sat at the table of super VIP celebrity club owner, David Tuo. Lara pleaded exhaustion and disappeared after the first karaoke session.

Enid was shocked to see Faye whip out her black Centurion card on nearly every occasion. She paid for everyone — even when they sat at a table with some acquaintances for less than twenty minutes and drank only bottled water. It was at Shilin Night Market when they stopped for a supper of stinky bean curd that they finally managed to intimately chat.

The alcohol unlocked Enid's tongue, "Faye, I feel so guilty. I would never be able to host you like this in Hong Kong, let alone in Zhabei. You are really kind to bring me out. I have never, ever had a night out like this. I feel like a celebrity! Thank you so much!" Enid could see how touched Faye was by her sincerity and honesty, but, as close as they were, she knew deep down that that her friendship with Faye could never be as strong as the bond between her and Angela — their worlds were too different and disconnected.

Faye gave a long and drawn-out sigh, "I am only telling you this because no one will ever believe you if you betrayed me and broadcasted it. My father does not give me a single dollar in cash so he can control me. Rothesay's salary goes straight into a joint account that I share with my mother. I pay for other people's bills so that I can get cash back. Otherwise, I would not even have the 50 cents to pay this *chou doufu* street vendor!"

The floodgates opened; Faye divulged how her parents relentlessly controlled her. They were obsessed with their image of an ideal family and, of course, a perfect daughter. When she was seven, she was sent away to Canyon Ranch in Arizona to lose her baby fat. It was a dismal failure. Homesick and the youngest patient there, the nanny who accompanied her took pity and consoled her with mountains of See's Candies. Frustrated, Faye's parents continued to wage war against her undisciplined growing body. Until today, Faye was required to weigh herself every morning under her mother's strict supervision, "if they could put me in a jar like a Bonsai Kitten, they would have."

The much-desired weight loss finally came much later during the one and only time that Faye decided to assert her independence. In a brave act of teenage rebellion, she insisted on reading fashion design instead of economics. Her parents reacted by cutting her off completely. In Michigan on a student visa, with no way of earning money, she survived by pawning family heirlooms to pay for school fees and sneaking into the catered halls for meals. With not enough money for basic necessities, she swiped toilet paper from unsuspecting friend's homes and used a five-finger discount for basic necessities.

In the end, she capitulated and chose economics as her major. This was her life. Her draconian parents made all the decisions for her, ranging from whom she should date, where she should work, and where she could go. "My mother doesn't even allow me to wear thongs — she says they're for sluts and strippers. I am 26-years-old, for heaven's sake, and I don't even choose my own underwear! They treat me like a puppet. Even my sister's pet poodle has more freedom than I do! I will get married to escape from that house!" Enid burst out laughing to think of the ultra-glamorous Mrs. Tsai conducting a compliance inspection of her daughter's underwear drawer.

Faye spoke without pause, "I know, it sounds crazy. My life seems like a dream to strangers. I don't know how long I can keep this up. I was hoping to find Mr. Right through this job but, so far, I have only met wannabes and boring Trustafarians who are as dependent on their parents as I am on mine. I guess my parents were right when they told me to pick one of their friend's sons, and that by now I know everyone that I am supposed to know. It probably sounds silly to you, because you are so independent, but I am nicely settled. I love this lifestyle. My parents have already warned me that they will cut me off as soon as I am married, so I need to find someone who can take care of me and loves me. My priority is in that order — cash is king. My parents constantly remind me that I am only a daughter, so I won't inherit anything and that, as it is, I am fortunate to have a no-limit credit card."

They chatted long into the night until Faye had to rush home in time for her morning weigh-in. Back at the hotel that night, Enid took great pleasure in her bubble bath. As usual, she used up every single grain of bath salt that the hotel supplied and packed away the remaining amenities. There was so much to digest. It was at Rothesay's that she had truly begun to know people like Mimi, June, and Faye. In the past, rose-colored impressions were built from gossip magazines or from seeing them stroll around Landmark armed with glossy full-to-the-brim shopping bags. At that time, her immediate thoughts had always been to enviously wonder what it would be like to be one of them. *Why are they picked to be so rich, pretty, and lucky while I stuck as plain old Ma Yi Nin? My entire month of groceries can't even buy one of their sandals, let alone a pair.*

Too many champagne cocktails dulled her mind and perhaps she would not feel like this tomorrow, but for now, Enid felt that they should be the ones envying her. Her parents always provided unstinting support, even when she had accepted this job in Hong Kong despite their reservations. She never, ever feared that their love was conditional. She was their only child, and they had never once wished for a son or told her that she was inadequate. And the same could be said of Luca and his unstinting affection. Enid felt momentary stirrings of guilt before her thoughts galloped ahead. *Whatever I make of myself, at least it is within my control. Every single decision is mine, so I only have myself to commiserate or congratulate! What is the point to have a fancy surname and wear the nicest clothes if I don't even get to choose what I wear or what I do*

Over a year had flown by since Enid began working at Rothesay's. She did not instantaneously belong to the upper echelons of society as she had once dreamed of. But she was having second thoughts, her interactions with them dissuaded rather than galvanized her. In the very beginning, she had unashamedly promised herself to be a social climber or a gold digger. However, when it boiled down to it, she was much too clear-headed and far too decent a character to stoop to such depths. Faye's honesty unveiled to her how stifling a life like that could be. She realized that the unhappiness had been around her all along, she had just been blinded by the sparkle of luxury.

Now, Enid's mind ran to a long list of clients who came to bid for the sake of it. She did not have to ponder long on this unfortunate list of who's-who. It was an addiction; a relentless need to spend more and more money to earn a feeling of empowerment. Not because they truly appreciated or understood what they were buying. Some of them were so frustrated with their lives that they desperately needed the seasonal attention and validation from the auction house. Buying something beautiful and shiny temporarily satiated feelings of unhappiness and inadequacy, but it was sugar-coating bitterness.

Chapter 11

AUCTION-PACKED ACTION

———————ǁ   ǁ———————

*W*hat a relief to get back to the muggy streets of Hong Kong! It was early May, but the weather had already turned humid and hot. Enid was glad that she did not have to work the final leg of the preview tour. It was in China and, although it would have been so heart-warming to see her parents, Enid recoiled from the relentless push of being on the road for a whole fortnight. Plus, she desperately needed to sort out her situation with Luca; it was becoming untenable.

When she came home from Taipei, the house was in a revolting mess. The place stank of weed, and there were filthy plates and piles of dirty laundry everywhere. It was even worse than living in a *tong lau* with a bunch of strangers. Using her sleuthing skills, Enid knew what he had been up to — his character was at maximum level cap in World of Warcraft. Luca's dark circles and look of exhaustion were definitely not from applying himself at the office.

The morning of the flight to Beijing, Enid came in early. She had a lot of work to catch up on after being away in Taipei. There were plans to go through the interest lists with Cockroach. Rothesay's database was a masterpiece, and it appealed to a tactician like Enid, who loved the precision and detail of it.

I wish I could find a husband through a database like this! That would be the ultimate database. Right now, it's only good for reviewing, not for sourcing.

Enid witnessed single colleagues like Rita using the system to research if prospective dates were Rothesay's-worthy (i.e., date-worthy). If they did not have a client account, they were unlikely to be of any account. Of course, the professed reason was to see if the prospective candidate shared the same passions with you. Hopefully, in 6-carat diamond rings.

Each time a client placed a bid or expressed interest in a particular item, it was logged on to the system. A savvy specialist would know how to feign intimate knowledge of the client's every want and desire. That was client service at its finest. The notes on the database helped Enid to remember that Cecil Mao loved to play bridge, collect classic cars, holiday in the South of France, and hid a weakness for erotic automaton pocket watches from his wife. It also divulged essential and practical information such as his payment history, which was why Cecil had not been called this season; a purchase in the previous New York auction had only been grudgingly settled after an unfriendly lawyer's notice.

It was interesting to learn how the filters worked. Yesterday before leaving work,

Cockroach showed Enid how to use different fields to glean clients based on geographical location and bidding appetite, as well as more specific level sorting to extract clients that generally bid on Vacheron Constantin watches, then specifically diamond timepieces above HKD 100,000, and, finally, Vacheron Constantin ladies timepieces with moon phase above HKD 100,000 in value. The permutations were countless, and Enid liked the idea of having options at her fingertips. *Perhaps I could become a business manager? If I take that route, it'll be easier to find a job outside the auction world. Being a specialist is restrictive, but it'll be even more restrictive to my search for a husband if I do not meet any clients face-to-face. I would be stuck in the office 24/7 and never meet anyone. Urgh! Imagine marrying a Rothesay's colleague! All flash and barely any cash.*

The sound of a drawer slamming shut interrupted Enid's reverie. She was taken aback; it was Cockroach at Penny's desk —

Cockroach was snooping or stealing! She rifled through Penny's drawers and emptied their contents in a pile on the desk. Before Enid could utter a word, Lara walked in and sniped straight to the offensive, "Did you get lost? Your desk is over there."

Cockroach blustered, "I knew Penny was too close to Tom and not to be trusted, she resigned yesterday. Deliberately abandoned us right before she was supposed to leave for the China preview. Security escorted her out of the building five minutes ago, and I am checking for anything incriminating to make sure that she didn't steal client lists or take the reserve prices with her."

Lara visibly reeled with shock. Although she and Penny had polar opposite personalities and counteracted, they still worked together as a unified partnership. Now it was a mess, the team would have to change plane tickets, notify the clients, and someone else would have to travel in her stead. Penny had clearly left with the maximum amount of disruption in mind. It was completely bewildering as it was not her style to burn bridges. Everyone was shocked. They had barely got over Mimi's mistake in the Taiwanese carnet and now this. The department really was in shambles. Cockroach commanded Enid without a please or thank you, "I have already spoken to Florian. You head to China and help Lara. You have a plane ticket at noon, so there is enough time for you to get your passport. We can't spare Alison now that we are down to two watch specialists." Cockroach did not even bother to take Little F into account or ask Enid for her acquiescence. Despite her rose-tinted Europhile glasses, even Cockroach realized that Little F was incapable and, even worse, had little desire to make himself capable.

Enid did not know whether to feel gratified that she could be counted on to help the department in such a sticky situation or to feel annoyed that they expected her to work the China previews without asking. As she climbed up the stairs to the apartment, she heard the sound of laughter through the door. *That is strange, Luca told me this morning that he is having training all this week and would be finishing work on time. But it's 10 am now! Maybe robbers have broken in! But the lock looks intact.* Enid quietly unlocked the door and crept softly in, comically prepared to use her handbag as a club. She did not know whether to laugh or cry. Luca was stretched out on the sofa, playing World of Warcraft and in-game voice chatting with some teenagers. Slouched in a disheveled, half-buttoned work shirt and boxer shorts with a joint between his lips. He was so engrossed with multitasking that he did not notice Enid come in until she switched the T.V. off.

Luca was so stoned that his first reaction was to whine about getting cut off mid-game. Then it slowly dawned on him that he should have been sitting at his desk at work instead of sitting stoned in his underwear. "Cara mia!

I can explain. I am taking a day off work, to relax, you know. Work has been so stressful lately."

Enid was furious, he was clearly lying. It was not solely because he was at the end of his joint that he could not make eye contact. Slowly but surely the dismal truth spilled out. Luca had lost his job before Christmas. Without the nerve to tell Vittoria or Enid, he pretended to go to work every day. So, every morning for the past two months, he dressed himself in a suit and tie, walked with Enid to the MTR station, only to return home on his own to pass the rest of the day. Sometimes he waited at the Starbucks around the corner so that Enid would think that he finished work after her.

Enid was at a loss for words. She could not find the words to express her fury, and whatever modicum of sympathy she had for him vanished into thin air. He was actually sobbing, which angered her even more. *It is so pathetic. I can't believe I wasted months of my life on this complete and utter loser! What a poor excuse for a man.* Enid coldly stared at him. She did not have the patience, energy, or desire to engage with him. At the back of her mind, she knew she was behaving immaturely, but she could not be bothered to hash it out. "There is nothing more to discuss. I don't want to talk to you. You are not worth the spit in my mouth. Our relationship is not worth saving. I am going to China for work; when I return, I will move out." She retrieved her passport and packed her bag, her whole body trembling with rage. In the living room, she could hear Luca gasping for breath through his torrent of tears. The upsetting scene did little to sway her on the way out of the front door.

The next fortnight passed by in a blur. Enid was more upset than she let on. She was so relieved to be traveling with Lara, who asked no questions and had little curiosity about anyone's personal life. Lara kept her busy with the preview set-up and a steady flow of clients. But each night Enid dissolved into a miserable state of tears and regret. She wailed to Angela and downed bottle after bottle of Tsingtao beer from 7-Eleven. The bedroom was a shimmering sea of bottletops and empty Calbee packets. The refrain ran on — he was not the kind of man that she imagined herself with... she had deliberately ignored all the warning signs... she knew that he was holding her back... but she still stayed on for months, all because of the rental contract. She had savings, she could have sucked it up, so on some deep-rooted subconscious level, she must be deeply in love with Luca. It did not make sense otherwise.

Angela tried to reason with her. "Aiyah, Enid, you cannot plan everything and expect life to fit into place like a jigsaw puzzle. Enjoy the relationship if he makes you happy. Not everyone has to have a purpose, and not every action has to be of use."

Enid knew that Angela was trying to introduce some rationality into her troubled state, but it was hard to think straight. She was running on an MSG/caffeine/alcohol high and not sleeping or eating properly. Enid had not even dared to let her parents know she was in China because they would be able to tell straightaway that something was wrong. Perhaps Angela was right, expectations of herself and others around her were too high.

There was a chance that her relationship with Luca could have been salvaged if he possessed the impetus to contact her. Radio silence. Not even a single red rose. That should have been the bare minimum, but there was not a single real or emoticon petal in sight. Nor telephone call, WhatsApp or Instagram messages, Facebook Messenger, or email. Enid checked every single app on her phone constantly, even paying the ridiculously expensive data-roaming bill. It was silly for that entire fifteen minutes when she was out of reach from the hotel's complimentary Wi-Fi signal. She was such an emotional train wreck that she could not take the risk. How could she be at ease deliberating between her comfort cravings of green tea mousse or banana milk Pocky at 7-Eleven if she feared missing his call? Over and over again, Enid recollected the scene of how completely shattered Luca looked when she walked out of the door.

By the last night of the preview, there were fewer tears and more sniffles, but Enid was still wallowing in her misery. Angela was visibly at the end of her tether, "If he were a real man and really in love with you, he would have apologized and called you. He could have flown here to Guangzhou and look for you. He can see our preview dates and venue on the Rothesay's website. What kind of man is this? Those stupid articles like the 'Five Stages of Relationship Grieving' that you keep reading are not for women like us! They are for female versions of Luca. Get it together, Enid! Always remember that your worst day is someone else's best day. There are so many girls on the streets of Sweden to

Singapore who would love to be you in your fake Chanel ballet flats."

At this cold splash of water, Enid laughed and laughed. Angela was truly a good friend. *Why should I allow myself to be swallowed up in the same quicksand of lethargy as Luca? I am better than this, I deserve more, and I WANT more!*

The apartment was empty and quiet when Enid returned home after locking away the Baby in the office safe. There was a note on the kitchen counter.

"Dear Enid,

I never meant to hurt you, but my situation spiraled out of control. I love, respect, and need you in my life but I am an undeserving mess. Please forgive me for running away, but I need to go back to Italy for a while to sort myself out.

P.S. Please, please don't move out, I can't bear to make you feel worse than I already have. I have settled the rent for the next three months."

There were even a couple of tear stains on the letter. Pure respite flooded through her veins. She did not have to face any immediate confrontation or conclusion. Now her priority could swing back to doing, well, this auction. If she were offered the permanent position, her decision to continue living with Luca would not be clouded by the financial incentive of having someone to split the bills with.

With no one to rush home to, Enid placed the sale first and foremost. She threw herself into work, and it was numbingly satisfying to have the distraction. At least whatever effort she put into her work, she was rewarded. With Luca and Vittoria, each effort had been rebutted or gone to waste. Finally culminating in a dead end. Now that the previews were over, the pressure was on. It was a double first for the Hong Kong market — a vintage-oriented auction, revolving around a single brand for its star lots. International interest was exceptional. The Bids Office had to bring in an extra staff member from the London saleroom dedicated to handling the Watch Department.

What made this season interesting was that it was not the usual array of clients. There were new bidders attracted by the press — watch geeks who usually traded with each other and shunned the commercialism of the auction house, as well as long-forgotten clients whose interest was reignited by the prospect of owning such rare timepieces. It made Enid chuckle to see Little F's reaction to some of the clients. He had not been tutored by Edward's fashion insights, so he was noticeably shocked the first time that a nondescript VIP client, carrying a worn supermarket plastic bag, asked to view the top five lots.

The plastic bag was the year-round accessory of choice for the low-key affluent Asian male. It could contain anything from dim sum lunch leftovers to a USD 9,000 Vertu Signature Touch customized phone and wallet, weighed down with numerous black cards. The logo-ed plastic bags were disposable and interchangeable; they did not divulge anything about the incognito owner who insouciantly swung the rustling plastic around like a *tai-tai* with this season's exotic leather handbag.

Although Rolex was generally not viewed as the most prestigious or elegant of brands, they were highly regarded as one of the most reliable manufacturers. They were lauded for their technical complexity and innovation, from the anti-magnetic Milgauss to the 12,800 feet waterproof DeepSea. Enid enjoyed memorizing the various reference numbers and learning how to take the bracelet off so that she could check the serial number against the certificate. The head of watches from London explained, "You are either a Patek Philippe or a Rolex specialist. These are the big two, and if you want to be a specialist, you need to focus on either to make it your strength." Enid straightaway decided on Rolex. Their robustness appealed to her, and she genuinely felt that they were a wearable investment. She promised herself to start saving for one. Her eye was on a simple Air King with Domino's Pizza logo, which she would customize with a hand-stitched scarlet leather strap.

Florian was back in Hong Kong for the auction and visibly energized about standing at the rostrum. It promised to be a phenomenal sale, seats were so sought after that they were not allowing spectators without a paddle to be in the room. Anyone authorized to bid on the top lot had placed a sizeable deposit. A new practice, this initially created a furor and sparked off threats of boycotts from clients. Some clients even criticized it as being racist as the HKD 1,000,000 deposit was being launched for the first time in Hong Kong this season as if Asian clients could not be trusted to honor their paddle raises. This was actually true as the majority of clients who defaulted were Asians. It was an honest to goodness cultural misunderstanding. They believed auction bidding was akin to going into a luxury boutique, trying on something, and saying you would come back later. Country reps were left with the arduous task of explaining the bidding process. Some clients were so inexperienced and misguided from Hollywood movies that they were too terrorized to cough or blink in case the auctioneer mistook their actions for a bid.

To make matters more confusing, this was also the first time that the Irrevocable Bid was introduced in Asia. Denoted by the symbol "" in the catalogs, it effectively meant an irrevocable bidder had placed a secret bid on the lot, and if someone else were to bid above that, the irrevocable bidder would profit from the difference between the secret bid and the final winning price. Irrevocable Bids helped auction houses like Rothesay's and consignors, as it meant that the lots were guaranteed to sell. For clients not in the know, it added an additional layer of confusion to the opacity of auction house dealings. After all, the "" symbol had to be in place when the catalog went to print, which meant that the irrevocable bidder had the inside track on auction lots. It was a sure punt for the irrevocable bidder; he or she stood to make money if someone else bought the lot. Rothesay's and the consignor stood to benefit the most — they were guaranteed the reserve price, which was the minimum the lot would sell for, and backed up by the higher irrevocable bid undisclosed to the public.

It was confusing enough for the staff to wrap their heads around it, let alone for the clients to understand. Thankfully, only the top lot (the Royal Oyster as it became known) enjoyed the distinction of "". The only known example of the reference 2288 ever to exist, it was a custom order of the last Emperor of China. So legendary was this watch that people had doubted its very existence. It took all of Florian's wheeling and dealing to convince Giovanni Giorgi — G.G., the most notorious of Italian dealers — to part with the timepiece, as well as the Emperor's reclusive descendants quietly retired in La Jolla to come forth and testify to its provenance. Even Lara, Alison, and Mimi did not know the seller's terms, let alone who had placed the irrevocable bid. Cockroach and Florian kept the paperwork on a strictly need-to-know basis. The watch had not traveled to China for fear of it being seized as belonging to the people, but the Mainland Chinese private interest on it was tremendous.

All the European dealers and consignors arrived in Hong Kong the day before the auction. The mood was already slightly celebratory, even though the auction had not yet taken place. *I guess I would be pretty happy too if I were given 0% commission and an all-expenses-paid holiday to Hong Kong.* Enid had helped Cockroach to type up the contracts, so she knew that G.G. and another dealer, Ricci, were being granted unprecedented terms at Rothesay's. Florian had also provided comp rooms for seven other industry stalwarts. It was curious that he felt the need to when the auction was oversubscribed several times over. Many people were flying in for the auction despite not having been allocated a seat in the saleroom.

In the pre-auction meeting when the book was discussed, it looked optimistically like it would be a White Glove auction. The Bids Department had done a stellar job as usual. The top quarter of lots was covered several times over with confirmed absentee bids and telephone activity. The adrenalin amongst the team was palpable; now it was all up to Florian to bring them over the finish line with the maximum of flair and pizzazz. Enid imagined the outfit she would wear one day if she were standing up on the podium. Lady auctioneers were the most eye-catching in their power play dramatic outfits, but gentlemen had to be content with a brightly colored tie.

Being an auctioneer was not easy, even with an auction like this that was covered in the book. Florian would have to multi-task between the book, room, telephones, and Internet. In the event that bidding failed to hit the reserve price, the auctioneer had to do a quick mental calculation to see how much leeway he had to bring the hammer down. This was especially difficult in auctions like last season's when so many lots had failed to sell at reserve. A seasoned auctioneer like Florian could keep his cool, juggle the bids, and still keep a mental tab on the running total to ensure that the overall auction was sustainable.

When lot number 88 rolled around, the hall was perfectly silent. Enid was sitting next to Elena, the Swiss specialist, and she could hear the regular ticking of the F.P. Journe on her wrist. The catalog stated in no uncertain terms that the estimate was "in excess of USD 2 million." With ten serious and committed bidders, the set increments of 10% were completely disregarded. Enid sat transfixed as three enthusiastic room bidders shouted out sums in the millions against the more sedate specialists on the phone. Those active on the telephone bank held their paddles at half-mast to signify continued bidding participation. Elena had the most active and suspense-building paddle; she was on the phone with Rolex Museum. She was the one to watch. Anyone in horology circles knew how close she was to the curator, so it was widely expected for her to be on the phone with them.

Bidding shot sky-high, "HKD 19,616,0000; USD 2,500,000; SFr 2,469,000... HKD 31,386,000; USD 4,000,000; SFr 3,950,000. Multi-currencies were announced, hinting at the geographical origins of the interested bidders. The sum of money changing hands was astronomical. Enid had seen a great deal of money transacted during her year at Rothesay's, but nothing prepared her for this unmitigated display of wealth. Eventually, only two bidders were left standing. At USD 5,000,000, all previously known records for Rolex at auction were smashed.

Everyone waited with bated breath as each bid became a carefully considered decision. Florian tried to ease the situation by quipping, "It's only money. You can make it back, but you can't make another Royal Oyster." Nervous tension and laughter filled the room. He sank his voice to a whisper as the bidding stalled between Elena with Rolex Museum on the telephone and Ricci. Then, with a sudden firm shake of her head and an offer of "Going once, going twice" and a "Fair Warning," the hammer came down in Ricci's favor for USD 5,090,000.

Enid saw a split-second cloud of worry cross Florian's face before it dispersed into the perfect smile of a consummate showman. Applause erupted and echoed throughout the hall. Ricci sat there, thoroughly stunned, a static grin on his face. Enid was one of the many people clapping her hands together.

I don't get it. If he wanted to buy the Royal Oyster, why didn't he buy the watch directly from his buddy G.G. and not pay Rothesay's commission? She could see from the countenance on Lara and Alison's faces that the same thought crossed their minds.

The rest of the auction went smoothly, and it took another five hours before it drew to an end. It went wonderfully — 97% sold by lot and 90% sold by value, at a grand total value of USD 25,000,000. Comprising 232 lots, it was one of the smaller auctions in the department's history but the highest total value for any watch auction ever held in Asia. Collectors from over 56 countries across seven continents had participated, and the watch department could now claim to be the most popular online auction, having attracted over 500 online participants. Florian and Cockroach had finally proven that they were the winning team. Even Rupert Bosewell deemed the achievement worthy enough to stop by to congratulate the whole department as they were packing up for the night.

Lara, Alison, Enid, and Mimi toasted each other with Earl Grey Caviar Martinis at Quinary. It was far enough from the HKCC that colleagues and clients would not interrupt or overhear them. Enid and Alison could not help questioning the legitimacy of the Royal Oyster winning bid. Lara was straight-to-the-point as usual, "Have you two got *tofu* for brains? It's obvious that Florian and Ricci were trying to sucker-punch the Rolex Museum. World record high, my ass! Huh! They thought Elena being all buddy-buddy with the curator, Dr. Borer, would mean that she knew their maximum ceiling. Even without the irrevocable bid, G.G. was going to make a ton of money anyway. They were driving up the price for everyone's benefit — the auction house, the consignor, the irrevocable bidder. Well, nearly everyone, that is. Now Ricci is well and truly stuck with his hand in the cookie jar. He has to fork out

USD 5,090,000. Luckily, it is Ricci and not some duped innocent underbidder. Ricci knows the way this business works. Ricci has that kind of money to blow anyway, his family owns half of Cap Ferrat. He really could have bought the Royal Oyster privately. It doesn't add up, he obviously wasn't meant to win. He overshot his hand. Ricci doesn't want or need that kind of fame."

Mimi shrugged at Lara's monologue and blew at the airy foam on her cocktail.

"Seriously, why are we even discussing this? It is so over, and we have to deal with post-sale and payments tomorrow. Urgh! Why not enjoy tonight?" Mimi stuck her tongue out. "Check out that cute bartender over there!" she said, grinning and waved. "Lara! You are too obsessed with work!" Mimi nudged Lara when she started to protest. "They aren't paying you to think about work when you are out of the office. Stop behaving like you have a stick up your arse. YOLO!" Mimi laughed as we all started nodding our heads, visibly loosening up.

Trust Mimi to lighten the mood. Enid and Alison smiled fondly at her. *I am going to be so sad to see her go. Mimi is right, anyway. Why does it make a difference to us who buys the lot or where the money comes from? As long as we make our number, get our paychecks, and the bosses are happy.* Mimi asking the bartender for "shots that are sweet but punchy like us" was the last sober memory Enid had that night.

Chapter 12

GRIT IN THE OYSTER

———————ll   ll———————

The morning after the sale was unusually quiet. Enid expected Florian and Little F to strut around, crowing like roosters, fluffing their feathers to appear larger in stature and status. It was perplexing that they were nowhere to be seen. Cockroach was in her room with the door shut, attacking the keyboard as usual. She did not look as ecstatic as she should have been after such remarkable auction results. Enid and the rest of the team expected a hectic rush of clients for collections and payments, but it was a surprisingly manageable trickle as people came in one by one. There were not even any out-of-the-ordinary requests like strap changes or claims of inaccurate condition reports.

When Enid and Alison went downstairs to Starbucks to get a pre-lunch caffeine fix, they bumped into Carl. Wearing reflective aviators and his usual Jermyn Street bespoke suit, Carl attracted admiring stares from women around. Even here, he looked as hot as the coffee that the mesmerized and distracted women were scalding their tongues with. Until he took off his sunglasses and stood next to them. He looked worse than he stank and that was no easy feat. His eyes were bloodshot, and his breath stank like a stale ashtray.

"Did you come straight from Lan Kwai or Wanchai?" Alison teased.

"Gawd, don't speak so loudly! You're making my headache worse. I can't believe they don't know what a Green Eyes[49] is and

---

49 For those looking for caffeine jitters, this drink comprises regular drip coffee with three extra shots of espresso.

I am too fragile to explain it to the barista... Anyway, you would not be laughing at me if you two had bothered to show up last night. You missed an amazing party!"

It was the best party in the history of Rothesay's. From Rembrandtplein district to the Las Vegas strip, Carl the consummate party animal had seen and done it all. For him to be impressed, it must have really been something.

From his stumbling account, no expense had been spared — champagne trains of Dom Pérignon, bottles of Patrón Tequila, Macallan 18, basically everything on the bottle menu. And more interesting items which were off the menu, from Carl's description of the drinking companions and other substances. Table One at Dragon-i, of course, followed by a series of after-after parties, ending up at Florian's penthouse suite in the wee hours. Generously hosted by the Watch department. Except not everyone in the Watch department had been invited. It was no wonder that the Cockroach was fuming. Not only was the invitation not extended to her, Florian's loyal sidekick, the night's tab was a whopping USD 60,000.

Florian had invited all his dealer buddies and billed it as a client event, and the staff were deemed unworthy of an invitation. The sad truth was that everyone knew he would get away with it. With such spectacular results and as the only global head of watches, who could say no to him? *Those hotel rooms and that party could have paid for two years of salary, bonus included, if they were feeling generous. It is so obvious Florian really doesn't care about us underlings. I work like a dog and they don't even give me a permanent position, let alone a party invitation! There is apparently no headcount and budget, but they can spend USD 60,000 in one night on a stupid party. If anyone deserves to drown their sorrows, it's me!*

That afternoon, the office cleared out on the dot at five. They felt too demoralized and unappreciated to stay past normal working hours. Florian and Little F floated into the office in the late afternoon. Not a word was said. No "Congratulations" or "Thank you" or "Well done." Florian behaved like he had singlehandedly accomplished the auction. His arrogance led him to believe that he was a one-man band, circus ringmaster, and star act rolled into one. To add insult to injury, his air of entitlement encouraged his mini-me, Little F, to delude himself into thinking that the record results were also because of him. Only Cockroach and Carl knew the truth, but both of them knew which side their bread was buttered on. There was no need for them to rock the boat; as far as they were concerned, it was every man for himself.

Dinner at Causeway Bay was quiet and downbeat. To cheer everyone up, Mimi had secretly invited Penny. When Penny showed up, everyone realized how much they missed her. It was wonderful to see how carefree and lively she looked, she was glowing with happiness, and it was as if a weight had been lifted off her shoulders. And settled on her tummy...

"I have happy news to share if you haven't already noticed! Tom and I are expecting a baby! I could not stand to be in that toxic environment any longer, unbalancing my chakras, and I did not want people to judge us. In the last weeks before I left, I was even wearing black to look slimmer so that people wouldn't spot my growing tummy."

And then the second piece of good news was announced, "Tom has finally left Blake!" Enid was ecstatic for Penny.

The grand plan was to form a husband-and-wife team and start an online watch business once the six months of gardening leave[50] came to an end. With a set-up like that, they could be anywhere in the world,

---

50 Typical gardening leave for auction house specialists is six months unpaid and six months paid leave. A long amount of time but two seasons of auctions ensure that you are sufficiently out of the loop. It is possible to contest your right to earn a living during the six months unpaid leave, but no one typically complains after a half year paid holiday.

but they were settling on a farm in Bowen, Queensland. Listening to Penny wax lyrical about the benefits of raising a child in the country away from unhealthy influences and how cute lambs are, Enid felt a stab of envy. For the first time in weeks, Enid missed Luca. Out of sight and out of mind had been a relatively easy feat, which probably meant that she was not that into him. Having said that, out of all the men she had ever dated, he was the only one that she had ever imagined settling down and having babies with.

Dinner felt like the good old days. It was a shame that Tom could not join them, he was already in Australia scoping out farms. Enid could imagine flower child Penny milking cows and cuddling piglets, but she definitely could not imagine Tom driving a tractor, let alone shoveling manure. This was a man whose routine demands included a standing monthly Shanghainese pedicure appointment at Mandarin Barber and seating in row 1 for all his flights. The flights were Chairman's Flights, of course, flying in the middle of the day and frittering away valuable work hours. Any later and it would be inconvenient for a decent dinner reservation. From fine dining to farmhand, it was amazing what love could do to a person.

Back in the office, Enid felt flattered that Cockroach seemed to trust her and take her under her wing. On top of teaching Enid how to work the client system during the run-up to the auction, Cockroach asked her to take the minutes at the high-level post-auction meeting. Only management was typically allowed. *This must mean that they are going to offer me a permanent position if they trust me this much.* Until Cockroach popped her bubble, "Sit there in the corner — I want you to be invisible. The only sound I want to hear from you is the click of the keyboard! I would take the minutes myself, but my rheumatoid arthritis is flaring up again. You are the least gossipy of the team and you have the most to lose as a temp staff, so I am taking my chance with you." *Pop goes my bubble.*

Florian was every inch the Machiavellian manipulator. He astutely maintained the fine balance between toadying up to Jean-Pierre and unflinchingly standing his ground. Particularly when it came to his expense account and personal benefits. It was no wonder that the USD 60,000 party was glossed over. In comparison to what Florian was spending elsewhere, it was negligible. When Jean-Pierre questioned Florian if was really necessary to continue drawing Tom's expat salary package, as well as his own salary in Geneva, Florian brushed it aside. "Better to keep it in the budget for when we get a suitable candidate." But there was no way that Florian would ever vacate the seat now that he had maneuvered his way onto it.

Even more interesting was that the team's bonus was given as a lump sum and it was up to the Head of Department to portion it out. It was not fair, and what seemed even worse was that Little F's was earning a guaranteed bonus for his "hardship posting." *What a complete joke! How is it a hardship to vanish at five on the dot, leave cataloging incomplete with a mess of xxxx, and jet off every weekend to Boracay or Halong Bay? The unfairness of valuing expats over locals and men over women!* No wonder Rothesay's had been called out on Glassdoor so many times. Upper management had recently issued a press statement about the 50% disparity between male and female wages. "The disparity is due to senior management positions being held by men who have earned leadership positions. We plan to offer more management training opportunities to women." *I wonder if this high-level meeting constitutes a "training opportunity." The only women invited here are Cockroach and me, and we are here to take the minutes. No one is asking our opinion about anything.*

Enid was on the edge of her seat, waiting for the discussion to turn toward the department's expense account. How naïve she was. It did not even warrant a mention. The bosses were bigger picture people, and what interested them was the bottom line of the income statement. Despite not being invited to attend the festivities, Cockroach had come up with some creative accounting and written off the USD 60,000 as a mixture of team-building and marketing. But Enid could see that Florian was deliberating. He repeatedly brushed off imaginary specks of dust and adjusted his shirtsleeve so that the correct half-inch of cuff emerged from the suit jacket.

Sure enough, the aha moment came when Jean-Pierre asked if there were any issues anticipated with client payments. If this was a poker table, then Jean-Pierre was the mark. From her seat in the corner, Enid could see Cockroach secretly communicating to Florian by repeatedly pulling on her earring. The cards were in play and the duo laid out the unpalatable news that Ricci would be coughing up his USD 5,090,000 for the Royal Oyster in installments.

Jean-Pierre spluttered, "Why didn't you do your homework and weed out the deadbeats who couldn't afford to bid? This is why clients needed paddle authorization and deposits to bid on this lot!" The situation was best summed up in Jean-Pierre's words, "beyond ludicrous," as he punctuated his sentences with piercing thumps of his signet ring against the glass table. Ricci was offering staggered payment over two years or payment over a year, but with negotiation on the buyer's premium. As it was, they had taken in the Royal Oyster at 0% seller's premium. It was very astute to put the ball in Jean-Pierre's court; if they took the two-year payment period and Ricci defaulted, the onus would be on Jean-Pierre. If they took the cut in buyer's premium for a year, Jean-Pierre was the one to sanction the loss.

Jean-Pierre was too irate to notice that Cockroach had calculations at the ready to decide on the buyer's premium cut that Rothesay's was willing to take. It was so obvious that the dynamic duo had already come to some kind of agreement with Ricci, but they were going through the motions with Jean-Pierre. This was clearly not the first time this had happened — Enid could see it from Jean-Pierre's weary reaction and Gallic shrug.

The Royal Oyster was to remain in Rothesay's possession and legal agreements were to be drawn up. If Ricci defaulted, he would incur a life ban, and the lot would come under Rothesay's possession and be auctioned much later. Having recently achieved a world record high, it would be completely dead in the water if it became known that the buyer had defaulted. This was on a strictly need-to-know basis. In the meantime, press releases continued to laud the auction's magnificent results and the world record high of the Royal Oyster.

It seemed like everyone was getting what they wanted, but it did not sit so well with Enid. Nothing was illegal, but there was something fishy about all these machinations running beneath the glossy, pristine surface. Enid had always wanted to be an insider but now she felt drained and sullied to be party to these schemes. She knew that if she wanted to get ahead, she had to be as wily and scheming but right now, the idea of living on a remote farm like Penny and Tom seemed a more idyllic option.

Mimi was offered an administrator position, and Enid was finally asked to join the team as a junior specialist. It was a huge release to finally become a permanent staff member, but at the back of her mind, Enid knew that this was not the right course of action for her. The typical auction house career path led an administrator into a choice of business manager or specialist roles. Enid knew deep down that she was better suited to be a business manager. She honestly did not have the passion for watches that Lara or Alison had. *Will there be a headcount if I say I want to be an assistant business manager? And do I want to be in the nexus of evil with Florian and Cockroach jiggling and juggling figures? At least as a specialist, I have a higher chance of meeting a prospective husband.*

At the moment, Enid preferred the company of inanimate objects to live people. She should have been turning cartwheels down the hall and celebrating, but she was plagued by a general melancholia. Her parents tried to be happy when she broke the news to them, but their immediate response was "Hah? Yi Nin, I thought you were coming back to live with us. Your mother and I miss you very much. They are opening HSBC branches all over Shanghai now." Her career train was finally exiting the station, but it was the guilt express. This was compounded by blasts from the past, Ping and Jill, who had come to the preview. They had invited her out every day since then, trying to mend the rift between her and Luca, hoping to give unsolicited relationship advice. She did not want to attend a pity party in her honor, so she avoided them like the plague.

Surprisingly, there was not much of a celebration when the job offers were made. No one seemed to be in the mood and even Enid, who had wished so fervently for this day, was feeling downbeat. Mimi moaned, "I am so crap at organizing, and they offered me an administrator position. Should I accept it?" Mimi asked Enid as she bounced on her heels. "It is far more relaxing to work for my family, but I will be so lonely without my darling sister-wives!" Mimi's shoulders slumped as Enid rubbed her back sympathetically. "My parents will get to nag me at home and in the office! Urgh!" Mimi was so frustrated. "Plus, this job makes me sound so much more interesting, and I love giving out my business card to hot guys." At this, Enid giggled. "They don't get intimidated, and I ALWAYS get a call within 48 hours." Mimi winked as Enid kept giggling. Even Lara could not resist being amused by Mimi's first-world, rich kid problems. In this industry where everyone kept their cards close to their chest, Mimi was an anomaly, she was so authentic and entertaining.

Nearly all of the watches had been shipped out, and Ricci had remitted his first installment. It was generally agreed that the season was a tremendous success. Enid did not dare to breathe a word about the post-auction meeting, and they had the courtesy not to enquire. Attempts to start working on the mid-season auction were half-hearted. Lots that failed to make the cut for the higher value May auction were allocated to the upcoming online sale as Enid started cataloging. The workload was not overly strenuous with low-to-middling value lots, so they were able to keep to regular working hours. The cycle had begun all over again.

Chapter 13

I Spy

————————— ‖   ‖ —————————

Everyone was in the mood for summer — the weather was hotter, work was leisurely, tans were darker, and clothes were skimpier (by conservative Rothesay's standards, this meant no panty hose and three-piece suits). It was Enid's turn to do the frozen yogurt run for the team, and when she was leaving Red Mango, she noticed four missed calls. *Urgh, how annoying! I bet you it is someone changing their order again and adding extra toppings.* When Enid called the department's direct line back, Mimi's voice was so shrill with emotion that she could barely understand a word she was saying. After several requests for her to calm down, finally Enid understood what was going on. "The police are here, a whole squad of them showed up and cleared out Ah Fai's desk. He was arrested at American immigration when he landed at JFK airport."

Enid's first thought was of a list of items that Ah Fai could have stolen. After all, he was so close to Mimi, he was frequently in and out of their office. More often than he needed to be. *Oh God, what if he has stolen the Royal Oyster? The warehouse guys are so diligent about not letting anyone into the secure room. Please, please let it not be something that I signed out!* Her instinct for survival was so strong that Enid's first thought was saving her own skin, not Mimi's breakdown or Ah Fai's imprisonment. The toxic office environment ensured that Enid's immediate reaction was to make sure it was not her neck on the chopping block, and her second consideration was to think about what Ah Fai could have done wrong. There was no presumption of innocence whatsoever, only who was going to take the fall. Rothesay's had taught her how to master the blame game.

Enid sprinted back to the office in full survival mode. The frozen yogurt did not even have an opportunity to melt in the 39-degree heat wave. She did not want to have anything *tai chi*-ed onto her. The whole office was abuzz; everyone was out in the corridors, walking around and speaking in hushed voices. Was it rumor, fact, or conjecture? It sounded too strange to be true. Enid could barely get a word in edgewise — Mimi was hysterically crying, big fat tears rolling down her face, head down on the table. She knew that Ah Fai and Mimi were friendly but not that up-close-and-personal. Apparently, they were buddies with benefits. It was Mimi's walk on the wild side, seeing a man from the wrong side of the tracks, or, in this case, the other side of the harbor.

Trust Edward to have the scoop. He alleged that Ah Fai was a spy, but no one knew what mission this apparent spy had been on. Enid struggled to believe any of this. She thought of Ah Fai as the helpful security guard who accompanied them on preview trips and even assisted in holding viewing trays when they needed an extra hand. The more everyone discussed it, the more ludicrous and impossible it sounded. No one got any work done that day, and it was widely expected when Jean-Pierre called for an all-staff meeting the next morning.

The pointless meeting was one big yawn, as Jean-Pierre had nothing more to say than what was reported in the South China Morning Post and the Rothesay's official press statement. The principal purpose of the meeting was to caution everyone against gossiping, particularly to the press, and a stern reminder that violating confidentiality clauses on their non-disclosure employee agreements would result in termination without notice or severance. Enid felt everyone's eyes on their department. The close friendship between Mimi and Ah Fai had already been the focus of much office gossip before his arrest. Everyone was judging Mimi, who showed up at work disheveled with swollen and red eyes. Cockroach gently took her aside and asked her to take the week off. *Luckily, Mimi is from a Hong Kong Establishment family, otherwise, God knows what they would be saying about her. Imagine if it were me the police would probably have arrested me side-by-side with Ah Fai.*

Days went by before the police finally released the charges. Not that it revealed much "mishandling classified information." No one knew what it meant. After all, he was merely a security guard in an auction house. There were no state secrets or covert spy network here. The most secretive that they had to be was about reserve prices, which were typically at the low end of the estimate anyway. Eventually, all the talk petered out, as there was nothing left to fuel the fire. Everyone was getting busy setting the sale to "Ready" and putting finishing touches on condition reports.

Finally, Mimi came back to work. Ah Fai was a guest of the U.S. government on Rikers Island and not permitted any visitors except for his lawyer. What should have been a routine training session in the New York office was now a desperate nightmare. After too many sleepless nights, Mimi had been so desperate to find out information that she had caved in and contacted his family even though she had never met them. She even deliberated hiring Pinkerton's detective agency and Alan Dershowitz to represent Ah Fai, but everyone told her that it was the stupidest idea and not to get involved.

The US government alleged that Ah Fai was spying on an American multinational company, on behalf of the Chinese government, to find out which clients were money laundering, avoiding taxes, and receiving bribes. It sort of made sense. As one of the security team, Ah Fai's job was to hover in the background at previews and observe when clients were inspecting lots. Since he was not attached to a particular department, he had a general overview of the various auction interests.

Nevertheless, it seemed like tenuous evidence-getting. *Wasn't it better to hire a specialist or business manager as a spy? I am not being a snob, but how is a security guard going to have access to hard evidence like client bidding records and bank transfer receipts?* Enid questioned the feasibility of the case, and not just because she was automatically on Mimi's side. The allegations seemed so shaky, but the prosecutors had apparently found evidence of Ah Fai's spying. Raids on his home and desk at the office uncovered pages and pages of notes with clients' names, purchases, and even shipping information for purchased lots. They were written in a complex code that had taken a while to crack, which was why news of it was only surfacing now. The case against Ah Fai was building up beyond a shadow of reasonable doubt.

Matters escalated when the Chinese customs conducted raids on art handling companies in Beijing and Shanghai. The raids seized invoices and import documents, which declared how much clients had paid for their artworks. Now the pieces of the puzzle were coming together. Art handling companies typically did not question the value that clients put on incoming shipments; the onus was on the clients to declare genuine values and pay the duties. With usual duties amounting up to 35% on fine art, it was the norm to under-declare. A Gauguin was declared as a Polynesian portrait. Overnight, the art market went entirely quiet, and interest slowed to a standstill. People whispered that art handlers, shipping companies, clients, and staff could be subject to charges of smuggling, which carried a sentence of life imprisonment. Enid shuddered — she could not imagine herself, let alone any of her fancy-schmancy colleagues, stuck in a crowded prison cell in China.

Evidently, Ah Fai's arrest by the American authorities was warranted. God knows what other information he had amassed during his undercover stint. He must have been the one following the trail of cookie crumbs and confirming the Chinese government's suspicions about the shady art world. The crackdown sent a clear signal that corruption would not be tolerated. It was evident that the authorities were clamping down on art as a means of hiding and storing wealth, and, of course, auction houses as the elegant conduit. A few of Rothesay's top clients were forbidden from leaving China whilst under investigation. There were whispers of a witch-hunt, and it looked like choppy days ahead. Rothesay's management self-serving response was to count their blessings that this all had happened after the major May auction.

China was the fastest-growing art and antiques market, surpassing the rest of the world, and now things slowed to a standstill. The Head of Paintings, Cedric, was extremely stressed. As it was, he was losing his hair rapidly. The last hurrah attempt to camouflage his bare scalp with straggling strands greatly diminished his gravitas. It was made even worse when he disastrously decided to get hair plugs. The new Paintings Specialist, Ines, joked, "He should have taught those buggers a lesson and exterminated all of them. Now he has invited some random mourners who don't know how to behave at the funeral of the dead hair strands. They should be sitting quietly in the pew, but they are holding a carnival for the Festival of the Dead." The newly implanted hairs swerved crazily in all directions. Their department had all the time in the world to joke about Cedric's hair now that their department was silent as a tomb. No one was interested in buying or consigning at the moment.

The clampdown on imports had severe repercussions on the art market, and its rippling effect reached watches and jewelry. For starters, Chinese collectors were less keen to bring their art home, let alone consign in Asia if they were being spied on. Enid messaged Angela, but there was no reply as she was obviously tearing her hair out in doing damage control. Everyone thought the situation was catastrophic, but it was the tip of a colossal iceberg. The next development was met with disbelief and skepticism. An announcement that Rothesay's and its competitors would "fully co-operate with the authorities."

To the dismay of every client and employee, the management of every major auction house agreed to hand over all invoices involving Chinese citizens. Initially, Cockroach and the Watch department were unaffected as they assumed that the handover would constitute only invoices that matched shipping documents. The assumption that watches and jewelry would remain unaffected was foolishness and naivety in equal measures. After all, brands like Rolex and Patek Philippe were regarded as a better medium of exchange than traceable dollar bills.

The investigation escalated rapidly into a wide-ranging full-frontal attack. All invoices in the Shanghai and Beijing offices were handed over to the authorities. Decades of auction house secrecy and client confidentiality were completely violated. No wonder Angela had completely cut off contact and could not be reached. Enid prayed that she was not holed up in a prison cell somewhere being interrogated... or worse.

Working for a multinational behemoth like Rothesay's looked wonderful on LinkedIn and was a subtle way to show off that you did not actually have to do something as horrid as working for a living, but when the Mouton turned mouth-puckeringly sour, no amount of razzle-dazzle offered protection against the might of the Chinese government. All day long, the telephones rang nonstop as every Rothesay's employee fielded calls from irate clients demanding to know what was happening and if all records would be released to every government and tax department around the world.

As a low-ranking employee, Enid could not understand why management decided to contravene the most basic tenet of the auction house, that of discretion. Hundreds of years of opacity and anonymity had built an exclusive mystique around auction houses. Dealers and commercial galleries with price tags were typically sneered at and considered crass. It did not make sense for Rothesay's and its competitors to give all this up with one fell swoop.

Transparency had always been present, albeit to a certain extent; for example, the limit on cash payments. Enid herself had flatly refused a famous Malaysian client who offered to settle payment for his USD 1,000,000 Vacheron Constantin in cash. She was relieved that she had given an unequivocal refusal without consulting Cockroach when the news came out a few months later about his kleptocrat ties. Her gut instinct had told her that he was a shady person from a sunny place. The client's requisites of meeting incognito at small cafes and hotel lobbies had rightly made her feel uneasy.

How the lots were paid for also came under tight scrutiny. Bank account names had to match bidders' names, but that was basic anti-money laundering supervision. What was left to great ambiguity was where the lots ended up, who sold, bought, and sold them on later. Benjamin Wallace's famous book *Billionaire's Vinegar* exposed how wine was traded round and round in circles — OWCs[51] in an apparently untouched state, leading to counterfeiting and people not knowing exactly what they were flipping. Ah Fai's low-level spy work skimmed the surface because no in-depth espionage was required —

51 Original Wooden Case

everyone who was anyone already knew what was going on. It was as obvious as stating the fairy tale ending of every Korean romance drama.

Open season was declared in the historically tight-lipped art world, as protective armor assembled over years of illustrious existence was cast aside. Headliner after headliner filled the gossip tabloids and financial broadsheets. Everyone from an ordinary citizen or a government official found it impossible to comprehend the art market and its volubility, where prices could swing from thousands to millions over a short period of time. Insider capitulation or a whistle blower was required to scale the insurmountable barrier of knowledge — knowing the clients and knowing the art. For hundreds of years, Western auction houses had preserved their Chinese walls, but these were no longer impenetrable to the Chinese government.

Chapter 14

GETTING WOUND UP

———————|| ||———————

Mimi's distress was evident for all to see. She continued to drag herself into work, appearing in a daze with stringy, unwashed hair and saggy Lululemon yoga pants. Enid tried her best to be sympathetic, especially as Mimi had been so sweet during the Luca breakup, but it was getting on her nerves.

When Mimi moaned, "We would have had such an amaaaaazing life together. He showed me a whole new world, he was so real."

Enid's eyes rolled. *It was weeks since Ah Fai had been charged — they had not even been together in a real relationship! Besides,* Enid reasoned, *she can 24k gold facial away those worry lines and dry her tears on her hand-embroidered shatoosh. A relationship like that would never have worked out anyway, they have nothing in common. The novelty of slumming it wouldn't last long...*

The patience of the team was wearing thin. Mimi was in too much of a frazzled state to be meeting clients, which was her only forte. She could not be trusted to catalog or do any administrative work, particularly since the Taiwan carnet debacle. Cockroach and Lara rolled their eyes and looked askance when they passed her cubicle. As protective as they were, Enid could not blame them. Mimi passed hours with her chin on the table, doodling in the margins of condition reports instead of proofreading them.

Enid did not know whether she was being paranoid because of the heightened security measures at work, but she felt like she was being watched. She was very particular to the point of obsessive-compulsiveness about keeping her desk tidy (the mark of a good and precise watch specialist). On a few occasions, she had come in to see her work journal open at a random page and her computer in sleep mode, but she dismissed it as exhaustion from taking on Mimi's workload. Years of Confucian self-discipline in school meant that Enid had an infallible routine at the start and end of each workday. Powering off her computer and stacking her loupe and stationary neatly on top of her journal gave her a sense of order after whatever shenanigans transpired during the workday.

Her suspicious were confirmed when an irate client told her off about not replying to a valuation email. The emails were tracked as "Read," and the time log stated that they had been opened at 7:09 pm. Enid had definitely left work by then, and, as a junior member of staff, she did not have a Blackberry or out-of-network email access. It was old school, and she had seen it on cheesy detective shows but Enid had to know for sure. She plucked a few of hairs from her brush and laid them on her keyboard, in her drawers, and between the pages of the work journal. Sure enough, by the third day, they had been moved around.

Alison dismissed it as the office cleaner until Enid pointed out that the computer cables were sprouting dust balls the size of desert tumbleweeds. "It can only be Cockroach. There is no one else, it is certainly not me. Mimi can barely function, and you are not in the way of Lara's plans for total world domination." Enid did not know what to do, and she could not think of any reason why Cockroach needed to carry out surveillance on her. There was no way she could confront her. She begged Alison to find out from Lara or Cockroach directly.

It was no surprise when Mimi simply stopped showing up for work one day. A terse email sent to the whole department offered her resignation, with no reason or notice period given. Florian and Cockroach were not even individually addressed, and the email was sent to "Dear Watch Department." Mimi clearly had no intention of coming back to the grind at Rothesay's, or she would have paid the illusion of respect. When Lara criticized Mimi as "burning her bridges," even fence-sitting Alison came to her defense. Mimi did not need the job and they had not been kind to her. "Why does she need to be fake about it when we couldn't even be bothered to fake concern about her either? We have been bad friends when Mimi is clearly in the midst of an emotional breakdown."

Separately, Mimi sent Enid a WhatsApp message explaining that she had endured enough of the bullying at Rothesay's. Her parents were beyond distressed to see their darling daughter so heartbroken and despondent. Mimi and her mother were checking into the celebrated Ananda spa in the Himalayas for an Aryuvedic wellness program. Overlooking the Ganges River in a 100-year-old Maharaja's palace, it was hopefully the place for Mimi to recuperate. Enid missed Mimi's joy and vitality, but she knew that it was best for her to leave. In all honestly, Mimi's departure provided Enid with relief tinged with guilt, now that she would not have to feign sympathy.

In an effort to expand her friendship circle, Enid took to socializing with Ines from the Paintings department. Ines was French, and, with her hipster insouciance, did not fit in with the ritzy Hong Kong Second Generation crowd. *I feel blessed to have so many friends at work. I used to worry that no one would want to be friends with me because we don't have clubs and credit card limits in common, but Angela, Christine, Mimi, Ines, Edward, and Francesco are my real friends. I don't have to put on any airs or pretenses, and we have so much to talk about. They have such fierce individuality and strong characters. They aren't impressed by the cookie-cutter clique like I am!*

Ines delivered witty one-liners with a sardonic smile. Most people did not know how to react to her, so for the most part, they avoided her like limp supermarket sushi. Enid guessed that she must be extremely connected. When Jean-Pierre came back from France, he always brought back Ines' favorite Calisoon d'Aix bonbons from Léonard Parli. Enid was shocked when Ines casually referred to Jean Pierre as "Tonton J-P." When Enid asked if she missed France, Ines shrugged, "Boh! I don't need to. I can walk into Jöel Robouchon or the many Francophile La restaurant, La boutique, La Le La places around the world." And when asked if she had a boyfriend back home, Ines' hilarious reply was, "Love the accents, not the attitude; love the handbags, not their baggage."

That was precisely the way Enid felt about Luca, summed up in one word. Baggage. Thankfully, Jill and Ping's squirm-worthy invitations to meet were now few and far between. Luca had completely disappeared, and the next time she heard news about him was from an entirely unexpected source. A scatterbrained message from Mimi: "OMG!!! Luca is here for the yoga and mediation program. Bad reception. Love it here ▢ Coming back in 1 or 2 weeks, speak then. Xoxo." Enid was infuriated. *At least it sounds like Mimi is feeling much better. But WTF? He is beyond absurd. Why is he spending USD 1,000 a night in a spa? Instead of working on his Lotus position, he should be focusing on an employment position! What a loser!*

Enid was too practical and ambitious to stomach this kind of self-indulgent behavior. Her parents had brought her up to believe in hard work and conscientious effort. When she was younger and her classmates brought her to the temple to pray before exams, Enid's mother would rebuke her, "God helps those who help themselves! Instead of going with your friends to burn incense, you should spend your time more productively by studying."

Unless she found a housemate, there was no way she could afford to continue staying where she was. The apartment cost a great deal but if she got rid of the queen size bed and put in a partition, she could easily fit in a couple of twin beds. She asked all her friends, even Alison, although it would be too close for comfort to live and work together in the same department. *No takers...yet! I'll advertise on Craigslist, Asiaxpat, and hk.58 when Luca's share of the rent runs out. It is so typical that he left me hanging like this, and I can't plan ahead.* Enid's goodwill for Luca had completely evaporated. She increasingly drew sweeping comparisons between Luca and Little F. Underworked and underwhelming.

Enid's antagonism toward Little F was compounded by her financial situation. As she had finally become a permanent staff member after the auction, the trade-off was no bonus. *I should be content with job stability but my hard work at the auction literally does not pay. One thing that I can really learn from Little F — less work, more ME!* To be honest, the lack of pay out mattered more to her than the prospect of being under surveillance. She had nothing to hide anyway, so she gave up amateur sleuthing to find out who the perpetrator was.

With her imaginary bonus, she had planned on treating herself to a coveted Chanel 2.55 handbag. Everyone at work had one, it was *de rigueur*. Enid envied the way that they indifferently stuffed it into a crammed office drawer or hung it casually from its chain strap on a chair back. She particularly felt a pang of resentment when an undeserving owner negligently threw the revered caviar leather bag underneath her desk. Right now, all she could afford was 0.05 of a 2.55.

Her bank account was at an all-time low. Most of her savings had gone toward the plane ticket back home and presents for numerous relatives. It was so gratifying to see the look of delight on everyone's faces when Enid treated them to a seafood dinner or gave them a simple gift of imported chocolates. *What a wonderful long weekend at home! It is so liberating to wear what I want and behave naturally without stressing all the time about someone judging me. I feel so loved and appreciated.* The summer was drawing to a close and still no sign of Luca. Mimi had gone straight to the Hamptons from the Himalayas, so there was no update from that end.

The environment of the Watch department was now the same as, if not worse than, in Jewelry's. Everyone was grouchy and she felt like she was walking on eggshells, despite the summer lull. Although she was relieved to finally have a full-time job with benefits, Enid began dreading going into work every morning. *I don't know whether it is better to be abrasive like Lara or neutral like Alison. At least I know where I stand with Lara, but with Alison, it's so hard to get any response or opinion out of her. I don't know what she is thinking. She is like a bowl of white rice, bland and goes with anything! Still, at least she doesn't gossip or backstab people.*

Pressure was steadily building to have a December auction to match last season's USD 25,000,000 value. The team was a victim of its own success as the inches of press coverage and minutes of interviews translated into a deluge of appraisal meetings. Random walk-ins with antique market finds and clients with family heirlooms demanded unreasonable reserves. It was hard to explain to them that the Royal Oyster had a unique provenance and that the other vintage Rolex pieces in the auction had benefitted from its star appeal.

The new intern was of little help. At least Mimi had been helpful and charming. Her replacement, Simon, was aloof and uncommunicative. Everyone knew he was trouble when he wandered in on the first day of work at eleven in the morning, with a Starbucks cup in hand.

He looked like he had lost his way to Harvey Nichols, and when he arrogantly handed his empty disposable cup to Cockroach without a word, everyone could barely contain their laughter. Cockroach took it without reprisal, confirming everyone's suspicions that they had to tiptoe around this young princeling. The wrist candy (the latest Audemars Piguet Royal Oak Offshore Ceramic Diver), preppy Ivy League accent, and Church shoes were further corroboration.

Enid could not help being intimidated by Simon. He was good-looking and, despite Lara's dismissal of him, everyone acknowledged that he was passionate about watches and had a great deal of knowledge. If only he was a little less condescending to clients and colleagues. Naturally, he was absorbed into the Second Generation clique. Whenever there was work to be done, he could usually be found chatting to his latest giggly target in another department. *He's the kind of guy that I dreamt of meeting before I started working at Rothesay's. Now, I have zero interest. It's not because Simon is out of my league, I am sure I can hook him if I really want, but he is so superficial. Imagine bringing him home to Zhabei.*

Fortunately, after last season's excellent results, sourcing consignments came extremely easily. Although Paintings and Works of Art were still reeling from the backlash after the release of client information, more liquid and portable interests like watches and jewelry fared better than ever. A few private wealth management funds and banks asked Rothesay's to speak to their clients about collecting watches. Florian was sourcing in Europe, so everyone was taken aback when Cockroach committed the department to a talk on "Wearable Investments." Lara immediately excused herself as she was in China sourcing and Alison unfortunately had a date clash with a cousin's wedding. Asking Little F if he was willing to present was not a question for debate.

Surprisingly, Cockroach offered herself as a suitable candidate. That took guts. The specialists promptly went up in arms about her presenting herself as a horology expert. Lara took it upon herself to email Florian, citing the line-in-the-sand separation between specialists and business managers. As Lara vented in after-work drinks, "Cockroach is an expert in manipulating numbers and people, but how dare she presume that she can do our job?" Lara pounded the table and the wine glasses wobbled precariously, "The only thing she knows about watches are their prices. The only balance she knows is one on an Excel sheet, she wouldn't know where a wheel fits or functions in a watch movement. She wants to stick her feelers into everything. Next thing you know, she is going to ask to be Head of Department."

Alison and Enid kept quiet. If anyone was positioning himself or herself to be Head of Department, it was Lara. However, as caustic as Lara was, she honestly deserved it. She commanded everyone's respect and could marshal the troops when needed.

As expected, Florian decisively declined Cockroach's desire to speak to Coutt's VIP clients. He was too much of a stickler for the status quo. He put Enid's name forward, despite her lowly position as junior specialist. The emails bounced back and forth as Cockroach tirelessly argued in favor of herself and reasoned how disrespectful it would look to have Rothesay's represented by someone so subordinate on the totem pole. After the increasing trust of last season, Enid mistakenly believed that she had earned Cockroach's respect or, at the very least, faith in her capabilities. The email chain that she was CC-ed in contradicted that. Cockroach did not even bother to be cordial; it escalated into a personal attack.

One particular gem that sent Enid seething read, "Enid is incapable of representing Rothesay's to Coutts' clients. It would be fine if this were a talk in Mandarin to China Merchant's Bank, but she does not carry herself well, and her English is unrefined."

Cockroach was so antagonistic that even Florian, with his Swiss policy of neutrality, reached his limit. It was childish for a senior business manager in her 50s to launch such a caustic attack against a newly minted specialist. Florian calmly replied with a succinct command to end the furor, "Enid, proceed."

The day of the talk, the whole department, even Little F and Simon, wished Enid good luck and reassured her that she was going to put on a superb show. After all the fuss and unnecessary antagonism, it turned out that half of Coutts' twenty guests were Mainland Chinese whilst the others were from Hong Kong and Singapore. At Coutts' request, the talk was conducted in Mandarin to put all the clients at ease. Enid enjoyed herself and managed to ignore Cockroach staring daggers at her. One of the most satisfying aspects of her job was interacting with clients. People were easily drawn to Enid as she did not put on any airs and graces.

Enid knew that Cockroach would not swallow this easily. Particularly when the Public Relations Director at Coutts emailed Florian and Jean-Pierre to thank them for hosting such an engaging and informative talk. He was so impressed by Enid's performance that he even suggested spinning the talk into a global series that would include other categories such as ceramics and precious stones. Enid was over the moon, it served her well to be recognized by Management. The one aspect of auction houses that she liked was how small the teams were. Even though the workload increased exponentially when you had a slacker like Little F on your team, the plus side was that it was obvious who was a contributing team player and who was not.

Despite her naked ambition and pretensions at ruthlessness, Enid responded well to praise and petting. She worked even harder than ever, responding to the general appraisal emails and meeting with brand-new or walk-in clients. Thankfully, the other specialists were too busy making their own targets to resent her success. Enid helped this camaraderie by continuing to humbly behave like she was still a trainee specialist. She remained on hand for late-night cataloging sessions or to attend any appointments that the others did not want to prioritize.

Chapter 15

STRIKE ONE

—|| ||—

The yearly *Wristwatch Annual* is the bible for horology buffs. Glossy photographs accompanied by complete specifications and list prices. Enid took to studying it on her lunch break even though Simon teased her for being such a geek. She thought he was full of himself, but she could not help blushing and getting completely tongue-tied around him. A couple of times when he tried to be friendly and asked what her weekend plans were, she awkwardly stuttered. *Urgh! I'm soooo lame! I can't tell him I have no plans! Quick, Yi Nin, make up something fun and fabulous... it's so hard to concentrate when he is so good-looking, though. Those big brown*

*eyes, that toned body and debonair style —
oh, he could be in an ad for Theodent or Ralph
Lauren or Audemars Piguet...or Vilebrequin...
Mmmm. Wait! Did he just walk off? OMG, he
must think I am a freak!* After a while, Simon
stopped trying to flirt and make small talk.

Simon was better at cataloging than entering
in consignments and creating contracts, so it
was entirely left to Enid. She may have been
promoted to junior specialist in name, but in
reality, she was still the dogsbody, picking up
the work no one else wanted to do. *They will
definitely give Simon a specialist position if
he stays on, so why can't Cockroach hurry up
and find a real administrator? I'm sure she's
doing this on purpose to punish me.*

As Enid tagged contract numbers on
the watches, her mind bounced back and
forth between work and fantasy, envy and
longing. *His forearms are so tanned — is it
from taking his parent's boat out or from the
Sunday Morning Drive Club with clients? He
is the first one from this entire office to land*

an invitation to the Club! I wish I could be his plus-one. He must look so incredibly hot in that McLaren 12C Spider that he uses as his screensaver.

Enid was so distracted thinking about Simon that she had to retag the watches after she was finished. This was really not up to Enid's usual standard of work, but she casually shrugged it off. Management liked her, and she was now part of permanent staff. She was effectively working two roles, anyway, so she permitted herself some slack. Cockroach, on the other hand, was not so willing to go easy on Enid. She sent her a list of possible consignments from her husband's boss.

In all honesty, and it was not solely because she wanted to embarrass Cockroach, but the collection was a load of old junk that did not remotely qualify as auction-worthy. At less than USD 2,000 each in value, they were not worth cataloging and photographing, even for a mid-season online auction. They comprised thirty modified ETA movement wristwatches and antique shop pocket watches that had seen better days and deeper pockets. Enid rolled her eyes when she replied for the second time that she "DEFINITELY" did not want the consignment unless it was a group lot at No Reserve. It was nearly midnight when she shut down the computer and left the office.

As she walked up the two flights of stairs, there was a whiff of patchouli from Luca's Acqua di Parma aftershave. She steeled herself that it was not her overactive imagination, so she appeared calm and collected when they met face-to-face outside the front door. "Hey" and a watery smile. There was no attempt to hug or effort to touch from either of them. Enid frowned. *At least he's not presumptuous enough to let himself in. Thankfully, he didn't, or he would have been hurt to see all his belongings (and that Nespresso machine) packed up in boxes.*

Conversation was stilted but Enid began to feel stirrings of emotion sneaking up on her when she saw how attractive and relaxed he looked. *Is it physical chemistry, yearning for the familiar, true affection, or downright desperation?* Enid did not know what to feel, but for once, it was clear that Luca was leading the way.

"Enid, there is no easy way to say this. Over the past few months, I was back in Europe with my mother and brother. We spent a lot of time discussing our fractured family dynamic; we even went to therapy together. Afterward, I traveled around India alone, to spend time reflecting. I bumped into Mimi; I am sure she told you." He paused to take a sip of tea and cleared his throat. "As happy as we were at the beginning of our relationship, I realize that you think of me as inadequate. Much like how my mother and brother regard or, hopefully, used to regard me. But I don't believe I am inferior just because I am not as driven or scrupulous as any of you. I have to try and change their perception of me because they are my family. But for us, trying would be too much of a leap of faith."

At this point, tears were free-falling down Enid's cheeks. She had always held the upper hand and assumed that she would be the one to walk away from Luca. From the hurt in his measured words and his calm composure, she finally realized how cruelly and condescendingly she had treated him with snide remarks and bossy commands. Unperturbed by her quiet weeping, Luca continued with tears in his eyes as he stroked her hand. "We have had some wonderful moments together, but I don't think we are good for each other. We have passed the point where we can make each other into better versions of ourselves."

They spent the rest of the night chatting in bed, where Luca collapsed from jetlag. It was a very amicable break-up, and Enid would have expected nothing less from such a gentleman. The next morning, they ventured together to their neighborhood coffee shop for iced milk tea and Hong Kong-style French toast with peanut butter and condensed milk. Enid was full of regret that she was letting such a wonderful man slip through her fingers. She honestly wished that they could meet each other halfway. *Perhaps if I was less materialistic and practical, or if he was more of a go-getter. Sigh, here I am again, trying to transform him. He says transform, I say improve. But there is no wrong and right. It is true, we are from different worlds, and we will continue to head in polar opposite directions.* It was a swift conclusion to a whirlwind romance and dragged-out break-up.

Luca was moving to India to teach English. He had never willingly subscribed to city life or corporate culture, and now he was finally at ease with admitting that. Enid was genuinely happy that he finally knew what he wanted to do and what mattered to him most. She had never heard him so enthused before. He glowed when he spoke about the school in Baradapur village and his plans to volunteer at Charity Water to increase the number of clean water wells in the West Bengal region.

As solicitous as ever, Luca offered to crash at a friend's home, but Enid felt too guilty. After all, he was still paying the rent. Besides, it would take him only a couple of weeks to wind up his affairs in Hong Kong. This would be more than enough time for Enid to find a flatmate, plus she had enough savings to pay for more than a month of rent. No more tears and recriminations; they even made plans to meet up with Ping and Jill before Luca left. Over their casual breakfast, Enid was reminded of what was and could have been. Conversation flowed smoothly with no hidden agenda; they simply had a good time. As Luca accompanied her to the MTR station, she noticed that both of them walked slower than usual. It had been such a while since they enjoyed each other's company.

At the office, Enid struggled to keep her eyes open. In spite of an ache in her heart, she felt as if a burden had been lifted off her shoulders. *Single again! But I don't feel lonely. I am free to charter my course ahead! Strategize, strategize, strategize.* Unfortunately, she could not have chosen a worse day to show up to work with barely a wink of sleep. Everyone else was busy with appraisals, so she was helping the Marketing department with the overseas preview press releases.

The first email of the morning was a request from the Human Resources Department to report in immediately. There had been no interaction with the Human Resources Director, Julia, since the first day that she had arrived at Rothesay's. Enid perked up; it must be something big for them to call her in. *Maybe they are giving me a pay raise or added responsibilities since I am doing so well! If the pay rise doesn't stretch far enough to cover a handbag, maybe a pair of Roger Vivier shoes with the signature buckle.*

Enid was ruffled to see Cockroach sitting outside Julia's office. They nodded at each other coolly in greeting and made no attempt at conversation. Cockroach continued to wait outside when Enid was called in. It was unsettling to feel Cockroach's beady eyes trained on her. Julia began by warmly asking after Enid's welfare and if she was settling well into Hong Kong and the Watch department. Finally, she cut to the chase. "Enid, so far, you have an exemplary performance record. Feedback from clients and evaluations from colleagues praise you as confident, professional, and knowledgeable. The heads of each department that you have rotated in value your contribution and praise you as an enthusiastic team player."

Enid smiled in growing confidence. She had been feeling anxious, but now she felt some semblance of ease. Julia went on listing Enid's positive attributes, lulling her into a false sense of security. She was thrown off guard when Julia changed tack. "I was concerned when I received a formal complaint against you." Julia passed her the printed copy of an email that Enid had sent last night. "The watches are not suitable for auction. I DEFIANTLY do not want them."

Enid had to read it twice before she cottoned onto the word "DEFIANTLY." She was initially confused and then increasingly furious. It was hard to maintain her composure in front of Julia. "It's a typo — I truthfully meant to say 'definitely,' is this really what I am in trouble for? I was working until nearly midnight and I was exhausted!" Enid could tell that Julia was on her side and thought this was a pointless exercise. After all, it was not without justification that Cockroach had earned her nickname and atrocious reputation.

"I understand where you are coming from. Regrettably, you used capital letters. This is in black and white. Florian is in Geneva, and your direct supervisor firmly insists upon an official caution and an entry on your employee record. I am sorry, I have no choice." Julia paused and her brows furrowed with concern. "Please do not let this setback affect the good work that you are doing at Rothesay's; you are a valued employee." Enid nodded her head in response, trying to keep the tears of indignation welling up in her eyes.

I don't want to let Cockroach see me upset. She is obviously waiting outside so she can enjoy my distress. It is clear that Julia has sympathy for me, but the unfairness of it all! I don't want to shoot the messenger but isn't HR supposed to be looking after the employee's best interest or at the very least, neutral? Julia glanced through the glass door at Cockroach waiting expectantly outside. She shook her head with exasperation and softly told Enid to take as much time as needed to compose herself. Julia's kindness was enough to rouse Enid to her senses. *I am better than this. Why should I allow myself to be embroiled in petty politics? Cockroach would love for me to scream, make a scene in front of HR, or better still, resign.* Enid squared her shoulders and strode confidently out with a frozen smile and unhurried steps. Out of the corner of her eye, she saw Cockroach's look of stupefaction and suspicion.

Not an iota of work was done that day. Enid spent her time WhatsApp-ing her support network. Their wholehearted reaction of indignation on her behalf gave her strength to pass the rest of the day. As she was about to shut down her computer, Sean bounded over from the Marketing department to ask for the press release draft. The featured Patek Philippe 5002P had previously sold at their competitor, Thompson's, so Enid swiftly copy-pasted from their archive and marked it in bold with "***Placeholder from Thompson's. To be written by Alison***." Alison was better at writing descriptive technical essays, and Enid's usual role was to help with the research and translation into Chinese. Although Alison was tied up sourcing in Surabaya, a task like this would take her less than thirty minutes whilst it would take Enid a whole day. Enid wished she shared Alison's same easy flow of written language.

At five on the dot, she immediately vacated the office for (not so) happy hour drinks. Mimi offered swift poison and funding for a hit man, Francesco created hilarious memes, Ines sat in incensed judgment, Lara swore undying loyalty and protection. Despite the initial dramatic reaction, Enid was surprisingly calm. Cockroach's target practice was of little consequence; what mattered most to her was how her colleagues dropped everything to make sure she was fine. She would have done the same for them without question, and as she drank her fourth Bellini, she light-heartedly joked, "Hey, it's not too bad, at least you guys are buying me drinks."

It's been over a year since I started at Rothesay's. I am not going to let this setback bring me down, which is Cockroach's intention. She can't take away my permanent position, and I have more loyal friends at Rothesay's than she has in the whole of Hong Kong. Not bad for a little Miss Nobody from Zhabei. I have to keep looking over my shoulder, but at least I have friends to keep a watch out for me. Enid smiled at the good-natured faces around her and counted her blessings.

Chapter 16

COCKROACH BAIT

————————|| ||————————

"**H**e's either goddamn stupid or a goddamn great actor!!" Lara screamed out in exasperation at the catalog proofs. Alison, Simon, and Enid allowed themselves two minutes of amusement at Lara's apt description of Little F before turning back to proofreading. The three of them were checking case and movement numbers, the bold header text, and lot accompaniments. Since the Royal Oyster triumph, Little F was still strutting around like a rooster. His work ethic, like his personality, had sadly not improved in the least. XXXs were as common as vowels on his cataloging entries. The rest of the team had now settled into a tight and symbiotic relationship, but Little F seemed unperturbed by their disdain. He continued to leave on the dot at five every day, regardless of how much work needed to be finished.

Even imperturbable Simon, who tried to stay in his lane for fear of friendly fire, became involved in the cold war against Little F. Enid wondered if it was because he was desperately in love with Mimi and wanted a favorable report. Unsurprisingly, Mimi would not commit to an exclusive relationship with Simon. "I have the rest of my life to be with someone like him. Yawn. Why should I start now?" She clearly had not lost her taste for grittier men. Establishment men bored her, especially as she was now immersed in the family business or, to put it in her words, being nagged full-time by her parents and dragged part-time to the office.

Mimi wanted to move in with Enid but, as much as Enid adored her, she was not sure she could handle the drama after a long day at work. Plus, what if Mimi had one of her romantic entanglements? That would be awkward in a partitioned one-bedroom apartment. No, Enid firmly made up her mind; it was much better for Mimi to crash on her sofa whenever she needed to. Plus, Mimi was used to having an army of helpers picking up after her. Enid was devoted to Mimi but determined not to become her Girl Friday.

By process of elimination, Enid was sure that it was Cockroach who was rifling through her desk. No one else had a reason or a vendetta to pursue. It became a running joke; one day she came into work and there were a dozen Raid roach bait traps scattered around her desk. Ines and Francesco bubbled over with laughter, "We thought this was the best way to catch the culprit. To be honest, we expected to see her unconscious body collapsed on your desk this morning." It was moments like these that made Enid really love her job.

Increasingly, it was the people that made the difference to her day rather than the actual work itself. When Enid first started, she was so self-conscious that she had built an impenetrable force field of insecurity. Now that she was more relaxed and approachable, people were drawn to her amiable personality. Enid felt like a member of Rothesay's inner circle when she was invited to Rita's wedding she felt so honored! They had not had much interaction since Enid had left the Jewelry department, and Rita had quit as soon as she got engaged.

Edward nodded sagely, "Of course, darling, it's merely being practical to leave Rothesay's — her engagement ring was too heavy. She could barely lift her ring finger to type, and it was throwing off her catalog entries, all those typos."

Work itself was the same monotonous slog of cataloging and proofreading over and over again. Enid knew that she would never be a watch geek like the rest of the team. Perhaps even apathetic Little F liked watches more than she did. The pieces that attracted her most were still the enamel and gem-set bling-bling ones. As much as Enid tried to read *Revolution*, *Spiral*, *Hodinkee*, and the other watch publications, they sent her to sleep. Perfect bedtime reading. Lara and Alison rolled their eyes and nagged her to read up instead of relying on her looks, charm, and wit. By now, Enid was the go-to girl for any Mainland Chinese or European clients; she could switch fluently from dialect to textbook perfect language.

"You know, if you really applied yourself, you could even be an auctioneer. Your confidence and language skills are so valuable, but you are wasting them by being so complacent, sometimes you can be a bit of a doormat too!" Lara harshly chided Enid, but her words slid off like water off a duck's back. Enid wanted to coast along. Ever since she could remember, she had plotted, schemed, and worked her way upwards. She was exhausted mentally and emotionally after last year's failed relationship with Luca and the battle for her permanent position, she just wanted to give herself a much-needed break.

Enid knew that green-eyed colleagues remarked on her inappropriate behavior as she flirted with clients and played the sweet girl-next-door card. She dismissed them as being catty Rothesay's spinsters. *Jealous, dried-up prunes. Why can't I enjoy the empowerment of being single, attractive, and intelligent? I would never sleep with a client unless we were seriously dating! And I am not going to date unless it is going to be a long-term relationship. Who wouldn't want to do a Rita?* Enid was further motivated to move in the same social circles as clients after attending Rita's lavish wedding.

A grand affair at the Peninsula, eight hundred guests tucked into a delicious fusion menu of foie gras, braised abalone, and wagyu tartare. Edward closed his eyes in appreciation as he took a mouthful of the perfectly succulent lobster. "I am so delighted that I asked Rita to look after Pang-*tai*. I might even settle for this plate of lobster as my finder's fee." Rita's husband was a notorious mummy's boy first and foremost. When Pang-*tai* sanctioned the union by introducing Rita to her son, it was a mere matter of months before he put a ring on her finger. For Edward, it was win-win on all counts. He designed Rita's engagement ring and bridal jewelry gifts, and he was guaranteed to be their go-to jewelry designer for as long as the marriage (and hopefully much, much later, the alimony) lasted.

Rothesay's employment contract was strict about client-employee relationships. Gifts over USD 50 had to be declared, and these were put in a pool at the end of the year and raffled to colleagues. But all this was far from the actual practice. Enid was trying to get close to Mr. Tung because last Chinese New Year, he had given Lara and Alison USD 10,000 *hongbao* each! She knew of colleagues who became close to clients (not even the type of friends with benefits, either!) and traveled together on grand all-expenses-paid holidays to South Africa and Europe. For that kind of treatment, she was more than willing to play the role of court jester or unofficial aide-de-camp.

Now that Enid was single, newly confident, and eager to enjoy herself, she made full use of social opportunities in the Watch department. She went to every brand marketing event and accepted invitations to lunch, dinner, and charity fundraisers. No one objected as Enid kept up to speed with all her work obligations. Lara sarcastically joked, "Enid will go anywhere she's invited. Even to the opening of a handbag!"

Nevertheless, Enid did set some boundaries; she flat out refused to answer calls at all hours, whether business or personal. Once she was home, she switched off her mobile phone. She learned from Angela's example, giving out a personal number made clients feel like you were on call. She did not want to be someone's designated driver or shoulder to cry on unless he or she was a genuine friend. Despite applauding Angela's success as head of Beijing, Enid refused to be at everyone's beck and call.

The rest of the team did not mind Enid's rising popularity. Everyone concentrated on a niche market — Lara monopolized the ultra-high net worth collectors, Alison got along best with the watch geeks, Little F with the Eurotrash expat crowd, and Simon with anyone who was like him. Enid was happy to help with anyone and any task, from changing a quartz battery to meeting with a lonely old client who would waffle on for hours. Even Florian recognized her contributions, but it still did not deter Cockroach from searching for ammunition. "Why do you give out your personal phone number? Are you trying to steal Rothesay's client lists? Do you give them your personal email?"

Cockroach's efforts were fruitless, and her frustration was growing apparent. She took great pride in her ability to exterminate adversaries. So far, the noteworthy body count comprised one Deputy Head of Paintings and a Head of Watches, yet she still failed to eliminate a lowly junior specialist. Francesco took pleasure in needling her, yodeling Hall and Oates lyrics at the top of his lungs, "You're out of touch/I'm out of time/Oh oh oh oh," whenever she walked into the main room. If only these halcyon days could have lasted, but it was sadly not to be.

One afternoon, as Enid was putting together the group lots for photography, Cockroach dramatically scuttled out. Her voice was unusually low and dangerously soft, so everyone strained to hear. She behaved as if she were about to share a juicy secret with Enid, baiting and reeling her in slowly. "Enid, Legal received a letter from Thompson's about copyright infringement. It concerns a press release that you recently wrote for the Singapore preview. They cited two whole paragraphs copied from a catalog endnote that was published a year ago."

Enid's immediate reaction was to shrug it off. *This is another of Cockroach's ploys to intimidate and provoke me into making some sort of scene.* She shrugged her shoulders and blithely turned away, "Dunno what you are going on about."

Her blasé reaction sparked a spontaneous explosion. Cockroach turned redder than a stop sign, and she began waving a printed email about, "It's here, it's all here. In all my years at Rothesay's, I have never worked with such a scam artist. You stole someone else's work. In such a public way too. You put us all to shame. Even the cheap way you act with clients." Her voice raised several octaves as she continued to rant. "I am sure you and Ah Fai are colluding! You Mainland Chinese stick together. I am looking for evidence, and it's only a matter of time before I find it."

Shocked silence followed, and everyone stood still. No one knew how to react. Cockroach's dislike of Enid was apparent, but it had been no more so than her typical dislike of everyone. Now, this outburst cemented a personal full-frontal attack. *So, this is confirmation that Cockroach is the one who has been going through my drawers and computer. Why am I astonished? She is venomous. Now, I can turn the tables and report HER to HR.*

Alison grabbed the sheet of paper and turned carbon copy white, "It's your place holder that I edited. I emailed Sean directly and CC-ed you." Enid shook her head and Alison rushed over to check her laptop and clutched her stomach, "Oh my God, the lousy reception in Surabaya and the Rothesay's firewall. I can't believe it, that bloody email is still stuck in my Outbox."

What shambles! Cockroach was firmly entangled in the web of her accusations. Their voices must have been conspicuously raised because Enid could hear furtive whispers and see curious glances from various colleagues as they found excuses to walk past the Watch department. They had barely gained a semblance of normalcy since Tom Cat and Penny's departure, and now it was back to square one. Reticent Alison ended the stand-off; she called Julia and requested for an immediate appointment. Waiting outside the HR office, Enid felt like a chastised student about to see the headmaster. *What happens if I receive a second caution? I should have followed up with Sean about the press release instead of getting wasted on Mimi's tab at Sevva. This copied press release really isn't my fault, but I am sure Cockroach is going to find a way to tai chi it to me.*

Julia did not look as understanding this time round. She sighed audibly and chewed her pen as she took notes. Cockroach, Enid, and Alison went in one at a time. It took over an hour, and Enid's stomach was grumbling — she was starving. She would have given anything to take a break, have a Kit Kat, parachute out of Rothesay's. Her thoughts rambled on. *The severance package is better at HSBC than at Rothesay's. Everything I have done and have had to go through and here I am, at the edge of a precipice again. What right does Cockroach have to keep bringing me down? Who does she think she is to look down on me?* By the time it was Enid's turn to go in, she was anything but contrite. Now she was defiant, and it was not the result of an auto-correct.

"I am not going to apologize. I didn't do anything wrong. Everyone, from Florian to a random walk-in client, recognizes what a good job I am doing. How am I supposed to work when my supervisor has a vendetta against me? Every day it is open hunting season with a target on my back. Is it legal that she has been snooping through my stuff? She accused me of being a spy and she is prejudiced because I am from China. I think I should see an employment lawyer..."

Enid had not premeditated what to say; the words and tears flowed out in an unmeasured amount.

Enid's intense monologue finally petered out, but it was only because she ran out of politically correct criticisms to say about Cockroach before she descended into swear words. There was an awkward silence. Julia shuffled handwritten notes together; it was obvious she was deliberating over what to say. "I believe there is a lot to discuss and there may be structural changes required in the Watch department. However, Jean-Pierre is the one to communicate best to your team. We will reconvene at three; in the meantime, please head out to lunch." As usual, Julia was unwilling to stick her neck out for anyone. Non-committal as ever, she was so un-resourceful when it came to dealing with human problems.

Enid agonized. *Why don't they want me to go to my desk? Are they going to give me my marching orders today? God, I don't even have a housemate, and I was going to use my savings to pay for rent! What am I going to live off while job hunting?* She could barely swallow her noodles as she sat in the corner of Canteen. Her phone rang and rang with missed calls from Alison, Lara, and Ines, but she could not bear to hear any advice or sympathetic platitudes right now. She stirred the soup around and stared into the bowl despondently.

"Hey, it's not a crystal ball."

Enid looked up to see Ines' gap-toothed grin and promptly burst into another round of tears.

She was deeply touched that Ines had made the effort to find her. Although she liked Ines, their conversation had never delved deeper beyond jokes and complaints about life at Rothesay's.

Perhaps that was why it suddenly became easier to unburden herself to Ines. Enid sensed something of a kindred spirit. Ines was always on the fringes and never seemed to fit in. She shunned the Francophile crowd and stood out like a sore thumb with her wacky sense of humor and penchant for wearing grubby, off-white sports socks with all her outfits. What interested Enid was that Ines deliberately chose to be an outlier. She thought that it was perverse, the way that Ines swam against the current. If she were in Ines' shoes, she would be exultant in belonging and not acting like a rebel without a cause.

Ines admonished her. "It is all in your head, this desperate need to fit in to Hong Kong and Rothesay's. Hierarchy is what you build up in your head. You need to learn your Bourdieu. You yourself are inviting, legitimizing, and reproducing the status quo. Everyone can speak three languages, is good-looking, and comes from whatever they consider is a good family. You are so much more interesting because you aren't another Rothesay's stereotype! Don't ever let anyone think they are better than you because they were handed the advantages of money, education, and exposure. People who earn their status based on their own merit are the ones who should be looked up to. You are selling yourself short."

Chapter 17

DECISIONS, DECISIONS

—————|| ||—————

E asy for her to say, speaking from high-above and looking down on us normal people like a sociology project. Enid struggled to keep Ines' well-meaning advice in mind and keep a neutral expression on her face as she took a seat in the conference room. Unfortunately, she was opposite Cockroach and had to avoid eye contact by staring at her ridiculous PVC outfit. The ensemble was undoubtedly by some *avant-garde* designer, but it looked exactly like a full Hefty garbage bag.

There was radio silence as Julia, Cockroach, Alison, and Enid waited for Jean-Pierre to show up. After twenty long drawn-out minutes, Jean-Pierre arrived. It felt like a scene from *The Apprentice*. He did not look amused. He silently removed his spectacles and massaged the red marks on the bridge of his nose. Looking around the table, he rapped his signet ring, signaling that he was about to speak.

"The Watch department. What can I say to you? Once again, we have a problem. Why is it that the lowest-earning department gives me the most trouble? Regardless of if you have been here at Rothesay's two decades or less than two years, we expect a certain level of decorum and professional behavior from our employees." He looked pointedly at Cockroach and then commenced to give her a rap across the knuckles, "I see and I know everything that is going on. I dislike effort spent playing politics and fabricating intrigue between colleagues when it could be better directed toward building client relationships, getting consignments, and earning more money for this company!"

Cockroach immediately appeared contrite. Or at least she appeared to be, hanging her head and looking downcast. Enid was beginning to feel like she was off the hook when Jean-Pierre turned in her direction and sarcastically asked, "Boh, Enid, where is your team of legal advisers? Do you think they will mediate and come up with a mutually beneficial solution to this situation, or will this be a long drawn-out legal battle?"

Enid was stunned. Julia must have reported everything word-for-word to Jean-Pierre. She did not know how to respond when put on the spot, but she was the wronged party and perfectly within her rights. There was a long pause as he waited for her answer before continuing. "Silent now, eh? In the future, please do not make accusations and demands before considering the consequences."

He narrowed his eyes and examined her closely, like a pinned specimen underneath a magnifying glass. "I have heard many good words about you. You are a worker and a contributor. But at Rothesay's, we do not tolerate this unproductive harboring of negative feelings and ill will. HR and I have discussed, and we have two options for you — resign with 3 months paid gardening leave or transfer. Let Julia know your decision first thing tomorrow morning." With that bombshell, he rapped his signet ring on the conference table and walked out without a second glance.

Enid was stunned. She resented being called out as if she were to blame for this situation. *Why don't they transfer Cockroach out? Perhaps to some Outer Mongolian representative office. Why am I the one being penalized?* This was a company that thrived on competition between colleagues and here she was, being blamed for a toxic environment! Jean-Pierre was upset because it was queen-bee-versus-worker drone. He sanctioned, even encouraged 'healthy competition' between specialists. This office was never about holding hands around a campfire, braiding each other's hair, and singing Kumbaya.

Head upright and using all her willpower to keep rein over her emotions, Enid looked up to see Julia and Alison's sympathetic looks. The mistake was undoubtedly Alison's, but because she always flew under the radar, the powers that be had no need to make an example of her. Mousy Alison. Even when she walked down the corridor, she moved sideways like a crab so as to not get in anyone's way. *Sigh, perhaps that is the key to survival.* Julia kindly told her to take the rest of the day off to consider the options and to collect whatever personal items she needed. At least she was not being frogmarched out of the office, but Enid could read between the lines — it was a polite command not to lay a finger on anything work-related.

The last thing on her mind was stealing client lists anyway. *They are so ridiculous. Anyway, all the client phone numbers are on my phone. What are they going to do?*

Make me hard reset my iPhone before I leave? Confiscate it? Enid was exasperated to find Ines waiting at her desk. *Great, this is really what I need now. Another condescending lecture from someone who doesn't know how good they have it.* Cockroach was already firmly planted at her desk, staring fixedly at her computer screen like it was the window to her soul. No one made eye contact with Enid as she grabbed her handbag and left the office. It was as if she had a scarlet letter marked on her chest.

Ines would not take no for an answer. She grabbed her by the arm and practically pulled her kicking and screaming to Sevva. Not a word was said until after their bottle of Merlot had arrived and Enid had downed her first glass of liquid courage.

"Everyone is coming to join us. I rallied the troops. Enid, cheer up. You have many friends and colleagues who appreciate and treasure you."

God, I want to go home, cry like a baby, and have a six-pack of Tsingtao to myself in a bubble bath. The last thing I want is a pep rally of Net-a-Porter outfitted cheerleaders. I am so sick of this world.

Enid kept silent as Ines went on, "I know you asked me not to get involved but I couldn't help it. I told Tonton how important you are to building the Mainland Chinese market, how quickly you learn, and how the clients are drawn to you. To be honest, they can't fire you; they are covering their arses after your gutsy confrontation about Cockroach being prejudiced. If you leave voluntarily, you lose! All your hard work would have been for nothing, and Cockroach will dance on your grave." Ines paused to sip her wine and compose a compelling argument, "Please, please consider a transfer to the China office, or you could even transfer to my department. You were top of your class in Art History at Guangzhou University, and the Paintings department has the headcount. Cedric is a better boss than Florian or Cockroach. He is more interested in publishing scholarly essays and hooking up with interns than playing office politics to get ahead."

It felt good to hear Ines say these reassuring words. And it felt even better when, one-by-one, all her friends (and even the people that she did not really consider her friends) came to meet them for drinks. Lara, Alison, Francesco, Edward, Christine, Sean, Simon, and even Little F joined the party convincing her to stay on. There were so many people that it could have been an end-of-season drinks celebration. Enid was buoyed by their positive energy and wondered whether they truly wanted her to stay or if it was to rub Cockroach's face in the mess.

Christine offered the most logical advice, "Listen, Enid, I am a veteran. You must pick the position that is either parallel or a promotion. If you switch departments, go to Contemporary Art where you will be a junior specialist of a higher value sale, or if you transfer offices, go to China or New York, not some tiny backwater rep office. You owe it to yourself to aim for the stars. This forces you out of your comfort zone, and you can realize your full potential." As the oldest colleague there who had survived so many economic downturns and corporate power struggles, Enid knew that Christine's advice was worth its weight in gold. Enid hugged the older lady tightly and told her how much she treasured her warm mentorship.

It was a relief that the whole night was not about Enid's trial. Enid did not like being the center of attention, and the spotlight was taken off her by the arrivals of Mimi and Little F's wife, Som. They were so exuberant, doing impressions of everyone in the office, mocking the trashy expats, and attracting cocky finance types over to treat them to rounds of drinks. It took the whole night for them to go through all thirty-six of the specialty cocktails on the menu. Christine, Edward, and Francesco were prescient enough to make their excuses and left before the serious drinking got underhand.

Chanting "Eating is cheating," Mimi, Som, and Ines did not allow anyone to grab a bite to eat. Enid managed to slowly sip and spit out her cocktails into an increasingly revolting-looking glass of wine. Not that anyone cottoned on, as they got progressively drunker. Simon had his hand in an attempt at familiarity by association on Mimi's lap and hung on her every word. He ignored her making come-hither-buy-me drinks eyes at everyone in trousers, waiting like an eager lap dog. *Sigh, they make such a cute couple; I wish I had a guy like that. He ticks all the right boxes. OK, maybe someone with more street smarts than Simon would be ideal. I miss having someone special to hug me, hold my hand, and talk to about which path I should take.* Looking at the both of them made Enid wistful but, deep down, she eschewed dependency. She took pride in making her own way, despite only making decisions after the judgment of a full court of public opinion.

Despite Enid's best efforts to secretly discard the drinks, it was still a terrible idea to mix wine with every single cocktail on the menu. Ines and Mimi were convinced that getting drunk would help clear her mind, separate thoughts from emotions, and she did not want to be a spoil sport. Her departure from the Watch department was now a given, and it was a foregone conclusion that Simon would be offered her position. Enid was not resentful of him in the least; he was more passionate about watches anyway.

She flamed with shame when recalling her pathetic efforts to get close to Cockroach. It made her furious thinking about it. *I thought she could be my mentor for the business manager's role. This makes me even more determined to be in a position where I can't be bullied, used, and discarded.* Everyone eagerly shared their opinion on her next course of action but none of the prospects particularly thrilled her. With the sole exception of Christine, they thought that she should transfer to Paintings and work together with Ines under the protective and perverted wing of Cedric.

Enid tossed and turned the whole night, drafting and redrafting a list of pros and cons over and over again. She had three options — junior specialist in the Paintings department, Shanghai representative, or perhaps a posting to Geneva or New York. The idea of moving to Geneva or New York appealed to her, especially the latter. The more she dwelled on it, the more she realized that there was nothing tying her to Hong Kong. Luca was happily living his dream in India; she received an occasional postcard. He did not even have Internet!

As a teenager, she had religiously watched every single episode of *Friends* and *Sex and the City* (the source of her pseudo-American accent), so she was thrilled at the prospect of living in New York. It would be a dream come true. So what if she did not even have a tourist visa for the US and had never set foot there? *I just know I will love it there. People always said that if you can make it in New York, you can make it anywhere. This could be my American dream!*

As usual, Enid's over-active imagination was putting the cart before the horse. New York would take a miracle and a half. The other options were more realistic but less appealing. She did not relish the thought of working directly under Florian in Geneva. It made her cringe to think of a whole city of big and little F uptight clones, with perfect manners and stiff posture. All the chocolate and raclette in the world were not going to change her mind. She had earned Florian's respect, and he would be eager to groom her to become a top watch specialist, but at heart, she knew it was the wrong career path.

The second option was to work together with Ines under Cedric. To be honest, Enid liked watches as much as contemporary art.

It was the people and the auction business that truly fascinated her and made her want to get up every morning. She did not have the passion and drive to become a first-rate art expert. Jewelry was her true passion, but Vera had passed on her during her graduate internship and it was unlikely that there would be an offer forthcoming.

Everyone could not stop freely weighing in on her transfer. Edward chided her, "Why do you want to go to New York? The English keep, Americans sell, Asians buy. Where are you going to earn the most money? And meet good marriage prospects? Actually silly, silly me, they are one and the same."

Perhaps becoming a representative was not a bad idea. It did not call for the savvy acumen of a business manager, but at least it was a role that allowed her to continue building client relationships. It was now abundantly clear to everyone that Enid would stay to fight for survival. She certainly possessed the skills to build further on the already influential network put together after a year in the business. Imagine what she could achieve if she stayed at Rothesay's for longer. There was now no doubt that she would defend herself instead of slinking away with her tail between her legs. Enid was determined to prove to herself as well as to the Cockroaches of the world that she could not be easily stepped on and discarded.

Chapter 18

BIG APPLE, BIG DREAMS

———————ıı   ıı———————

"Seriously, these are your entire possessions? Are you sure you don't have a huge van waiting 'round the corner? I can't believe that all your stuff fits into two cardboard boxes and a single suitcase. What about shoes? Or books?" Enid was helping Alison carry the boxes up four flights of stairs to the apartment. Alison was going to be her new housemate and eventually take over the lease.

It was the perfect solution; they knew each other so well from hours spent working together, and their friendship had survived extreme moments of stress and jubilation. Alison was as quiet as a church mouse, but she was solid and reliable, someone who could always be counted on.

Around Alison, Enid felt like she was the main actress and not the supporting sidekick. Enid valued her both as a friend and colleague. Then again, Enid was currently in the mood to love the whole wide world. The boxes felt as light as Enid's heart.

At long last, all the jigsaw pieces were finally falling into place. Jean-Pierre and Julia agreed to a transfer to the New York office. Enid put this as the third biggest event that had ever happened in her life; the first when she won the Sorbonne scholarship, the second was the internship position at Rothesay's and now, this — the promise of life in the Big Apple. Her cup runneth over with blessings. More so, when she managed to push her parents' plaintive questions deep into the recesses of her mind. Their decided lack of enthusiasm almost popped her bubble when she told them the big news, "Aiyah, Yi Nin, why would you move there? You haven't even visited America before. What if you marry an American and never come home? They have guns, everything is so fast and big there, you don't like even eating cheeseburgers!"

It made Enid roll her eyes with annoyance and clench her phone hard with frustration. *I wish I had one of those prehistoric clamshell phones so I can dramatically slam down the phone! No wonder they've lived their whole lives in Zhabei. As much as I love them, they are so provincial! Village chickens! I don't want to grow up marrying the boy next door, both of us remembering each other's awkward adolescent acne. I am reinventing myself, and the American dream is going to get me places!* At least her colleagues and friends were happy for her. Everyone she told elicited the promise of a pull-out sofa, visits to Woodbury, and the Hamptons.

To Enid's wonder, it had not taken much persuasion to convince management that a move to New York was in everybody's best interests. She knew Ines had played a significant role in the process and wished she could show her how grateful she was for her support. Since her first day at Rothesay's, Enid learned that most people operated with an agenda in mind. Which made her more appreciative of true friends like Mimi and Ines because she had nothing to offer them.

Mimi was already offering the use of her parents' Hamptons home whenever Enid wanted. It was a generous offer, but Enid was more elated about Mimi hosting the leaving party. From research on Instagram and online forays, Enid did not see what the fuss was about. The Hamptons looked the same as in Hainan — just mucky brown water. Mimi had to explain, it's the scene. "Everyone from New York heads up there — in the Hamptons, more people are relaxed, better dressed — even the sex is better in the Hamptons!"

Carl was delighted at the prospect of Enid's move to New York. Lara warned her, "Gosh if you think Tom Cat was lazy, Carl puts him to shame! He probably makes his one-night stands tie his shoelaces and zip up his trousers before they leave." Lara looked at her fondly, "You can always come back because I will miss bossing you around." The solitary individual who could not mask her misery at Enid's upcoming promotion was the Cockroach. She practically gnashed her teeth with displeasure when Julia informed her. In an effort to smooth over hard feelings, Enid took it upon herself to apologize for any real and imagined misdemeanors. Cockroach's reaction was true to form, "Don't expect an apology from me. There is nothing to apologize for, my mother always taught me to be responsible and sincere in my actions. I have no regrets and nothing to feel sorry about."

Cockroach held her greasy head up high and stared dismissively as Enid put away her outstretched hand and shrugged her shoulders. Extending the olive branch had not been a big deal to her, and the gesture had purely been at her own initiative. Enid was humble and still eager to please, despite the turn of events. This rejection took place out in the open, so Enid knew that it would spread like wildfire throughout the office. It would be to Cockroach's detriment.

No wonder she eats lunch alone at her desk every day. People will do absolutely anything to avoid being stuck with her. It was sheer genius of Cedric to deliberately spill red wine all over his white shirt so he could escape the Cockroach trap.

Philosophical Ines naturally had theoretical evidence to analyze Enid's experience. "I knew Cockroach had BPD. This confirms it! Borderline Personality Disorder! She won't apologize because she wants to maintain the upper hand. She does this to maintain control and feel better about herself despite getting a dressing down from Tonton. Typical BPD dysfunctional self-image, lack of empathy, hostility, and intense volatile moods." Ines gloated with satisfaction over her psych analysis while Enid motioned the waiter over for another delicious KGB cocktail that she could ill afford. It was her turn to buy drinks too. *Ah well, I am going to get the rental deposit from Alison. Rothesay's is paying me three months of relocation allowance and rent, so why should I worry about money right now?* Enid's mind flicked guiltily to the soft calf leather Fratelli Rossetti boots that she had recently treated herself to — a must-have for those New York City snowstorms.

As she fiddled around with the yellow duck floating on the gin foam, she confessed to Ines that she was lying awake at night worrying about her US visa. "What if Cockroach does something to sabotage me? I should have heard back by now; it has been two months since we sent the papers off. What if I don't qualify for a visa?" Ines told her off for being too pessimistic and changed the subject to discuss Enid's upcoming leaving party. As host, Mimi had invited the entire office, and, Enid was sure, the whole of Lan Kwai as well. Mischievous as ever, Mimi had taken the trouble to add a postscript to Cockroach's invitation, "Look forward to celebrating with you! ☺"

Enid had told Mimi that an e-invitation would have been perfectly sufficient, but Mimi made the effort to print out embossed invitation cards. Mimi was superb at working out the finer details, just not when it came to work.

The family home was on Plantation Road, of course. It was actually the first time that Enid was visiting Mimi's home, even though she crashed so often on Enid's sofa that she left a spare change of clothes and toothbrush. "I am so embarrassed by my home; do you think it's weird if I ask the guests to go straight through the side gate to the poolside? I don't want them seeing all this mix-and-match, it looks like a flea market," she motioned with a sweeping hand. Compliant as usual, Enid nodded her head as she ran her fingers down the smooth marble medallion of a carved rosewood armchair. *She really has no idea how fortunate she is. My parents think Ikea is fancy; they would faint if they came here.*

The home had been in the family for over four generations, and each succeeding affluent generation had introduced furniture and decorations from their era. Enid tried not to look around too obviously. In the corner of the sprawling living room that she was standing in, an opulent stained glass Tiffany chandelier dimly lit up a pair of Le Corbusier chaise longue, reclined next to a Qing dynasty opium bed. Admittedly it was a lot to take in visually, but Enid unsympathetically thought of Mimi's social anxieties as poor little rich girl problems.

In her Rothesay's life, everyone constantly made casual references or jokes about their parents, "Argh, my mother thinks she is on the set of Dynasty, she still wears Versace with shoulder pads...I can't lunch on Sunday, I need to play tennis with my high maintenance parents...Aren't these cannelés delicious? I am so lucky that my sister trained at Cordon Bleu..." So much of the day-to-day conversations swelled with entitlement and privilege. Thankfully, everyone was considerate and well-brought-up enough to not ask Enid any prying questions about her family, but she had to grin and bear the unspoken burden of being an outsider.

The party was everything that Enid could have wanted and more. In all her social-climbing fantasies, she had never imagined that all these people would show up. They knew her name! She felt completely at ease chatting to people without constantly wondering if she was making the right kind of small talk or if her hand gestures were too crass. Exposure to different and diverse clients had given her personal confidence. She used to think of herself as a NINJA that faded into the background —No Income, No Job, or Assets — and now here she was, at a fabulous party surrounded by well-wishing friends and garnished with Mimi's entourage that usually graced the society pages.

As she walked around the party, making conversation and getting tips from guests about the best blowout bar, sushi restaurants, and galleries in New York, Enid felt a little sad. She was getting reluctant to leave this all behind and start all over again. Flashback to her first months at Rothesay's with her acrylic manicure and tongue rolling that ridiculous American accent, throwing French phrases around like confetti, and wearing a Michael Kors logoed beret to the office on Friday. It made her cringe and cold sweat prickle on her scalp to think of the many faux pas that she had committed and was still slowly discovering. The difficult aspect of this world was that there was no rulebook. The code of conduct changed constantly, and it was a steep learning curve. Up until today, she still had not figured out whether it was called a loo, bathroom, toilet, lady's, washroom, powder room, or WC.

Leaving to the US was literally and figuratively further than anyone in her family had ever been. She could not help wishing that her parents saw this as an achievement. They started playing the only child card. It was the first and only time they had ever used it, so it was extremely effective — "Now you live in Hong Kong and we see you less than a handful of times a year. If you move to the other side of the world to America, we will see you even less. We have only one child, who will pour tea for us during Chinese New Year?" She was the first one in the family to go to the US, the first one to get a job at an international company, and the first one to go to university. She had managed all these firsts on her own terms with her parents' steadfast support, so she could not help harboring proportionate doses of guilt and gratitude toward them.

Enid gave herself an A- in the personal development section of her imaginary report card. A+ would have been to show up with a Trustafarian fiancé or, at the very least, a devoted Richie Rich groupie like Simon.

That was what he was. Glancing across the room, she could see him juggling shot glasses in an effort to win Mimi's attention away from the very sexy tattooed bartender. When she had met the bartender, Enid was automatically suspicious of where Mimi had sourced him. She was reassured that he really was on loan from Quinary once he proved it with a few excellent Oolong Tea Collins cocktails. To no one's surprise, sour grapes Cockroach failed to show up. Which was just as well as everyone had made grand plans to accidentally on purpose push her into the pool. *What a beautiful night, the weather is turning crisp and to think, by Christmas, I am going to be looking out at a view of the Hudson River instead of Hong Kong harbor.*

Auction season was starting again, and consignments were starting to trickle in. Enid felt like she was in no-man's land, as she did not know if she should be sourcing for the New York or Hong Kong office. She spent her workdays mostly calling clients to let them know that she was moving on, and the rest of the time following New York social media celebrities so she could get her style right. They seemed so much edgier with their balayage hair and distressed, asymmetrical clothing. The deliberately disheveled look was so different from the Hong Kong-style gamut, which ran from the super put-together look of Hermes bags and Ferragamo shoes to the equally common white singlet and thong slippers ensemble.

As soon as Julia summoned Enid to her office, Enid dropped everything and rushed upstairs. She was fed up with being in limbo, it was already early October, and she had heard that autumn leaves in Central Park were a sight not to be missed. "Enid, I am sorry to be the bearer of bad news. The US authorities rejected your L1 application. We were very hopeful when we applied because you have specialized knowledge and multi-lingual ability. However, because of the new administration in the recent elections, they have based their objections on your not being at the managerial or executive level. I am very disappointed for you. Please know that Jean-Pierre and the rest of the team here at Rothesay's will do our best to come up with a solution."

Tears began to roll down Enid's cheeks, and Julia whipped out a box of Kleenex, continuing her speech, "Now, you know that you have been a junior specialist for around half a year, so that's likely the other reason why they dinged you. If you continue to perform to this high standard in Watches, we can definitely look into applying again for a visa and transfer in a year's time."

Enid lost all poise and mumbled in a small voice, "I've already had my leaving party. That's what I want to do, leave. I don't want to be in Watches anymore, having to constantly watch my back." Enid was exhausted to the point of collapse. She always tried to take a positive spin on everything, but now and then her willpower failed her. It truly was a weary uphill battle. She rambled on in disbelief, "Why would they reject my visa? Is it because I am a woman? Or I'm from Mainland China? Carl doesn't have a university degree and he managed to land a 'sushi chef' EB3 visa." As Julia unfolded details of a Plan C, Enid merely nodded and gazed longingly at the door, itching to escape.

Chapter 19

Reality Hits Home

It was mid-morning in Central, another hectic day. People were rushing to and fro, just running errands, on the way to meetings and social calls. Enid wandered around mindlessly. No one would miss her, and if they happened to be looking for the resident scapegoat to tai chi some work to, they would assume she was either sorting out her move with Julia or attending to a client. Her impulse sale shoes were beginning to pinch her feet. *I was going to throw them out because I didn't have enough room in my luggage. I guess I can keep them since I'm not going anywhere. Me or the shoes. Painfully stuck here.*

Enid could not help feeling bitter. It seemed to come easily for some people, but for her, everything she wanted always seemed to lie just tantalizingly out of reach. She treated herself to a high-calorie high sugar Vitasoy outside 7-Eleven and sat slouched on the concrete planter, kicking her heels against the rough edge. *Who cares if anyone sees me now, lounging around like a street kid? I am one anyway.* She tore the Rothesay's lanyard off her neck.

The perfect daughter, the perfect friend, the perfect student. Where has this taken me? I am, in fact, the perfect doormat, the perfect scapegoat, and the perfect target. And after all I've willingly put myself through, to send me back to China on a one-way ticket. Enid was furious and frustrated with the world, but more with herself than with anyone else. For letting her hopes swell so large and her dreams soar so high. She turned off her phone and threw it deep into her handbag. For the rest of the day, Enid walked mindlessly. She would have gone on foot to Macau if she could. She rambled past the glamorous fashion displays in Central, the fierce stone lions standing guard at HSBC, the sweaty booze-smelling bars in Lan Kwai, the Sai Ying Pun frogs jumping around in their tanks, and then came to a halt at the pier in Kennedy Town.

It had been one of the areas Enid considered living in when she first arrived in Hong Kong just over a year ago. Then, it was full of sleepy provisions and coffee shops, better known for its public housing estates. Rent had been reasonable then, but it was changing fast now that the new MTR had been announced. Red and white flags of estate agents everywhere offering places for sale, now that Kennedy Town had gentrified from a novel off-the-beaten-track destination to chic hipster hangout. People like Ines were attracted like magnets to Kennedy Town. *And me — how about me? I didn't fit in here before when no one could understand my China-accented*

Cantonese, and I still don't fit in with this hipster crowd. Here or anywhere in Hong Kong. Everyone and everything moves on and I am always playing catch-up. I am still the same Ma Yi Nin, no matter how much I try to cultivate and reinvent myself as Enid Ma.

Enid took great pleasure wallowing in her misery. She indulged herself with worst-case scenarios, that her next stop would be selling gold bridal pigs at Chow Tai Fook, or she could go back to floating around from department to department as a trainee specialist if Cockroach had her way. The whole afternoon, when she was wandering around with tears on her cheeks, stepping on the backs of her chafing shoes, not a single person took a moment out of their day to offer help. Not that she was looking for hollow words of sympathy, anyway, or she would have left her phone on. She did not want more of the same banal stock phrases. Julia's parting missive that things happen for a reason and have a way of sorting themselves was a sharp twist of the knife. There was no point in hearing more empty platitudes.

Was it remotely possible to reconcile the offered position in China with her shameful loss of face in Hong Kong? The countless number of times she had boasted and gloated about her move to New York! Thinking about the leaving party where she had been fêted and acted all Charlotte York Goldenblatt made her feel sick to her stomach. But this was Enid, and she had not come so far without the ability to pick herself up. Building fairy tale castles on wisps of imagination and threads of the truth was her specialty. The best thing about coming from nothing and nowhere was that the grass was truly greener on the other side.

Frankly, the brief package that Julia outlined was not too bad. As the Shanghai representative, she would be in charge of local client services, the aspect of work that she enjoyed most at Rothesay's. They were offering a housing allowance and a salary matching what she earned now. That would go much further in China than it did here, she would be able to buy better-fitting shoes, that was for sure! And perhaps enough to give her mother a little pocket money, so that she could stop her part-time embroidery job. *It is not too bad I suppose, and maybe I can eventually go to New York one day. Perhaps even on vacation, not as a worker ant! Perhaps it is time to give up on Hong Kong? I aimed too high, and maybe this is as good as it gets. I need to go back to where I belong. I am a guppy fish lost in a big koi pond.*

Everything in Hong Kong was so expensive, and it was a struggle to stay afloat. Each month started out with a budget in mind and the best of intentions, but by the end of every month, it was a scramble to settle essential bills. Enid felt plagued by continual calculations and the non-stop muzak in her head playing a sad song about how dirt-poor she was. She tried not to deeply resent the unfairness of her lot in life. No wonder it was often said that rich people get richer, and it was in part because they do not have to pay for anything, unlike ordinary people. When she went out with Rita, Mimi, or Ines, they got complimentary drinks, upgrades, and velvet rope treatment. Free clothes and skin care were delivered to their homes in exchange for social media mentions. They were even lent jewelry to attend events, like movie stars at the Oscars. In their world, it seemed like the easier you could pay for something, the more likely you were to get it for free.

Like the time that Mimi had thrown a tantrum when she was paid HKD 10,000 in-store credit for the Marc Jacob's opening, "I refuse to go. What's wrong with them? Don't they know that the other brands give me cash? Who wears Marc Jacob's nowadays anyway? Soooo passé!" Rita was another stellar example; Enid knew that she too had struggled to make ends meet before her marriage. She had witnessed, with her own eyes, Rita furiously rubbing a free perfume sample on her wrists and neck. Now she was kind enough to regift Enid complimentary boxes of facemasks and creams from Amore Pacific and Swiss Perfection. Not a day passed by without an example of special privileges for the already privileged. This morning, before her meeting with Julia, she had waived USD 300 of shipping costs for an entitled billionaire client who refused to pony up this negligible three-figure sum to consign his watch collection valued at seven figures.

Still rooted on the park bench, Enid finally turned on her phone. If there was one person on the same wavelength who could best advise her on the pros and cons of this course of action, it was Angela. She picked up on the first ring, bubbly and thrilled to hear from Enid. Angela had already reserved a spot on the imaginary New York sofa in the fantasy loft for the Christmas holidays. Thankfully, she had not bought her plane ticket yet, and as Enid broke the bad news and went into detail about her options, Angela grew quiet.

"Are you still there? Hello? Hello?"

"Yes, I am, you don't have to shout down the phone like a rural villager. I can hear you loud and clear."

Enid was taken aback by her gruff tone.

"Enid, you don't have much choice. Sure, you can take the job. You will be the Shanghai representative, and I will be your parallel in Beijing. But let me be frank with you. You should be reporting to me because I have more experience. On paper, I am the acting head in Beijing, but in reality, I am doing Liu-*jie*'s job and covering the whole of China. I thought that it was only a matter of time before they promoted me to become head of China. Now it is clear that they never had this intention, or they would have sounded me out before offering you this position."

It was at the tip of Enid's tongue to tell Angela how much she respected her at work and valued her friendship, but she held back. But the condescending attitude and icy tone were like speaking to a complete stranger, an enemy even. Enid swallowed a lump in her throat; she had never seen this side of Angela. One of the most positive aspects of the offer had been the opportunity of working closely with Angela. They had no pretenses in their friendship, and now it would be the same in their adversarial relationship.

Angela acidly drew the line in the sand. She snarled, "Yi Nin, you are green. I don't care what the bosses say, you will answer to me. One day, when I am head of China, I might make you my deputy. But never the co-head. Don't get ideas about pulling strings and using your NBFs[52] Ines and Mimi or whomever you have sucked in with your small-town girl act. You use all your tricks and scramble to the top like a rat, but I see you for what you are."

Angela's words hurt Enid to the core.

Over the next week, as the i's were dotted and the t's were crossed on her new employment contract. Enid kept checking her phone to see if Angela would get in touch. She was even

---

52 New Best Friends

more anxious about Angela than she had been about Luca when he went AWOL.

The Panglossian that she was, Enid could not stop hoping that it was all a horrible misunderstanding. People assumed Enid was moping over the move, and she did not dare to tell anyone else what had passed. There was a significant kernel of truth in Angela's harsh words, and no amount of Enid-style sugar-coating was going to hide it.

But I don't understand the distinction. When does ambition become greed? And networking turn into using people? And how does a social climber graduate into a yuppie? Am I too obvious about wanting to get ahead in life, and what is wrong with that anyway? Angela is as ambitious as I am, but I would never speak to a friend the way she treated me. Perhaps when we meet face-to-face, it will all be forgotten.

When news of Enid's role as Shanghai representative was announced, there were congratulations all around. She was bewildered that no one commiserated with her. On the contrary, colleagues who ordinarily ignored her now smiled toothily at her. Crafty Ines, who was miles ahead in the realm of office politics, teased Enid, "Of course everyone wants to be your bestest bosom buddy-buddy now. You are headed to our rice bowl! China is the biggest market and growing faster than any other region. After Liu-*jie's* epic departure, Rothesay's is loath to have one absolute figurehead in China, and since you are taking half that role, everyone needs you on their side." It was at the tip of Enid's tongue to tell Ines about Angela's verbal missiles, partially for advice and mostly because Ines was extremely protective and kind.

The next fortnight passed by in a flash. With Alison taking over the lease and furnishings in the apartment, there was not much personal business to sort out. *Anyway, there are over thirty-two flights a day from Shanghai to Hong Kong. It's not like it is sixteen hours flight away. I can come back to Hong Kong anytime.* She still thought wistfully of New York, but now looked forward to posing like one of those elegant Coffee Bitches she had seen strolling around Lujiazui district with Starbucks cups and Goyard portfolios (personalized with monogrammed initials, of course).

Shanghai would be easier to navigate than Hong Kong. There, she knew which blogs, style icons, and socialites to follow. Hong Kong was far too confusing. For example, Louis Vuitton's Damier, Empreinte, and signature monograms warranted eye rolls, but the Speedy was fine because it was an iconic bag. And it was considered cool to carry a grade AA Shenzhen fake bag, but only if you could afford the real deal. Ines and Francesco took delight in recommending their favorite shop in Lo Wu Shopping Plaza whenever anyone admired their accessories. Enid now felt relieved that she was going home to where she belonged, where she knew the lay of the land. It was time to move back and move on.

Chapter 20

BACK HOME

The plane landed with a thud on the runway, and Enid woke up to the thunderous applause of her fellow passengers. *Well, I am definitely back in China! People in Hong Kong are too jaded to be this enthusiastic.* Enid smiled at the kindly old lady sitting next to her who was cheerfully packing away everything from her seat pocket. Sick bag, safety-briefing card, complimentary peanuts, even the plastic toothpick disappeared into her cavernous handbag.

Enid admired her uninhibited enthusiasm; these were utilitarian (and free!) souvenirs. Enid vaguely remembered that her parents had also swiped the evacuation instructions during their trip to Singapore in the early 90s. It was still sitting at home somewhere, along with a cheesy photograph of the Merlion, carefully preserved for posterity in a yellowing plastic folder.

Enid could not have missed them at the arrivals gate. Her mother waved as vigorously as a landing signal officer, narrowly flipping away her father's toothpick. They were so happy to see her that they hugged her. In public! *That's a first.* Enid swore that her father had tears in his eyes. It felt right to be home, and Enid was pleased that fate had drawn her to this path. Her parents had come on foot and taken the bus and then the subway to meet her. It was nine in the evening, way past their bedtime, so Enid nodded her assent when her mother tentatively suggested spending the night with her. She could not say no, anyway, when she spotted their fully packed Pure Life promotional duffle bag.

It was so awkward that they treated her like a child, but with such deferential respect. Enid certainly did not feel better than them because she had a fancy degree or a higher paying job — she had met enough of that kind of people at Rothesay's to not let superficial qualifications get to her head. The very best of intentions were there but did not last long. After two hours, she reached her limit.

In the taxi, her mother snacked on roasted sunflower seeds and proceeded to leave a trail of shells behind like Hansel and Gretel. The click of each seed cracking between her overlapping teeth coupled with her father's slurping of his flipped toothpick was worse than nails down a chalkboard. Nevertheless, the irritation was coupled with happiness at being able to treat them to a stay at the Lanson Place service apartments. She felt such a burst of pride when her mother took photos of the marble bathroom and soft furnishings. Even of the well-stocked mini bar and hospital corners of the bed sheets.

Although it was way past her parents' bedtime, they could not sleep because of the thrill of Netflix. Local cable television paled in comparison to the entertainment of American reality television. That was the reason they were still awake when Enid got out of the shower. Dripping wet and screaming for a towel, her father grudgingly unpacked the towels he had filched. "I left that for you," he pointed at the bathmat on the floor, "since when are you so spoilt that you need one towel for your hair and another for your feet and one more for your body?" Enid rolled her eyes. *It's good to be home but now I remember why I wanted to leave in the first place!*

They started bickering when Enid mentioned that she wanted to move to West Nanjing, closer to the office. "Give me a good reason why you can't stay with us. I can change the Hello Kitty curtains and *maybe* you can have fancy blinds like in this hotel! Big Uncle Liu can make the same. He is working at a fabric factory now making car seats, you know. You can't live by yourself, like a Western girl. You can move out when you get married, what will the neighbors think?" Enid shook her head and turned away with a sigh. She had been through years of this suffocating mindset. She would do as she had always done, i.e. whatever she wanted behind her parents' backs. They would be reconciled eventually, just as they had been when she went on her year abroad to Paris.

Enid was so eager to be at work that she arrived at the Four Seasons Hotel two hours before the office was due to open. Of course, the office was closed and completely in darkness. Through the glass door, she saw leather wingback chairs and shelves of catalogs surrounded by wood paneling. It looked like an English gentleman's club, completely different from the sleek modernity of the Hong Kong office. She could count the number of times on one hand that she had dropped by during the previews, never imagining that she would be sitting behind one of the desks one day. Perhaps it was the two lattes that she had gulped down at Starbucks that made her heart race faster, but she felt nervous to meet her Shanghainese colleague Jade again.

At precisely nine on the dot, Jade huffed and puffed down the corridor. Wearing a paisley floral dress, she looked like an overstuffed sofa on the move. Enid was apprehensive because she did not know if Jade would be resentful about being passed over for the position once again. After the run-in with Angela, she was cautious around everyone. She need not have worried. Jade gave her a cheery wave by swinging a translucent plastic bag filled with *ci fan*[53]. "Real Shanghainese breakfast to welcome my new Shanghai colleague!" Jade announced with a toothy grin and a big hug. "Carb on carb, exactly

---

53 Shanghai breakfast rice rolls, a sticky rice ball stuffed with fried dough fritter.

---

what you need to celebrate joining the team. Now we are the dynamic duo."

Enid looked at the office in a different light now that she was going to belong there. There was a reception where Jade sat, one viewing room, and three desks at the back. They did not even have any gem-testing equipment or microscopes, just some well-used velvet trays and a loupe that visiting specialists had left behind. Jade joked when she saw Enid's look of disappointment, "This is an outpost, and you have been seconded on a hardship posting." Before the kettle had even begun to whistle, Jade began to gossip away. This was the first time they were spending time alone together, and Enid felt an immediate bond with her. Jade reminded her so much of Christine, with her wealth of warmth and experience.

"I'm so glad that you are a returning Shanghainese. We have had a revolving door of representatives here. Worse than musical chairs. Easily the worst by far was this random French expat with fancy connections. Family friends with J-P, of course. She claimed that she spoke fluent Mandarin after a three-month course at BLCU[54]. I am so glad that her time here at Rothesay's lasted no longer than the duration of her Chinese language course. I figured she couldn't speak Chinese when she ordered the same lunch every day because she didn't know any other words beyond *mapo doufu*." But I suppose she was very presentable even if she couldn't communicate with clients. We also had a well-known academic professor — a renowned scholar of ceramics. I had to constantly remind him not to pick his nose in front of clients." Jade laughed and continued, "but he was very good-natured about it. He said that for him, picking his nose is like

54 Beijing Language and Cultural Institute is the most popular and prestigious university for foreigners to learn Chinese. It is as known for its teaching as it is for its location in Wudaokou, close by to wallet-friendly nightlife and the notorious Propaganda club.

scratching his head, it stimulated his brain to help him with the estimates!"

Jade made Enid laugh until she had tears in her eyes. Her tales of the snobby Hong Kong specialists and clients were spot-on. She mimicked Jean-Pierre's hungover face as he pursed his lips and tried to focus on a meeting after his first *mao tai* drinking bout. Jade had been with Rothesay's for over two decades; she had even been with the house when Rupert Bosewell's father still held the reins.

"It's paid for all my kids' education. My son is working at China Construction Bank, and my daughter is an eye doctor. With Rothesay's regular paycheck and insurance benefits, there is nothing more I can ask for except to arrive at nine and leave precisely at four every single day. Especially now that you are here, and I don't have to be on call 24/7 for clients. My next goal in life is to marry my children off and have grandchildren!"

Enid understood that it was not for a lack of capability that Jade had not advanced to become a representative; it was simply not her priority. Her family took place first and foremost. Everyone knew that Jade had singlehandedly raised her two children; no mention was ever made of a husband. There were rumors floating around ranging from a tragic car accident to an unsavory departure with a karaoke hostess, but Jade was so highly respected that no one ever dared to enquire further. She was a bottomless source of gossip, but Enid was impressed by her good nature. During the day they spent together and the months to come, Enid never heard her speak badly or maliciously of anyone. Everything was said with good-natured humor. Perhaps this was the secret to long-term survival and popularity.

Files and files of paper records, it seemed like the office was stuck in the pre-computer age. *I suppose it goes hand-in-hand with the Victorian country club furnishings.* The paper trail included some of the famed records that had been handed over during the customs investigation. No wonder her first task at hand was to make electronic copies of everything. Ostensibly, it was to become eco-friendly and digitize the office into a paperless environment, but Enid suspected it lessened the risk and responsibility of another investigation. A simple spill of hot tea or a push of the delete button could get rid of any pesky information. As the new representative, it was under Enid's jurisdiction to decide what was storage versus clutter. To be honest, Jade should have been the decision maker as she was far better organized and had a memory like a steel trap.

Tacked to many of the client folders were Post-its with illegible scrawls. "Oh, that is Liu-*jie's* private business," and Jade clammed up. It took a fortnight of treating Jade to breakfast every morning before she elaborated further. Liu-*jie* had not solely been taking client bidding off-the-books, she had been conducting underhand business on astronomical terms. Unseasoned clients were given crippling estimates or poor seller's terms, followed by Liu-*jie's* ever so tender-hearted offer to help them sell their consignments privately. The perfect pop-up office was set up using Rothesay's database and resources, and it had gone on for over three years. Liu-*jie* had even hosted intimate cocktail parties displaying artworks for sale like a professional gallery.

All of this had been carried out with Angela and Jade's knowledge, and from the sounds of it, compliance. Enid could not help her reaction. She brusquely asked Jade, "How could you do something like this? It is dishonest and unethical. I thought better of you." The very instant that the words were out of her mouth, she deeply regretted it.

Jade visibly winced and looked so hurt by the weight of the accusations. "I know where my children's and my next meal is coming from. Who do you think is a more valuable

Rothesay's employee, Liu-*jie* or me? You are naïve and you have been away from China for so long that you don't respect the demands and benefits of the *guanxi*[55] network. How do you think I survived for so long at Rothesay's? Because I stay out of everyone's business. Everywhere has *guanxi*, look at how Vera's department consists of her relatives. And how do you think your best friend Ines secured her position?"

Enid backed down immediately and bowed her head, profusely apologizing. Jade was right. *Who am I to judge? It is true, I have made the most of my friendships with Mimi and Ines. And didn't I vow to myself from the very beginning to do what it takes to be successful? Jade is not even doing this for fame and fortune, she is supporting her family.*

---

55 The network of obligations, trust, and respect which greases the wheels of business relationships in China. It is about leveraging contacts, maintaining face, respecting hierarchies, and benefiting from social influence.

Enid felt horrible for flinging her judgments about and, true to nature, she immediately took it to heart. Noticing the remorse in Enid's eyes and her trembling lower lip, Jade patted her on the hand. "It's OK, it's OK, you and I are OK. We are good, don't be upset. We need to understand each other and be a team. You are young, same age as my daughter, so I sympathize that you react and act before you think things through."

After that episode, Enid and Jade's relationship blossomed into true friendship. They were completely up-front with each other. Testimony to the convivial atmosphere of the office was that Enid permitted her parents to visit so she could introduce them to Jade. Enid was settling in nicely. She was the frog that had been out in the world and was now content to stay in her well. It was such a contrast from Hong Kong, where you had to send a Thank You e-mail after attending a meeting held to chastise you. She could answer Alison and the rest of her friends with absolute honesty that she did not miss Hong Kong one iota. Enid recognized Jade's knowledge and experience, and treated her with obeisance, like a wise elderly relative.

Now that Enid was nicely settled into the daily office routine, Jade started lining up appointments. Enid's cursory knowledge was sufficient to meet clients from all departments and provide preliminary estimates if required. Her first appraisal appointment was with the self-proclaimed Saatchi's of Asia. The two brothers were the biggest collectors of Chinese contemporary ink painting. They discovered artists like Li Jihn and Wang Donglin when they were first emerging and had amassed hundreds upon hundreds of rare and important artworks. The unconfirmed rumor was that they had cornered the market by paying a monthly salary to struggling artists in return for their complete output.

Art was one of their many hefty portfolios. The Wang brothers had their fingers in every pie from fashion brand distribution to advertising agencies. But the real meat behind their fat bank accounts lay in chicken feet. An immigrant to the US in the 1960s, Wang Senior had worked at a poultry slaughterhouse in Kansas. When he saw how freely chicken feet were discarded, he astutely raised money from his clan association and began exporting the prized delicacies back to China. He packed his sons off to the toniest of East Coast boarding schools, and, as soon as they were articulate enough, dispatched them to travel around abattoirs all over the US to negotiate on behalf of the family's business. All manner of feet, from pigs to geese, sheep's testicles, goat brains, and other spare parts disgusting to the western palate found new leases of life as gastronomic delights in China.

Regardless of how many magazine covers they graced or the number of supermodels dangling from the arms of their gold-buttoned navy blazers, the Wang Brothers would always be popularly known as Chicken Feet Royalty. Any other conventional Chinese family would have been proud of a history of business acumen, but the Wang Brothers craved for a flashy veneer of sophistication.

The meeting took place in Putuo, close to M50 Creative Park. Winston and Elvis Wang had repurposed an old factory into climate-controlled storage with quarters for artist residencies. Strictly by invitation only. Not that any casual visitor could sneak past the burly Gurkha security force and top-notch security system. There were so many surveillance cameras everywhere; it looked like an Ai Wei Wei installation. Enid plopped ungracefully on the Tom Sachs polycarbonate chair; it was as stunning as it was uncomfortable. She stifled a yelp after tripping when her heel caught in the hole of the stainless-steel leg. The designer furniture had been launched at Art Basel Miami a mere couple of months ago and here they were, sitting in an old factory, an hour by subway from the Shanghai city center.

It was her first client appointment, and she wanted to create a lasting impression. Enid suspected that Jade had facilitated this appointment to ease her into client relationships. The Wang Brothers were known to be westernized and direct, so she would not have to bow and scrape too obsequiously. Elvis did not stand on ceremony, and Enid was taken aback by his easy familiarity. "Want a cawfee? No? Then let's go see some art, eh." She could barely understand his heavy Bostonian accent, but she was encouraged by his winning smile and open energetic manner. Clearly, it was not for his looks that he had a reputation as a bit of a ladies' man.

Enid expected an army of minions to do the heavy lifting, but Elvis bounced around, rolling open racks and racks of artworks. He shared his favorite and not-so-favorite pieces, joking about how he and his brother shared the same taste in beauty but not in beautiful women. Finally, they arrived at the pièce de résistance, it was a 200-meter-long ink brush painting and a modern-day interpretation of the classic Song dynasty scroll *Along the River during the Qingming Festival*. Enid was amazed at the technical finesse, exacting detail, and charming expression of the bustling scene. It took her breath away; it was a 21st-century answer to the original at the Palace Museum.

She was one of a dozen people fortunate enough to view this masterpiece in real life. Cedric had hopped around like an Energizer Bunny when Jade had told him about this possible consignment. However, he had cautioned that an artwork of this magnitude (and estimate) could only be purchased by a private museum or state institution. The astronomical price was a deterrent for the average collector, and it could not be squirreled away in some conservation archive, the delicate nature of the single-ply *sheng xuan* paper would not lend itself easily to storage. Tentatively, Enid voiced Cedric's reservations, but she was careful to mediate this with appropriate laudatory phrases about the rarity and desirability of the artwork.

Elvis' face temporarily darkened like a thundercloud. "It's not a bespoke suit, you can't order to size! How can you people say that? Bah, but I suppose you are the specialists in this matter." He turned away with a long sigh and then shrugged his shoulders. A long and drawn-out silence ensued as Elvis calculated and computed. She jumped when he clapped his hands and stated decisively, "*Mei guan xie*[56], no hay problema amiga. Let's chop it up. Three pieces. A triptych and then we sell them separately. If someone wants to buy 'em together, they pay me more. No siree Bob, no one is going to get a buy-one-get-two free deal from me. I am the one who should benefit. I buy one, sell three!"

---

56 No problem. Elvis is not actually multi-lingual but there is nothing he loves more than a few catch phrases in different languages.

Chapter 21

TRICKS OF THE TRADE

––––––––––––ǁ   ǁ––––––––––––

Back at the office and still completely flummoxed, Enid related Elvis's thoughts to Jade, who was amused rather than aghast. Her only advice was for Enid to consult Cedric before matters spiraled out of control. It was not without reason that Cedric was the Head of Department — he was cool, calm, and quick to act. As well as completely nonplussed at Elvis' suggestion. Thinking aloud in the conference call, "Hmm well, less than a handful of people have seen the artwork in real life. Who will say otherwise when it appears at auction as a triptych? Certainly not the artist, Li Shen. No one from the art world with an iota of common sense would dare to go against the Wang Brothers! Why not? Elvis is sharp as a tack. A smaller size will make it easier to transport to previews. Maybe we will only take the central piece viewing; this will whet collectors' appetites to see the rest of the panels. And of course, by invitation only viewings. If they want to see the entire triptych together, they will have to come to the Shanghai preview or attend the auction in Hong Kong."

Both Elvis and Cedric were consummate businessmen able to find an angle in every approach and a deal in every transaction. Enid was disturbed by their ethics and fragrant disrespect for art, particularly as one was supposed to be an authority on art and the other a patron. Nevertheless, she could not help but admire how shrewd and sneaky they were. *This is how to make it to the top. I need to take advantage of what is available and position myself to seize any opportunities that come my way. Luca made me too soft. It's good that we are no longer together. Imagine if I was looking for water sources in West Bengal instead of looking for apartments in West Nanjing! Elvis and Cedric are at the top of their game because they are so enterprising and proactive. I am just coasting along, and I need to do better*!

Enid was buoyed up by the energy in Shanghai. Finally, she was in a city with a voltage that sparked a connection with her. She met up with many of her old schoolmates from Guangzhou University, but they were all engaged/married/expecting their first or second babies. It bored and frustrated her in equal measures to sit down for hours of endless discussion on a reliable source of milk powder or pre-school applications. She thought their one-track obsessive conversations were downright rude, and she pitied them for having nothing more consequential in their lives.

After a handful of get-togethers, Enid dropped all contact with her schoolmates despite their thoughtful offers to match-make her with their husbands' colleagues, distant relatives, or neighbors. Basically, anyone single and random, they could easily be serial killers or con artists! Anyway, they were not in the kind of circles she wanted to move in or fitted in anymore. They were more outer ring road, and she was more central business district. Back in university days, she had daydreamed about living in a smart full-service condominium and driving a BMW paid for by a doting husband. Now she wanted more than this, and she wanted to earn it based on her own merit, not through marriage. She shuddered at the specter of turning into an ordinary Shanghainese housewife running daily errands, complaining about the nanny, and debating diaper brands.

Enid simply did not have the time or desire to fritter away in a yawn-making routine of afternoon cakes and strolls in shopping malls. There was a major snuff bottle auction on the cards, and Enid was negotiating a vanity catalog with the consignor, Dr. Bing.

Landing such a large-scale consignment would be career-defining. The last record-breaking Imperial Qianlong snuff bottle had sold for USD 3.3 million to Edward's client two years ago, and this collection had many similar examples.

Dr. Bing hosted a sumptuous dinner for Enid and Meng, the works of art specialist from Hong Kong. After nearly a week of twelve-hour workdays, Enid was content just escaping from Dr. Bing's environment-controlled storage basement. Her throat was parched from the dehumidifier, and her hand ached from tagging and writing consignment receipts for nearly one-thousand-five-hundred lots. Although Dr. Bing was very kind, he was also very old-school. Despite a week of seeing her every day, he still did not know Enid's name and either clicked his fingers in her direction or called out "wei ah..." What made the collection all the more impressive was that Dr. Bing was by no means one of the super wealthy, he was a state hospital liver specialist with a lifelong passion for snuff bottles. He had never married because there was no room for anyone or anything else in his life.

Now retired and in his seventies, his sole desire in life was to see his cherished collection documented in a single-owner catalog. "The Collection of Dr. Bing" promised to be a noteworthy tome, with plenty of detailed photographs and scholarly essays. Enid did not manage to build up much of a rapport with Dr. Bing because he proved impossible to hold a conversation about anything besides snuff bottles. Even a chance remark about the weather led to deliberations about whether the humidity control in his basement sufficiently protected his darlings. Thankfully, Meng was there to talk geek with him, and Enid devoted her full attention to wielding her chopsticks, chewing her food, and enjoying every delicious morsel of the meal.

Whilst the Peking duck was being delicately sliced, Dr. Bing elaborated to

Meng and Enid on his reasons for consigning with Rothesay's. Dr. Bing was adamant that everything in the collection had to be sold. With no direct descendants, he was fearful that his thirty-year-old collection would not receive adequate care and attention after his death. Auctioning them was a way to document his life's passion and for other enthusiastic collectors to access and applaud his taste. The total value of the collection had a high estimate of USD 32 million. It was undoubtedly a collection without parallel; no one had ever single-mindedly put together such a focused collection of Qing Dynasty snuff bottles.

Dr. Bing was a teetotaler since he dealt too often with cirrhosis patients, so they avoided the obligatory *maotai* bottoms-up session. Dinner ended early, so Meng and Enid went for a much-needed foot massage. Soaking her toes in hot water whilst the knots were eased from her shoulders was pure heaven. "You know, I remember the good old days before they introduced business managers like Cockroach, we used to expense foot massages if we went with a client. Sadly, those days are over now. Yet another reason to leave this pressure cooker industry." They chatted about their colleagues in the Hong Kong office but there was not much in the way of gossip, Meng was more of a bookish scholar. He lamented, "I feel sorry for Dr. Bing. I did try my best to convince the head of sale, Victoria, but you know how it is."

Enid had no idea what he was rambling on about, and she initially thought that it concerned the low estimates, but then Meng elaborated further. Victoria's plan was to accept the entire collection and then separate the lots into three sections. The most valuable would enter a prestigious evening sale, the semi-valuable snuff bottles into the day sale, and the average grade ones would be returned to Dr. Bing. Dr. Bing was fully unaware of this A, B, and C list grading and it would not be discussed until after the consignment was safely in Rothesay's hands. They were prepared to let him sign a contract under the misplaced assumption that Rothesay's intended to sell the whole collection in a single owner catalog. After the best lots had gone under the hammer, excuses would be given about poor market conditions and lack of client interest. Dr. Bing would be fobbed off with vague plans for a postponement that would never happen.

"But we won this consignment away from our competitors because they proposed to pick and choose the cream of the crop. How can we do the same thing to Dr. Bing? How can we shaft the client like this?"

Meng gave an audible sigh, "You don't think this kind of bait-and-switch hasn't happened before? You don't think it gives me sleepless nights? The day I get a job offer from an established museum, I am handing in my resignation letter."

Enid was crushed with guilt. Dr. Bing would never believe that both of them were not in on this secret plan. He may have been socially awkward and pedantic, but he was honest and truly dedicated to his collection. Rothesay's did not care to preserve the client relationship, because after the auction, nothing more was needed from the elderly gentleman. Enid felt self-disgust when she recalled how grateful he was to both of them and Rothesay's. The Peking duck treat churned in her stomach like an attack of Beijing Belly.

That night, she tossed and turned on the 1000-thread-count sheets of her service apartment bed. As Shanghai representative, Enid would ultimately be tasked with breaking the bad news to Dr. Bing. The key difference between the two collectors Elvis Wang and Dr. Bing was that the former would undoubtedly have an army of lawyers to go through the contract with a fine-toothed comb whilst the latter would get completely screwed over. It did not matter that Elvis was entirely mercenary and would do whatever it took to gain more money, more status, more anything. Dr. Bing, on the other hand, would never achieve his dream of deepening research and popular interest in snuff bottles. *Only in Hollywood do the good guys win. Maybe I can make an anonymous tip. Or hint to him that he should hire a lawyer to go through the contract.*

All these thoughts ran through Enid's mind, but deep down she knew any good intentions would evaporate by the next morning. Her strong sense of self-preservation would never permit her to jeopardize her own welfare. Meng was in the office finishing off the paperwork, so Enid was unable to get Jade alone to relate the full story. Not that she needed to, Jade was astute enough to guess the reasons behind the lack of concentration.

Jade was exasperated, "Aiyah, I know you have the best of intentions. But if you want to have this holier-than-thou kind of attitude, you are better off being an administrator like me. Is that something you want? Do you have the luxury of scruples? Please, you are too ambitious for that! If you want to stay as country representative and be a boss, you need to let go of this dreamy idealism. Dreams don't pay the rent and bills."

When am I going to grow up and stop having these pathetic principles? I can't keep having these touchy-feely existential crises. Enid was frustrated with herself for continually being led by emotions. And worst of all, for pretending to have principles but not having the guts to do anything. *I am sure Lara or Angela don't suffer from these self-imposed dilemmas.* Thankfully, there was no opportunity to get drawn into a vortex of philosophical self-recrimination; there was enough to occupy her. Not only was Mimi was coming to Shanghai for Fashion Week, but Enid also had two weeks left on the service apartment lease and needed to find a place to live. The absence of a swimming pool and hotel-monogrammed fluffy towels was going to take some getting used to in ordinary civilian life.

Plus-one. Enid did not mind it. Being a plus-one meant that she knew someone who belonged. Not so long ago, she remembered enviously reading about events like this in the Shanghai Daily and here she was, in the same party as Zhang Ziyi. *It is not too bad hanging on the fringes if you have a flute of champagne in your hand.* Enid smiled as she watched Mimi immersed herself in her usual routine — blowing rounds of air kisses whilst precariously balancing on ridiculously high heels. Enid had come straight from work and definitely did not look like one of this fashionista crowd. If anything, she probably passed for one of the dozens of ushers in their black suits. They were probably made at the same hole-in-the-wall tailor anyway.

In the limo on the way over, Mimi put in her two cents, "What? Still not dating? Come on, don't be a Rothesay's spinster! What is it going to say on your tombstone? Here lies Enid Ma, dearly loved and somewhat appreciated by Rothesay's, survived by fifty auction catalogs." Enid knew that Mimi was speaking the truth, she ought to be socializing but she did not know how or where to make new friends.

A profile on Meetup lay dormant as she made trivial excuses. *I make small-talk all day at work. Is this really how I want to spend my free time? Especially with people who are as equally desperate to make friends?* Her social life comprised solely cinema excursions with Jade's daughter, but they had nothing to talk about apart from their massive crushes on the Korean boy band, BIGBANG. *It is true — I'm soooo pathetic!*

Mimi's frantic waving at a stranger broke Enid's reverie. "Hey dreamer, meet Xia, we went to Chinese International School together. She recently moved to Shanghai to work for Vogue as a fact-checker/copy editor. She has no friends either, so both of you can hold on to each other for dear life." *What an introduction!* Enid and Xia muttered hi's and warily sized each other up. Xia was plain but passably pretty. In fact, if Enid were to be cuttingly honest, Xia did not look stylish enough to be a Vogue glamazon. Not to be superficial or anything, but they were both dressed in the same yawn-inspiring style of black suit.

Conversation was stilted and Xia was not a drinker either, so she became increasingly boring as the night wore on. *She is such a wallflower. Actually, she is not decorative enough to be a flower. More like a clump of moss. How did Mimi become friends with someone like her? Hmmm, I suppose people ask the same question when they see Mimi and me together.* At the very least, Xia was refreshingly direct. Vogue was paying her a pittance of a salary, so she was looking for a housemate to share her West Nanjing apartment. It sounded ideal and almost too good to be true. They made plans to meet up the next day before Xia pleaded an early morning meeting and made a rapid exit.

Even before seeing the apartment, Enid hoped that it would work out with Xia, despite Mimi's passionate protests. "You can't live with her! She is no fun at all. The kind of guys that she knows accessorize with a scientific calculator and multi-colored ball point pens in their breast pockets! We became friendly in school because she let me copy her physics and algebra homework. She is one big geek. I have no idea how she got a job at Vogue. She has no fashion sense, so you won't even be able to borrow clothes from her." Enid shrugged with relief. As much as she adored Mimi, she dreaded coming home after a long day at work to a party girl who thrived on spontaneous entertainment.

Chapter 22

FEEDING THE SENSES

————————II   II————————

Xia was the ideal choice for a housemate, Enid could not have asked for a better candidate. Once Enid's parents met her, they were immediately reassured by her simple and quiet manner. The list of rules outlined by Xia revealed that she was also wary of bringing a stranger into her personal space. It was clear that an introduction from Mimi was far from a recommendation. No overnight guests, no late payment of rent, no loud noise after 10 pm on weekdays and midnight on weekends. A cleaning roster supplemented these prohibitions, even though they were splitting the cost of a weekly *ayi*[57]. Enid should have found it annoying, but she was glad that their rules for living together were outlined from the very beginning.

Anyway, there were lofty plans to save up and buy an apartment as soon as her parents became reconciled to her independence. She found it silly that they had not once raised any objections about where she had lived in Hong Kong or Paris, but now that she was back in China, they were eager to preserve some notion of traditional respectability. They had antiquated notions that having a property would make a man feel like he was no longer needed. Enid tried to hide her irritation at their conservatism and the way that they quoted everything they read in *People's Daily* as the gospel truth. Nevertheless, she made an effort at Sunday dinner every week. It was one of the best aspects of moving back home, being close to

---

57 Means "Auntie," but not literally a relative. A respectful term for a domestic helper or nanny.

her parents. Subtle changes revealed that her parents were getting on in age. Aside from telling stale stories like a broken record, her father started using a magnifying glass to look at his weekly lottery tickets.

Despite their differences, her parents provided much-needed repose from the chaos at work. The special traveling exhibition of Elvis' *Along the River* was a logistical nightmare but a marketing dream. Attending to that was a job in itself, but Enid still had to be of assistance to the other departments. She suffered from a distinct lack of motivation since the artist Li Shen had cut *Along the River* into a triptych and agreed to sell them as a series. The shortage of ethics made her uncomfortable but, as Jade pointed out, who was she to judge if the owner and creator did not find any fault in it?

The silver lining in the clouds on the horizon was Dr. Bing. Enid practically jumped for joy when Dr. Bing came up with stipulation after stipulation on his contract. The big wigs at

Rothesay's had clearly underestimated him. At long last, in the battle of David versus Goliath, David finally won in real life!

Dr. Bing communicated with Victoria directly, and his emails were straight to the point, "I want everything sold in one day. A full-day auction with vanity catalog, full-color images of the rare jadeite, inside painted and glass overlay pieces. I am not in this for the money so I don't care what estimates you put, but I am sure you will make it worth your while." Dr. Bing even handpicked the scholars who would contribute essays for the catalog. Enid twirled Jade around the office when she read that email. Meng could not keep the note of joy out of his voice during Victoria's conference call on how to salvage the situation. There was no other option but to acquiesce to Dr. Bing's demands; it was too late in the game for the Works of Art department to put together another auction in time for early December. Victoria tried her best to involve Enid in the plea-bargaining, but Enid went through the motions without any genuine effort.

The good news continued when Ines called to say that she was coming to Shanghai for the YC (young collectors) dinner. Enid was really looking forward to spending time with Ines to discuss her moral quandary of the moment. *Am I too judgmental?* Enid could not wait to update Ines on how well she was settling into her role. At one point, it had looked like the YC dinner would be canceled, but it came through in the nick of time with Rothesay's Education as the sponsor. The YC dinner was the expensive legacy of the French ex-rep, and each year proved a struggle to find a new sponsor, as it was prohibitively expensive. The princelings and princesses in waiting expected to be impressed, and the event more than paid for itself in goodwill. Some of the clients even purchased contemporary artworks so that they could land an invitation to this ultra-exclusive event. Last year, they had sailed down the Bund, drinking gold-flaked vodka and enjoying caviar skin treatments extracted from a still twitching sturgeon. This year was a tough act to follow.

The excitement of dinner outweighed the stress of having to deal with the Head of Education, Eugenie. She was management's most prolific air-kissing ass-kisser and had attained her position by using her family's wealth. So, incapable of contributing in a concrete way without doing harm, she had finally been contained in the education department. Short courses on how to have a conversation about art at a dinner party and order wine without embarrassment were under her sole purview. It was widely known in the office that Eugenie braised sharks fin and goose webs at home to bring to Jean-Pierre. Ines sniggered, "He loathes the stuff, he passes it on to me, and I give it to Ah Sum, the tea lady." Eugenie was like Cockroach, always looking for someone to have lunch with. They should have stuck together like yesterday's congealed leftovers, but neither would have anything to do with each other.

This year did not disappoint expectations, with a series of private performances by Cirque du Soleil curated to integrate seamlessly with each degustation course. An excerpt from "O: The Aquatic" accompanied delicately seared Fourchu lobster, whilst a Mexican-inspired Mangalica pork taco was served during *The Iluvia* dance from *Luzia*.

Everyone was impresszed that Eugenie had managed to convince celebrity chef Daniel Hern to cater this intimate pop-up in Shanghai without any cost to the house! The cost was borne by Eugenie's house, as she had put her family's private plane at the chef's disposal in return for hosting this one-of-a-kind experience.

It was an epic night. Dressed to impress, Enid stared bemused at the place cards. Ines had somehow made mischief with Eugenie's carefully constructed seating plan. She was seated in between two extremely eligible gentlemen. This was due no doubt to Mimi telling tales in Hong Kong about her being a hermit/charity case that needed to be rescued. Seated to her left, Edison had paid the world record price for Andy Warhol's screen print of Mao. Sadly, this was the sole action in life that made him interesting, because he had zero conversational skills and interests aside from watching cat videos on YouTube. Enid tried her best, asking questions about where the painting was hung, inquiring if he enjoyed the Cirque du Soleil performance but to no avail. Edison stayed completely silent and stuttered into his fork every time Enid spoke to him. He was a complete washout. No light switch and not a slight flicker in the bulb when compared to the ball of energy on her left, who was holding court with travel anecdotes.

Zheng drew the attention of the whole table like a magnet, telling tales from the time he did target practice with a bazooka in Cambodia to when he was gored in the bottom at the

Running of the Bulls in Pamplona. "I had to carry a hemorrhoids cushion everywhere with me for close to a year. The life lesson here is, never take anything for granted. Even an ass, especially if it is your own!"

Everyone drew his or her chairs closer to Zheng by the end of the night, hoping to be illuminated by his glittery star power. The female guests tried their very best to win his attention by propping up their cosmetically enhanced cleavages in full view. It looked like a melon stand at the market.

Looking around at the table, Enid spotted so many familiar faces. Not that she personally knew many of them; she was there to serve. She felt anointed to be in such company, it was the crème de la crème from Shanghai's circles of privilege. Listening to snippets of their conversation, Enid was in awe of their easy elitism. "I lost so much weight at The Farm that Stefano had to make this haute couture gown all over again... it's only a second rate Lichtenstein, his collection isn't filled with up-and-comings, more like tried-tested-tired... yes, she signed the postnup and paid him back every cent he had ever spent on her, even the dry-cleaning bills for the outfits he wore on their dates... I had to buy my grandmother a Mercedes and give away the Maybach because none of her village friends know what a Maybach is."

Enid could not help staring, everyone was so good-looking and confident, their aura of entitlement was mesmerizing. And best of all, if she happened to catch someone's eye, they smiled at her. They actually acknowledged her! Ma Yi Nin from Zhabei. Of course, Enid knew that if she were to bump into them later, they would struggle to connect her face with a name. Perhaps confuse her with a receptionist from the office or one of their poor distant relatives who hovered like flies.

At the end of the night, as she was bidding farewells to the guests and handing out goody bags of La Mer and Bollinger, Enid was curious to find that Zheng was still there.

Surely someone like him has dozens of parties on the circuit to move to. But there he was, fully immersed in conversation with Ines. Enid awkwardly stood to one side, watching, they were getting along like a house on fire. She did not want to interrupt them. They would have carried on talking for hours more if Eugenie had not turned on all the lights and started shooing everyone out like a cinema usher. Enid honestly did not mind being the plus-one, but she was jealous of being the one left on the shelf, compared to quirky Ines. *What does he see in her? She has such mousy brown hair and snaggly teeth! God, I am such a bitch for being so competitive with one of my closest friends.*

Ines spotted her easily since the harsh fluorescent lights beamed down like a UFO sighting. "There you are, I was telling Zheng all about you." She clapped her hand on his back territorially. "We are friends from rich kid camp — you know, the Credit Suisse Next Generation program. You should have been sitting with us instead of giving out those goody bags! They are going to be tossed out anyway or, at the least, given to someone's grateful P.A. or *ayi*." Enid speechlessly nodded her head, too consumed by the green-eyed monster. Ines and Zheng continued to chat in a mixture of French, English, and Mandarin.

Zheng reminded Enid of a young Dr. Bing. Now that he was no longer in the limelight, he stopped playing the role of droll raconteur. Well-thought-out and critical questions were fired at Ines and Enid. He seemed interested in *Along the River*, with the idea of placing each panel in a different city hotel to attract clients. With all the marketing hype that Rothesay's was generating, it was a marvelous idea. He echoed Enid's thoughts by strongly declaring objections to the three paintings being sold separately. His passion for art was profound; his deep knowledge was evident from his comments about discovering new talent at Basel or Volta. Not in the least boastful, he casually mentioned the art schools and young students that he was trying to support.

It was obvious that Ines held Zheng in high regard — this was the first time Enid witnessed her speaking without a mocking and sarcastic tone. Ines did not care about a client's net worth, she held the most respect for clients who did their homework and collected for the love of it, not chasers of big names. Ines was the type of specialist who remained true to her principles. Her condition reports were lengthy exercises that described the most minute details from how many paintbrush hairs were adhered to canvas to the degree of restoration. Cedric repeatedly censored her reports because he feared that she was needlessly shooting down the artworks.

Contemporary art was not Enid's thing, as much as she wanted to learn more. Her mind wandered, trying to spot the sexy sous chef with the tattooed arms that had eloquently described each dish. He has a lovely smile that reached his eyes, better looking than any painting. Enid was reluctant when Zheng invited both of them to look at his latest commission, an artist collective's mural displayed in one of his hotel bars. She tried to give Ines a signaling eye that it was time to leave, but Ines ignored her and happily accepted. *Urgh, it's at the Shanghai World Financial Centre, so far away across the river. My heels are killing me.* She reluctantly followed in tow, hoping to spend more time with Ines before her flight tomorrow. She felt like the third wheel but, from what she gathered, their relationship was strictly platonic. At least Zheng made every effort to include her in his ponderously art-heavy conversation.

On the plus side, Zheng was very serious about bidding on *Along the River*. Enid was pleased. She no longer suffered from the pressure she used to as a specialist. Instead, her performance was now linked to the total volume of bids coming from bull marche

Shanghai. Zheng seemed confident that he would win *Along the River*, he had a whole marketing campaign planned — riverside cuisine with freshwater seafood served at his restaurants; displays of local willow, bamboo, and lotus blossom plants in the public areas; guided day trips to Kaifeng. He was going to milk maximum mileage out of all the hype. It was shrewd — Rothesay's with their exclusive previews and advertising campaign would build up pre-interest from the general public. Zheng would then jump on the Rothesay's bandwagon and ride it to his destination.

Only a handful of people around the world could afford to bid, but a night's stay at one of Zheng's hotels or a meal at one of his restaurants placed the paintings well within the reach of an ordinary middle-class person. Enid and Ines were in complete awe at Zheng's plans to make *Along the River* accessible. As it was, the public areas in his hotels were like private museums. Each room was tastefully decorated with editioned work by emerging artists. Artists enjoyed royalties from the merchandise sold online and in the hotel gift shop. Zheng strongly believed in sharing his love for art in a tasteful way and supporting artistic development. Enid understood why Ines respected Zheng, he combined his love of culture with financial acumen.

Zheng elaborated on the proposed F&B crowd-pleasers — a special seasonal menu with riverside delicacies like *jicai* and morel mushroom dumplings, steamed *shiyu* with rice wine, and black truffles. Delicious local comfort food amped up with notes from the finest European ingredients. "Did you like tonight's menu?" and before Ines and Enid could reply, Zheng warmly waved over someone behind Enid's shoulder. "Ladies, meet Fabien again, he's the Creative Director of all my F&B outlets."

Enid's heart skipped a beat when Fabien smiled sincerely in greeting. He did not say much, but his demonstrative hands and facial expressions conveyed his thoughts. *One of those silent but deadly heartthrob types,* Enid blushed. His awkwardness was obvious to Ines who pointedly rolled her eyes.

Zheng continued to chat nineteen to the dozen about his collection and his latest interest in Filipino contemporary art and design, whilst the rest of them slipped in one-word responses. Enid was delighted when Zheng invited her to lunch when he visited the previews in a couple of weeks. If she collected a bid from him, she would validate her position as Shanghai Representative. *Perhaps the invitation means that Zheng fancies me? But there are definitely no sparks flying."* Enid shook her head and mentally checked herself, *God, here I go again, I am supposed to be concentrating on my career but here I am, planning on throwing myself at the first eligible bachelor that comes along. Don't be a fool, Ma Yi Nin!*

Chapter 23

SERVICE WITH A SMILE

D espite the eye candy and scintillating
conversation, Enid was exhausted. She
had gone out of her way to help Eugenie with
tonight's event, despite having the Shanghai
preview preparations to finalize. *I don't
want to be the kiss-ass of a kiss-ass, but it is
strategic to have Eugenie on my side as she has
management on her side. Or, in other words,
Eugenie's self-appointment as unofficial
tattletale. I don't need another enemy.* Enid's
mind drifted toward her email exchanges
with Angela. They were professional and
very curt. She had not even asked Enid once
how she was settling in. It was as if she was a
complete stranger.

Enid tried to shake Angela's animosity out of her head as Zheng cracked another joke. With a herculean effort, she brought her attention back to the present. There was no point in dwelling on it when she was supposed to be enjoying the company of Zheng, Fabien, and Ines. Nevertheless, it was hard to shake a presentiment of doom that Angela wanted her to fail and would even go so far as to sabotage her. After all, Angela was the disciple of Liu-*jie*, the mistress of cunning. This made Enid extra cautious with the preview plans — triple and quadruple checking the specialists' flights, display requirements, and import permits.

One too many osmanthus flower cocktails and the next thing she knew, the alarm clock was shrilling away in her ear. She groaned, her head was pounding and with each throb, she listed an item on today's task list. It seemed endless but at least she fitted into this administrative and relationship-building role like a made-to-measure qipao.

This position gave her a complete picture of the running of the auction house. A good country rep could ensure the success of a preview and make a considerable difference to the bidding interest to the whole season, not just a single auction.

Ordinarily, Enid would have gone back to bed. She and Jade were now full partners in crime, taking turns to cover for each other. Most days, Jade left in the late afternoon for her *qigong* lesson. Enid had been tortured by too much hierarchical trash in Hong Kong, so she made sure that there was no such politics in her small local office. It would have been ridiculous to try anyway, with Jade's depth of experience. One of the managerial skills she had learned was to place trust in capable hands and allow the right people to proceed with their job. Vera's example had shown Enid how a strong team could be built through effective delegation and strict boundaries.

This morning's fabrication meeting was going to be one big yawn. Enid dismissed it as a waste of time. It was so old school and so China-style that the contractor had to meet her in person to go over the measurements, despite detailed email exchanges. Set-ups had the risk of going horribly wrong, but in today's final fabrication meeting for the showcases, she was merely coordinating and rubber-stamping. The exhibition fabricators had been doing this for over a decade since Rothesay's opened their offices in China, so she knew better than to show up and command everyone as if she knew what she was talking about. The contractors could do the job with their eyes closed, so there was no point in stressing about the small details.

The specialists were used to creating attractive displays from temporary set-ups anyway. The lots would speak for themselves. A preview style that was gaining popularity was the tableau scene. This was mostly done at the London and New York previews, but Enid thought it could gain traction in Shanghai. Especially if they had family collections like the recent estate auction, "Live a Vanderbilt Life." People were eager to buy into a lifestyle and the mystique of an eminent family dynasty. There was more cache to possessing a piece of tradition and legacy than a store-bought recent purchase. No item was too small, ancestral teaspoons to antique tiaras found eager homes.

The import lists showed that the preview was going to be spectacular as usual. Rothesay's well-tuned engine was revved up and running full steam ahead. Business managers had generated endless permutations of interest lists, and the specialists were targeting clients for specific lots. Enid contributed to the building momentum with appointment times and press releases to attract the general public. Part and parcel of her job was to be nice to everyone, and she relished not having to play the bad cop specialist by giving disappointing estimates or popping someone's bubble that they had inherited a priceless family heirloom.

Now that she was in a position of trust, some of the client requests asked of Enid were increasingly bizarre. They were the kind of highly personal tasks that could not be attended to by employees or family dependents. For instance, Enid helped to source extra-extra-extra-large Spanx for a male client and booked a Bro-zillian appointment for a client's unsuspecting teenage boyfriend who did not know he was in for a pejazzling session. The unofficial order of business included purchasing the new iPhone for a paranoid client and installing tracking software so that he could spy on his daughter. Forget black or platinum card services, the Rothesay's VIP card opened doors — top-secret platinum-plated diamond-encrusted ones.

Not that she stopped seeing her share of junk. Patek Philip watches, cubic zirconia jewelry with badly forged GIA certs, bronzes with sharply defined machine cut edges. They could have held entire auctions of bad fakes. *Oh wait, that is already being done by the dubious smaller houses. Stop being catty, Enid!* Despite all the wrangling and politicking at Rothesay's, Enid thanked her lucky stars whenever she met the earnest young specialists from the little shrimp houses. She honestly could not see the difference between them and her. It boiled down to luck, and she was grateful that her resume had been plucked out of the hundreds and thousands of applications that Rothesay's received daily. She felt like Career Cinderella with a gem-set, NOT glass, slipper.

There were some unforeseen lot-tery winners, such as the incredible porcelain discovery. The moment that Enid and Jade saw the Ming vase with its exquisite purplish-blue palette, they immediately recognized that they were in the presence of an inestimable masterpiece. A majestic, clawed dragon depicted in flawless traditional Chinese craftsmanship took their breath away. But that was not the sole reason they were left breathless— the consignor transported it in a white styrofoam fish feed box. The stench emitting from it was rivaled only by the malodorous aroma from the man himself. His fingernails were black with dirt, and his rough cotton trousers held up by a frayed gummy rope. The vase was discovered during excavations for an indoor toilet, and the value of his vase became apparent when dealers began paying house visits to his rural village home. It had been in his family since the fifteenth century and survived decades of family poverty and the Cultural Revolution by fortuitous concealment.

Jade took numerous photographs of the vase to send to Meng for appraisal. Exhilarated by their discovery, they suggested storing the vase safely, but the prospective consignor looked at their proffered receipt with suspicion. He could not read and write anything apart from his name, and he was taking no risks. Without a word, he grabbed the vase off the plinth and literally chucked the priceless vase back in the box. Jade's offer to professionally pack the vase with conservation materials was casually declined with a nod of the head. "It came in this box on a seven-hour train ride, it can come back with me the same way. Anyway, it's been intact since the Xuande period, I'm sure it can last a few more years." Enid smiled back at his toothy grin and took great pleasure in visualizing how his life would never be the same again once this family heirloom was sold. From *sampan* to Sunseeker. He was probably too much of a salt-of-the-earth type to indulge in luxury, so it would probably be up to his children to enjoy the newfound wealth. Their Lamborghini would probably be the first in their rural county.

Diamonds in the rough were the best. They gave the most job satisfaction. The most annoying clients were the crass show-offs who loved repeating in what they thought was a casual off-hand manner, "I haven't even worn/opened up last season's purchases."

These pretentious clients were usually the most demanding and high-maintenance. Yesterday, a client dropped by the office to buy catalogs and asked for twenty Rothesay's paper bags. Jade handed them over without batting an eyelid. Undoubtedly, these were the only high-quality items from Rothesay's that the client would ever purchase or use. The logo-ed bag would reappear in a flashy parade down Xintiandi, purportedly holding an expensive necklace instead of a thermos flask of tea. Real clients asked for nondescript brown paper bags because they were paranoid about being robbed.

Internally, it was referred to as the Napoleon syndrome, because of the client's financial stature. The smaller the wallet, the more desperate the need to compensate. Clients who purchased bargain No Reserve lots were typically the ones with the most demands. Enid learned from Alison to be solicitous to all clients, no matter who they were. Alison's client base included bread-and-butter clients that no one wanted to fight over, but they still constituted a significant bidder base. Moreover, this was China, and with a new billionaire created every five days, it was not prudent to snub anyone.

Some of her colleagues easily assumed the prestigious identity of the auction house like they had been divinely chosen and crowned. Enid would never be able to do this because she had seen the pitfalls of such assumptions. Anyway, her position was tenuous, like catnip on a string. Each time she settled down and made herself comfortable, it was a matter of time before she was clawed and then narrowly flicked out of reach. She still could not shake the premonition that her worsening relationship with Angela would lead to her downfall. *Angela would not hesitate to take advantage of my insecurities and weaknesses. I was naïve to trust her so implicitly. Anyway, what's the point of this after the fact self-immolation? What's done is done.*

One day, Jean-Pierre summoned all the country reps for an emergency conference call. Enid did not issue a peep, stunned by the anger reverberating from the speakerphone. She could visualize the veins on his temple bulging out. The signet ring rang repeatedly on the table like a heavy synthesizer rap beat, "Boh, once again I have to remind all of you. You are representatives of Rothesay's, and your behavior reflects on this house. Last season, Dewi snuck purchased lots into Jakarta in an effort to save the clients a couple of thousand in shipping fees and import duty. The result was that Rothesay's ended up spending tens of thousands in Indonesian customs fines." He seethed in anger, "Not that any of you have learned this valuable lesson by example. The latest shenanigans have reached my ears. Allowing a specialist to smuggle in artworks into Singapore without an import permit." The line crackled with static as Jean-Pierre shot out his sentences like machine gun fire.

So, the rumor about the Lin Feng Mian was true. The artwork had been consigned too late and missed the carnet deadline. Devoted as always, to hitting his target, Cedric had instructed one of his underlings to secretly import the painting into Singapore in his suitcase. Jean-Pierre listed the ramifications, "the painting could have been confiscated… no insurance coverage…illegal trafficking of high-value items…" The list went on, and Enid felt like she was the only one with the unspoken questions, *What if the junior had been caught and put in prison? Would Cedric have owned up to it or pretended that the junior had stolen and sneaked out the painting?* Enid shivered. If her supervisor had asked, she would have done the same without question. She recalled the tense uncertainty when she and Lara had been stuck at Taiwanese customs, they had been utterly alone and completely responsible. *What is it about the auction house that inspires such fear and loyalty?* It was a tantalizing and carnivorous Venus flytrap that drew you into its clutches.

That evening, as Enid sipped a second glass of Dom Perignon Reserve and nestled into the plush sofa, it was easy to drive foreboding thoughts to the back of her mind. She slipped easily into plus-one mode; it did not take much to get adjusted to this level of opulence. Hanging out with Zheng was very agreeable, with no obligations and no expenses. He casually signed credit card bills like they were autograph requests, and he was super fun to be around. Enid felt like a fool when she finally confessed her worries to Ines, "Are you kidding me? Enid, you are gorgeous but not enough for Zheng to fall for you. You are not his type. You aren't even the right gender for starters!"

Zheng laughed until he had tears in his eyes when Enid confessed her presumptions. "All I need to do is smile in someone's direction and they start selecting wedding theme colors. By the way, this doesn't work only for the single ladies. Their mamas get equally feverish at the possibility of an autumn romance and think I am trying to ingratiate myself into the sagging bosom of the family. Shudders."

It felt good to have friends around her again. Saying friends in plural was an exaggeration, considering the count came up to a grand total of two — Zheng and his boyfriend Fabien. Having someone to call at the end of a long day of work to whine or tell a funny anecdote to make a marked difference in her life. Sadly, Enid did not manage to build up much of a friendship with Xia. Xia kept to herself and communicated to Enid terse messages about whose turn it was to buy toilet paper and a reminder to double-bolt the door if she was the last one to come home. Making friends was not easy in Shanghai, as Enid did not fit into any clique. She was too much of a husband-hunter for the career women in the corporate multinationals, too common for the *fu er dai*, and too pretentious for old classmates with one-track baby brains. She resented being asked about her love life before any interest was shown in her work life (mainly because the former was dead on arrival). Men did not have to suffer the same mind-numbing torture.

Each day's work outfit was planned with great care. With previews a week away, there was no telling who would drop by the office or if a client would call up to invite the new Shanghai rep out for coffee and bidding advice.

Enid became so confident about her performance that she shifted focus to her appearance. Maybe it was back to the old bling-on-the-finger fantasies, but Enid could not help dreaming that she would meet Mr. Right through work. In an increasingly long list, HE would make people sit up and take notice when entering a room, be tasteful enough to love beautiful objects but only have eyes only for her, speak French as fluently as he spoke Mandarin, enjoy eating decadent meals but have washboard abs. The last gourmet aspiration was the newest addition to the list since Fabien had instructively treated her to a blind tasting, face-off session of Périgord vs. burgundy vs. Alba vs. whitish truffles.

Always the waiting and watchful plus-one in the corner, Enid observed and scrutinized. Now that she was frequently in Zheng's company, people speculated on their relationship. "Is he or isn't he dating her?" was the query on every Shanghai mama and daughter's collagen-smacked lips

Enid had been too much in the shadows to be deceived that the fawning attention was genuine. Did that maître d' honestly care about the room temperature when he had previously pretended that she had failed to make a table reservation? Or the compliment on her chain-store dress, when she accompanied Zheng on one of his numerous boutique buy-outs? Anyone more petty or vindictive would have unleashed insecurities, but that was not and would never be Enid. In Hong Kong, she had seen too many newly appointed young *tai-tais* throw temper tantrums or insult people who were just trying to do their jobs.

Enid marveled at her promotion from little anchovy in the sea to paparazzi-worthy mover and shaker. She found herself rubbing shoulders with established collectors and society doyens, but she never forgot her place in a complex world where money and a surname were still not enough to gain an invitation or win a friendship. At T'ang Court, when she was dining with Elvis Wang, one of his bankers sent over a bottle of wartime Margaux and settled the bill. Elvis was gracious enough to play the "Awww, you shouldn't have" game. Everyone on the table toasted the generous banker before he left, but Enid noticed that he was not invited to join them. Elvis's latest arm candy gave a harsh laugh, "What a suit! Elvis, doesn't he know that you only like your ass kissed by me?"

Everyone else laughed heartily and Enid shriveled up inside. *God knows what they say about me when I am not around. What makes Dreamy, second-runner up in the Miss China contest think she is better than that polite and generous man? He didn't do anything to her. No matter whether it is Hong Kong or Shanghai, why is there a persistent need to crush someone down to make you feel bigger and look better?* This kind of unpleasant behavior made Enid miss Luca's simplicity. Although Enid knew that she could never be as easily contented with a simple life, the harsh ugliness of the path she had chosen never ceased to trouble her.

Chapter 24

Putting on a Show

———II   II———

After months of preparation, the big week finally arrived. Although it was very cheesy, and she was sure that all the visiting specialists would kick up a fuss about the commercial tackiness, Enid had Christmas carols playing on loop.

She was sure that it created the right environment for bidding. In the season of giving, everybody loves a shiny, expensive present! Plus, she hated and did not understand classical music, it reminded her of dentists and elevators. Jade remained unconvinced but Enid reassured her, previews were changing. If they were practically doing what looked like show homes to display lots in

London and New York, Nat King Cole's "Magic of Christmas" album was hardly a game-changer. As expected, the most challenging display proved to be the 200-meters long *Along the River*. Enid had pulled off the logistics, press viewings, and marketing with great aplomb. Even Jean-Pierre called her by name now, instead of gesturing vaguely with his hands in her direction.

The long nights of socializing and rubbing shoulders with needy clients and tolerating rude comments paid off. Bidding interest on the books nearly matched Liu-*jie's* period of reign. Enid wished that she could have worked closely with Angela, but she still acted as if Enid was a total stranger. *Along the River* was covered manifold times over on the books, and there was even interest from as far away as the Abu Dhabi royal family.

Not one to rest on her laurels, Enid worked tirelessly, and Jade clucked over her like a mother hen, lecturing her to "drink chicken essence to keep your energy up" and "if you must wear those crazy high heels, don't forget to put Salonpas heat rub on your legs at night." Enid could only nod in response; she was too tired to argue with these folk remedies. At this point, the nights and days were a blur, and Enid had a persistent ringing in her ears from the endless phone calls.

Nothing was laid to chance. Management's eyes were on China and there were many balls spinning simultaneously in the air like a Greubel Forsey quadruple tourbillon; *Along the River* was pocket change compared to the bronze vessels from the Summer Palace.

Media coverage was intense; it was a magnificent opportunity for one of the Rothesay's clients to purchase a one-of-a-kind work of art from the last royal dynasty of China. Discovered in a small antiquities shop in Marseille, it had been part of Royal Marine Captain Percival's haul when he was stationed in Peking during the second Opium War. Accompanying diary entries from Captain Percival's descendants told the story of greed and power, how his commanding General supervised carts so crammed with treasures that they could barely exit the gates.

To many collectors, it presented a golden opportunity to personally possess a treasured part of China's culture, but Rothesay's was cleverly marketing it as a chance to purchase and patriotically return the vessel home to China. The State Administration of Cultural Heritage issued a multitude of official statements criticizing and demanding the vessel's repatriation and decrying the illegal and immoral theft whilst the Association of Auctioneers called on the public to boycott the sale.

Fears about protests and, more importantly, the danger of being impounded by the authorities meant that the vessels could not be physically displayed at the China previews. This did not deter Rothesay's marketing geniuses, and they produced an enticing exhibition complete with 3D projections and a CGI documentary.

Despite the heated outcry from all fronts, ranging from the popular press to government press statements, Enid was holding onto nine significant bids on the vessels. Background checks were being run on four clients, but the remainder were from serious VIP clients eager to show love for their homeland by returning the bronzes back to where they had been stolen from, over 150 years ago. It was incredibly heart-warming to Enid that there were people willing to commit millions of dollars in a show of flag-waving patriotism. *And I have a role to play in all this! This vessel belongs to us. Another item to add to the list of how blessed I am to be back home.* Although the vessels were not on display at the Shanghai or Beijing previews, Rothesay's had heightened security. Mudslinging critics made Rothesay's out as a greedy Western company out to profit from the people, a new form of imperialism.

Victoria and Meng nonchalantly shrugged off the claims. "Eventually the People's Daily will move on. Why should Rothesay's be the scapegoat when our competitor Thompson's sold those notable cloisonné censers without a hitch? It is an exaggeration that over 10 million antiquities were taken from China after 1840. Plus, no one has any records to back up the claims that close to 1.5 million items were really taken from the Old Summer Palace. Anyway, if the numbers were true, it would flood the market and we wouldn't be able to put any of it up for auction." Enid found this cavalier attitude distasteful; she expected Meng to have more integrity.

Money talks and bullshit walks. All around her it was the same nauseating bullshit. Enid remained eager to bend over backward to catch whatever steaming cow patties the clients could fling at her because she still felt a buzz of elation when closing a successful bid. It was the office politics that stank to high heaven. Works of Art had flown in ten specialists from offices around the globe at the expense of the China preview budget.

Their principal contribution was to show up to work in the late morning if at all, stinking of last night's vodka. Naturally, they were comfortable ensconced in their business class flights and club lounge floors at the Four Seasons Hotel. It was the junior and local staff standing on their feet all day, who shared rooms and flew on budget airlines.

Enid did not mind being a one-stop concierge service for the clients, but she deeply resented requests from her narcissist colleagues. She genuinely doubted if they would remember her name after the preview was over. James was a fine example of the brat pack. He rolled his eyes when Enid confessed ignorance of any underground gambling dens or illegal dog fights. The clients could barely understand his clipped tones and elongated vowels. Edward called him a "chinless wonder, he is only here because his father, brother, and uncle went to Eton with Rupert Bosewell." It had been two years since she first set foot in Rothesay's, and Enid had come a long way. She no longer suffered from social anxiety about fitting in with colleagues, and she had lost the ardent desire to curry favor. *If the clients like and accept me and they are the ones who actually have the means to bid, why should I stress if no one invites me for lunch? Pffff, anyway, James shouldn't be gambling with money he hasn't inherited yet!*

With Watches and Jewelry, it is relatively easy for an expert to spot a completely fake or Frankenstein creation. Certificates, laser-marked serial numbers, and engraved cases provided immediate verification. Enid did not envy the Paintings and Works of Art specialists — so much of their time was spent tracking provenance and even then, that was no guarantee of authenticity. There were some murmurs about this season's breathtaking Fan Guanzhang ink painting entitled *Cranes*. Consigned by a respected Taiwanese dealer, it possessed a stellar provenance. It had been sourced from the family of one of Fan's colleagues from Tsinghua University.

The soothing waterscape of dancing cranes on a riverbank worked thematically hand-in-hand with *Along the River*. Cedric marketed it as the consolation prize to underbidders of *Along the River*. It was savvy of him to place *Cranes* as the lot immediately after. Three of the clients, including Zheng, had written "either-or" bids, and it looked like it was going to be another record-breaking auction for Cedric. It was perplexing when Zheng suddenly amended his bidding form without explanation. Only after Enid's persistent inquiries did he finally confess that Ines had told him not to bid on *Cranes*. Apparently, the rumor that it was Fan's student's work gaining traction. Enid had initially dismissed it as sour grapes from Thompson's and the smaller local auction houses because they had not landed the consignment, but if Ines was whispering in Zheng's ear, there must be a grain of truth to the tale.

The clients bidding on *Cranes* were closer to Angela anyway, so Enid absolved herself of any responsibility. There was no point in fighting fires on so many fronts, particularly as this was not her battle. Enid operated in a by-the-book style. If Angela was so clear about monopolizing her clients, then it was up to her to look after their interests. She was deeply possessive of them and, if she could, she would have given them golden showers to mark her territory. All Enid had to do was stand next to one of them, and before she could utter a word, Angela paused whatever she was doing and ran clean across the ballroom. Jade timed it at an average of a minute before Angela claimed the client and gave Enid a poisonous glance before diverting away her quarry. *There are so many shui yu to be caught, the net is wide enough for both of us. She is behaving like a petty amateur.*

Enid rolled her eyes at Angela's departing back. It was childish and short-sighted. They could have been a great team together; Enid had the specialist knowledge to back up bidding recommendations whilst Angela admittedly had far superior social and tactical savvy. *She really knows who's who and who's worth what. Not only is she a human calculator, that photographic memory helps too. With a single glance, she remembers every lot and the current bid so she can egg on the bidders.* At this point, Enid had given up on ever building a bridge with Angela since they could not be cordial to each other, not even in front of clients.

Despite ever-increasing competition from local houses, the bids flowed in at Rothesay's. Enid never ceased to be amazed at the support structure and how the global tentacles of Rothesay's ensured that even the ugliest or tackiest object could be sold, provided it had some measure of rarity or intrinsic value.

Naturally, specialists and representatives from the other houses came to check out their preview. Enid could differentiate them from the clients so easily, with their thin veneer of shabby respectability. She was all too familiar with the ensemble of an overused suit and worn but well-polished Ferragamo shoes. It was the norm for competitors to make their rounds, but she personally never did. She thought it was in poor taste to sniff around like a stray dog. The competing house that most fascinated her was China Prestige. Everyone assumed that it was backed by the government and hence a sanctioned way to launder money and spend fast and ill-gotten gains. Even the specialists there looked like civil servants with their buzz cuts and plastic leather briefcases. They reeked of garlic, soya sauce, and earnestness.

With the groundwork in place, previews went by smoothly. Enid traveled to Beijing to help, although Angela made it clear that her presence was unwanted. At client dinners, Enid was deliberately and uselessly seated next to younger sons, wives of miserly husbands, social media celebrities, and clients who spent a fortune on their appearances and not much else. Not even the D list, she was relegated to the Z list. These minor clients had managed to scrape up a place at the dinner because they were seat fillers. The latest addition to the management team had come up with this guest list without consulting colleagues on the ground, the reasoning being that Rothesay's had to strike a balance between discreet old money and the flash cash of the newly minted. Jade quipped, "Fine, if these people had any money at all, but the only thing they have in the millions are Weibo and Instagram followers."

The day after previews ended, Enid delighted in no makeup and Pleats Please baggy trousers. She had finally learned how to dress. And shop. At sample sales and secondhand luxury stores, of course. How to wear brands that were clearly brands without the logo. It made her cringe now to think of her once-treasured Coach bag. However, she never let herself forget how gauche she once was. She hung the bag on her room door as a reminder to double-check her appearance before setting foot out into the world.

Appearance was image, and image was perception. Enid had been subliminally groomed by her Hong Kong friends. When Mr. Bai showed up at the preview newly single and ready to mingle, she no longer looked at him with stars in her eyes. The shiny H belt buckle and sequined Gucci jacket were so ostentatious. Now, she felt like she had a lot to teach him rather than vice versa. Gone were the days when he had to explain that risotto was not undercooked stale rice. Her aloofness was tantalizing, and he came every day to the preview. Enid was sure it was because he was not used to hearing the word no.

"Hey Bai-*gege*, I'm not saying this because I work for an auction house, but why don't you collect something aside from watches and jewelry."

He grinned cheekily in response, "But that means I actually have to know what I'm buying. That's so boring. Are you trying to turn me into some wannabe smartie pants show-off so I can start going to lectures with you and Professor Zheng? Sorry to disappoint you dear, but I only like spending money on stocks, watches, jewelry, property, and you, of course."

Enid knew negging was the worst kind of flirting, but she could not help it. Bai reminded her too much of her simple parents, they had zero desire to expand their horizons. Well, sort of like her parents. Except with many more digits in his bank account

Despite being equally at ease slurping a bowl of street noodles or twirling a forkful of al dente tagliatelle al tartufo, after a few first dates in Western restaurants, Bai unilaterally stated a preference for simple street food. Roaring up to a roadside stall in one of his super sports cars was not her idea of fun. Nevertheless, she appreciated the simple pleasures they had, like going squid fishing at night and sharing Sichuan popcorn chicken in the cinema. "This is the first time I have ever dated a girl that enjoys spending as much time with me as the Cartier saleslady."

Enid felt sorry for Bai, she liked him, but she was definitely not feeling the same butterflies in her stomach that she had with Luca.

Playing the Chinese courtship game, Enid introduced Bai to her parents even though they had not gone past second base. She was careful not to become of his many gossip-magazine flings, and she remained unsure if she wanted to be Mrs. Bai numero quattro. Enid was not particularly attracted to Bai, but she still went through the usual girlfriend routine — checking his phone when he went to the bathroom, leaving a cutesy (territorial) stuffed toy in his car, and calling him at random hours to see what he was up to. Enid skillfully staked her claim even though she did not know if she wanted ownership.

Zheng and Fabien teased her endlessly, "You have him wrapped around your little finger, so stop playing coy. The more you say no, the more he wants you. You are that edition unique Richard Mille that he needs to get his fat paws on. Give him a chance; we would welcome the challenge of a makeover. First plan of action: burn those striped polo shirts and flashy gold buckle belts. Then maybe a couple of months on the Paleo diet or, better still, boot camp. He needs to learn that a massage doesn't count as exercise. And that no one, under any circumstances, should have a long pinky fingernail. Yuck!" Enid stifled a giggle and gave a feeble attempt to defend Bai.

After all, it was thanks to him that she was enjoying her new social status. It seems like her days of being the consummate people pleaser were drawing to a close. She was tired of being the designated driver, the one who accompanied girls to the bathroom, the dinner party invitee forced to sit next to the most boring guest. It was refreshing to finally be the individual that people had to tiptoe around and be solicitous toward. One rung up the social ladder was a very comfortable place to be.

Bai fitted in with a certain set of Enid's clients. Amongst them, he was charming and eloquent and moved with ease. Around the more westernized crowd, Bai clammed up and sat by himself in the corner. "Why do we need to spend time with these people? They have Western names they can't even pronounce that they picked up from TV. And they speak Mandarin with a fake accent even though it is their mother tongue. And the way that they mock normal people slurping noodles or squatting by the road! What makes them think they are better than everyone else? Their grandparents were working in the fields alongside mine. We are so blessed to be where we are and yet they look down on others who aren't as fortunate."

Enid rolled her eyes and changed the subject. She knew deep down that Bai was making sense and, for the first time, she realistically saw herself having a future with him. *Perhaps it is better to have a comfortable life without trying so hard and putting on airs all the time. All the magazines say that it is better to be with someone who loves me more than I love him. He even gets along with my parents. I am an expert at the art of faking it, look how far I've come. He doesn't have to know that I am not head-over-heels-in-love with him. Over time, I am sure that I can truly start to love him, at least I respect him.*

Fortune smiled on her love and work life; it was clearly an auspicious time, and Enid felt blessed. The previews had gone so well that Jean-Pierre was even thinking of getting a foot soldier for Enid and Jade. There was no doubt in her mind that the auction would do well. At each interest meeting with the heads of department, all seemed like smooth sailing. On paper, more than three-quarters of the auctions were covered. Even the fishy *Cranes* flew high with overwhelming interest. With a low estimate of USD 200,000, it was a bargain when compared to *Along the River*.

Cedric's reputation for being a bull shark in a red sea was a well-deserved one. Liaising to schedule his appointments and tagging along, Enid was taken aback to find him not just wining and dining clients. Galleries and dealers were high on his attention list. Cedric was cold and distant when he did not need to switch on the charm offensive, so he did not babysit her at the meetings. It was left to Enid to observe and learn by example, she watched him pit the galleries against each other, feeding dealers information about which client was interested in collecting the work of a particular artist, as well as who was selling off their collection. Again, Enid experienced the cold-water shock of how the game was played by the players who made the rules. So much for conflict of interest, it was literally and figuratively a game of Chinese whispers.

Enid was glad when all that was left was personal preparation for the Hong Kong auctions. "Two inches higher please, and then take it in here and here," Enid motioned to the tailor. She had a week's worth of new outfits, designs copied off Ray Li and Yoka. com. Thinking back to when she had first started at Rothesay's, wearing those Chanel knock-off tweed jackets that left a trail of fluff behind. Not to mention the plastic gold double C buttons with rhinestone finishing.

It was so crass, no wonder no one wanted to make friends with me. Sure, I still can't afford the real deal, but if I really wanted it, Bai would pay for it without question. He already offered me a supp card. But why should I? It matters more to me that I can have it when I want it. And I only want it if I can buy it with my own hard-earned money. I am in this for the long term, not to get a new pair of shoes that will be outdated in a few months. Bai knows that I am not using him for his money, but who knows how long before the novelty of me wears off? I don't want to be another cliché, a client cast-off, discarded like last season's catalog.

In Hong Kong, the taxi driver made her repeat the Grand Hyatt address over and over again. It was so annoying; she knew he understood her perfectly even though her Cantonese had an obvious Mainland accent. She knew the type, resentful of Mainland money and political power. There was no time to rest, and after a quick change of clothes, Enid headed next door to the HKCC. The preview displays were remarkable; she made mental notes and took photographs. There was always more to learn. Even Enid, who had been CC'ed in the hundreds of email set-up discussions and logistics arrangements, was blown away by the spectacle.

She could not wait to show Bai what money could really buy. This kind of display spelled out for clients the lifestyle and surroundings they could aspire to. All of it could be theirs with one paddle raise and one swipe of the credit card. *Of course, it is unashamedly wannabe, but keeping an open mind is half the battle! I want Bai to broaden his horizons like the Mimis and Zhengs of this world. So many possibilities are waiting, like a magic carpet ride. If I had even a tenth of Bai's bank account, how different my life would be. This is not merely about possessions; it is about experiences.* There was a difference between owning a Sèvres porcelain dinner service and storing it in a display cabinet and eating your daily meal off it so that you could savor the gilded pattern appearing as you cleared your plate.

Unsurprisingly, Bai was resistant to change but he doted on her, so Enid knew she could coerce him into anything. After all, he was coming to Hong Kong to keep her company, even though he was not bidding on anything. She had been clear to dissuade his interest this season. More and more, she was of the mindset that he was for keeps. It was imperative that he did not feel like she was dating him to fill up a couple of bidding forms. The effort worked both ways; he truly tried his best to make her happy. Even the choice of hotel on this trip, she appreciated that he reserved the suite at Grand Hyatt instead of staying at the usual Four Seasons where the staff groveled over him and his HKD 1,000 tips. Of course, the plus side of this was that he would be on full display. Angela and her minions would never dare to bully her as long as Bai and his *fu er dai* circle were eating out of her hand.

Perhaps she was a veteran after a mere two years in the business, but she did not suffer from the usual nervous attack or nerves. *I guess being a rep, especially for China, is different. People are spending money left, right, and center. With the paddle guarantees and signed bidding forms, the old days of clients defaulting are long gone.* Enid wandered through the previews, not disturbing any of her friends or the people who pretended to be her friends. She had more clout as a rep than she ever had as a specialist, particularly as the gatekeeper to Chinese bids. Colleagues who would have previously blanked her acknowledged her with a half-wave or passing eye contact. Even if they disliked her on a personal level, they had to respect her professionally.

She made absolutely sure to do a thorough job — she never missed a single interest meeting or ignored a single email or telephone call from her colleagues, no matter how trivial. Enid was too humble to realize it, and at no point did it dawn on her that she had singlehandedly earned her new status, it had not rubbed off on her by association.

The halls were a hive of activity, everyone counting lots, setting up the displays, and marking their catalogs with any recently adjusted reserve prices. The earliest hours of the preview were the most crucial, as this was when the more serious collectors arrived. Not the desperate to-see and be-seen types. Although paparazzi courting clients were not completely without merit, the specialists sincerely appreciated clients who really make the effort to understand what they were bidding on. Senior management was behind-closed-door meetings, and Enid made a mental note of who was absent and who was strolling around like a headless chicken. It paid off to scrutinize who were the chosen few that made the big decisions. Enid went to deliver some candy to the Bids Department from the famous Xiaochengguang Snacks Shop. In her first season, the jewelry administrator had taught her the importance of keeping support staff happy. It meant getting an updated auctioneer's book slightly faster than other departments.

The bathroom door slammed, and Enid heard Angela complimenting Lara on her shade of lipstick. Enid shuddered and lowered the toilet seat cover; she was going to hide in the cubicle until they left. "Oh, I'm shocked you like it, your frenemy bought or, more likely, stole it for me last Christmas." Enid could hear Lara snickering before volleying the bitchball back, "She is such a cheap gold digger. Did you hear that she dragged Bai to Hong Kong? What is she hoping, that he will bid on the pink diamond as an engagement ring? Please! He will throw her out like yesterday's newspaper once he is done with her. She should probably try to get herself pregnant. You know how fertile these peasant-types are." Not even a pause for breath, "Little Miss Popularity doing that cutesy act with the bosses and the clients. Absolutely no dignity. I can't wait for her to get what she deserves."

I thought we were friends! Enid was shaken to the core and trembled with anxiety. *Is this what everyone thinks of me? I really do my best at work! Does dating Bai give people ammunition and make people take me less seriously? I thought that it would make everyone sit up and take notice (in a good way). Or at least be happy for me.* Enid put her head in her hands, her tears making rivulets down her foundation and staining her white collared shirt. *They are mean girls. So mean. I don't think I have ever been this mean to anyone. Mean. Mean. Mean. Why can't they be happy for me instead of trying to step on me? Even if Lara approaches me for a favor in a few hours, I will still help her. Maybe that's my mistake,* she thought grimly. *I am such a sucker. It is true, I am stupid for trying to get everyone to like and respect me.*

Once the coast was clear, she was unlocking the cubicle door with shaking hands when she heard a barely stifled sob. "Hello?" Whoever was inside the next cubicle had already heard her bawling her eyes out. Anyway, her cubicle neighbor was clearly as miserable as her. It was Cockroach. Sobbing so hard that she was wheezing for breath. She looked as bad as Enid did. Without a word, Enid gave her a hug. With so much bitchiness and nastiness permeating the air, there was no point in crushing another person's soul.

Enid did not want to ask, but Cockroach stuttered, "It was a mistake, I was trying to email a preview reminder to all the VIP clients and forgot to put the addresses in the BCC field. Now everyone has everyone else's email. It is a free-for-all mailing list exchange.

Jean-Pierre and HR asked to speak with me tomorrow morning. I might as well pack up my bag and leave now, instead of giving air kisses at the opening cocktail party to people who will be thrilled at my misfortune."

As much as Enid would have liked to console her, there was nothing to say. She stared, her mouth agape.

"Shut that mouth," Cockroach said coldly. "You look like you are catching flies. You have nothing to say? I was once like you, always eager to please. I was at everyone's beck and call, booking manicures, walking the dog, feeding the fish, scratching an itch. Yes, people actually wanted to call me once upon a time. If you are lucky and smart enough to get to where I am, you will realize how jealous people are of success."

Enid turned away in horror and avoided eye contact by scrubbing away at the smeared mascara. *How deluded Cockroach is — people aren't jealous of her; people don't like her because she is unpleasant! She is notorious for stepping over anyone and everyone to get what she wants. Even her sissy husband has his shrunken balls in her handbag. Could I become like Cockroach? I always have the best of intentions and genuinely want to help people. My agenda is my own, not at the expense of others.*

To Enid's dismay, the awkward silence did not last. "Yoohoo ladies, no one sent me a calendar invite to this meeting? Count me in for a team building session!" *Oh God, just what we need, Eugenie. Now it's the three most unpopular people in the whole of Rothesay's.* Eugenie lined up with them in front of the mirror, checking her teeth whilst simultaneously unpicking her thong wedgie from doughy butt cheeks.

Enid was horrified at Eugenie's up-close-and-personal behavior. *Both of them have no boundaries and I do! Why would people tar me with the same brush? I know I care too much about what others think of me, but it is in my nature — I can't help myself. I am a much better person than I am given credit for.*

Enid patted her pocket and pretended that her phone was buzzing. She swiftly excused herself. The last thing she wanted was for someone else to come in and think they were having an intimate pow-wow. The Three Witches of Macbeth. She could not help herself and patted Cockroach gently on the back as she left. *Wow, that's some death stare. I guess she doesn't want my sympathy. OK, OK, maybe it came off as a pity pat!* Enid shrugged. *Enough of that, I have bigger problems. I wish I could speak to Ines or Mimi. If anyone is really my friend, it is those two. Alison is too much of a fence-sitter to give me any comfort.*

As glum as she was, it was relatively easy to put the unpleasant episode at the back of her mind. Head high, back straight, hair flip, and dimpled smile. The cocktail party for VIP clients was a splendid success. All her clients that had promised to attend stayed long after the hors d'oeuvres were served, placing bids. They gave her a tremendous amount of face, mentioning to some specialists that had specially come to Hong Kong to support Enid in her first auction as Shanghai rep.

Enid took so much comfort in her client relationships *(dare I call them friends?)* and she was deeply grateful. From the bathroom debacle, she knew for certain that some of her colleagues laughed at her role as trusted sidekick. Nevertheless, this was how she built up relationships and got people to rely on her. She played a hand with the only cards at her disposal — being a sincerely nice person. They trusted her, and their trust was well placed. Only she knew which client's daughter was in rehab instead of studying art history in Florence. Or the multi-millionaire client that was too cheap to buy retail and would only bid for his many girlfriends at auction if Enid promised the condition was "as new" and sourced boutique packaging, so the lots appeared store-bought.

The clients respect me more than my colleagues do. Honestly, if I were to go to another auction house tomorrow, I am sure they would continue to support me. They wouldn't delete me from their phone book, which is more than I can say for half the people working in this office. Now I understand why Liu-jie behaved the way she did. Wallowing in her misery would mean that she was throwing in the towel, so she plastered on her brightest smile and make small talk throughout the party. Rothesay's had certainly trained Enid well; she even had a conversation with Lara without revealing a single twinge of discomfort.

Only when the lights of the display cases were turned off did Enid self-indulge. She deflated like a punctured helium balloon. Perched out of sight on the window ledge, she massaged her calves and ignored the messages from Jade and Ines inviting her to a late-night supper of satay beef noodles at Tsui Wah. Bai was arriving after midnight and she wanted to meet him. Out of everyone, he was the one who knew her best, and he clearly liked what he saw! He made no attempt to change her, although it was unfortunate that she could not say the same herself. *If I regard him as my security blanket, I am no better than his ex-wives, and I deserve the lowly opinion that some of my colleagues have of me. Look what happened with Luca. Stop and take a breath, Yi Nin, you don't need to always be moving onwards and upwards.*

Surprise, surprise, the flight was delayed so Enid had no other choice but to head to the hotel bar to meet Ines and Mimi. As soon as Ines saw her facial expression, she called for a fresh round of lychee martinis. "Seriously, you were leaving us to get drunk by ourselves? Mimi came to the preview to support us. The least you can do is to buy us drinks on that big fat expense account of yours, Miss Rainmaker." Enid smiled wanly.

She barely sat down before her reddened eyes started to tear again. After relating her pathetic tale, she saw the look of genuine concern coupled with exasperation on both Ines and Mimi's faces. "Seriously, put on your big girl panties and deal with it," Ines said as Mimi nodded. "You signed up for this bitch fest but then you act like it is an eye-opener when someone draws a bull's eye target on your back. As much as we love you, please stop playing the damsel in distress!"

"Amen!" Mimi lifted her glass.

"You are so much better than that." Ines continued, "Find the strength in yourself. You, and only you, are responsible for this season's highest client turnout. You trumped all the other reps. Plus your clients are putting their money where their mouths are and putting in bids. Management is singing your praises." Ines paused to give Enid a high five, "Come on, you have to realize that's what made them turn on you. Pure envy. Bullies, that's what they are. If you are foolish enough to feel sorry for yourself instead of celebrating, you deserve the opinion they have of you!"

Enid felt a little silly after Ines' rousing speech. Mimi piped in, "All I can say is that I am glad that I left that toxic place. Bad vibes, bad karma. Enid, don't let the place change you. You need to be stronger than this, or you need to move on."

Enid was startled by Mimi's advice. The truth of it echoed with her for days. Easygoing party girl Mimi practiced what she preached, and she was so much the happier for it. Everyone has something to learn from someone. *I can be so childish and overdramatic. So what if a few people don't like me? From the outset, they dismissed me as a Zhabei peasant. They never gave me a chance to start with, so why do I keep seeking their approval? I am Enid Ma Yi Nin! I am more than someone's girlfriend, employee, or friend.*

Chapter 25

HAMMER TIME

—ıı—   —ıı—

Multiple alarm clocks shrilled at the crack of dawn. Enid checked to make sure that Bai was not in the room before proceeding to unleash the most guttural swear words in Shanghainese, English, French, and Mandarin. *Why do I do this to myself? Urgh, I will never remember that drinking is only a good idea at the time.* Her last concrete memory was of Mimi taking over the drums at the Champagne Bar, so it must have been Bai who set all the alarm clocks. Berocca and Alka-seltzer, stirred not shaken, chased with a couple of Asprin.

After the night she had, liver damage was the least of her worries. As Enid swallowed her hangover cocktail of choice, she spotted a note lying on top, "Thought you would need this. Gone for a meeting, see you later."

Enid smiled and then winced from the effort. She had never imagined that Bai would be this kind of boyfriend. When she had first met him, she had looked up to him as a sophisticated princeling but with such a playboy reputation; she had not expected him to be this tender-hearted. When she confessed all this to Bai, he unequivocally assured her that no one else had ever made him want to be a thoughtful and better person. If good relationships were about making each other into better people, then they were the perfect pair, yin and yang.

Enid increasingly believed that they ticked all the right boxes together. He made her feel secure about her family, her capabilities, and the kind of person that she was trying to become. It was hard to verbalize and explain, especially since Bai was not a touchy-feely kind of person. Being a typical Asian male, he was so practical, and he waved his hand dismissively, "Enid, you are perfect to me until you start talking about your feelings. I mean, I won't even ask you to get a boob job." Enid smacked him when he said that. He could be such an idiot.

It was going to be another long day and an even longer week ahead. Try as she might, sky-high heels were an impossible task for her. Moving at an elevated height was enough to set the nausea rolling in. She was impressed with herself that she stomached it when Lara waved her over to join breakfast. After yesterday's pep talk and calming reassurances, Enid felt stronger than ever. *So what if Lara doesn't like me? I have been nothing but supportive and helpful to her. If she does not want me as a friend and backstabs me, then it is her loss. She may laugh at my background but, at least where I come from, we don't treat people like this.*

They shared a pineapple bun while going through the big lots that Enid's clients were bidding on to make sure that no one was adjusting or withdrawing their bids. Enid patted herself on the back for being so calm and professional.

The previews were going smoothly. Enid enjoyed touring the preview with her clients and spending time with them. She picked up a few extra bids on her rounds. Seeing objects in real life was always better than two-dimensional images in a glossy catalog, no matter how wonderful Francesco's work was. The earliest auction was handbags, which always sold like hotcakes. An easy auction for the beginner auctioneer, it passed without a hitch despite the backlash against the former First Lady, now Bag Lady of Malaysia. Many of the Southeast Asian clients did not want to be seen with an ostentatious display of wealth on the crook of their elbow after the ex-Prime Minister's wife was arrested for spending the country's money on baubles and branded goods. She was this century's answer to Imelda Marcos, minus the fabulous hairstyle.

The repeated striking of the auctioneer's gavel was sweet music to Enid's ears. Snugly ensconced in the telephone bidding bank, Enid did not miss being a specialist in the least. She had the best of both worlds now, client interaction without having to stand behind the display cases for hours. It was much more thrilling to sit next to the more experienced reps. She learned to adjust the cadences of her voice and how to encourage bidding without sounding desperate. Even when she was not taking a bid or waiting for an upcoming call, she acted busy by doodling in her catalog and frowning furiously in concentration at the auctioneer. Psychologically, it would not do to have the Shanghai rep absent from the action, so she rarely took a bathroom break. All the consignors were in pursuit of Chinese money, and Enid was responsible for rounding up the fatted calves.

An added plus of sitting on the telephone bank was that she got to take off her shoes. Despite a platform at the front and the addition of a Dr. Scholl's cushion pad, pain radiated all the way from the ball of her foot to the front of her shin. Honestly, she hated wearing high heels. It did not say anything in the employee dress code about wearing heels, but there was peer pressure from everyone. If you wore flats, no one said anything, but if you wore heels you warranted a compliment and a second glance.

The same rigorous presentation applied for the men with their pocket-handkerchiefs and tight suits. The Thai rep was dressed to the nines in a very elegant houndstooth suit with contrast stitching. He grumbled in a low whisper between lots, "I am trying not to get up so often because if I sit and stand up too fast, my trousers may burst at the seams. Damn my vanity for asking for hand-basted silk gauze seams. I can't even look at carbs in case my eyes absorb the calories." His patent shoes were even pointier than Enid's, they were so narrow they looked like racing skis. So, it did not make a difference if she wore heels or not, everyone was uniformly pimped out and uncomfortable.

Yet another record-breaking season for Rothesay's. The more confident specialists were already patting themselves on the back. Enid did not allow herself the luxury of relaxing. Too many people were poised with knives at her back or breathing down her neck. Nothing unforeseen occurred...until the Paintings auction.

Enid was in such high spirits about *Along the River* that she barely slept the night before. Li Shen was expected to achieve a new record high for work sold at auction, and it was widely anticipated that a landmark value for contemporary ink brush painting would be attained. A hush stole over the auction room when the lot number was announced. At least a dozen paddles in the room and on the phone bank popped up like a game of Smack the Gopher.

Enid was on the telephone with the Collections Curator from the Shanghai

Art Museum, so she was fully occupied. Bureaucrats to a T, it was achingly slow to eke out a bid from them. By the time they agreed to an increment, the auctioneer had already moved on. The Curator was getting antsy, and Enid could tell that at USD 20 million, their budget ceiling had been hit. It was a relationship worth preserving, so Enid graciously stayed on the telephone to keep him abreast of the bidding progress. Now that she had time, Enid scrutinized the room. As expected, Zheng was quietly sitting at the back of the room, poised to pounce like a panther in a sleek black velvet blazer.

"Oh!" Enid exclaimed out loud and then tried to deflect her note of incredulity as part of an increment update to the Curator. To her astonishment, Elvis' brother Winston as well as Li Shen's gallery manager had their paddles raised. It was not a casual flick of the paddle either. They were strong-arming it. Enid mentally counted off the number of people who had seen the painting in Elvis' possession. No wonder she had never met his brother. And why Cedric had been so keen to keep the contract strictly hush-hush. Even Jean-Pierre did not know who the consignor was; it had been logged in the system under a company name. Both of them did not bother lowering their paddles as they steamrolled bidding to USD 40 million. People in the room craned their necks to see who was bidding and blatantly pulled out their phones to record the frenzy. The high estimate had already been surpassed.

What is the deal? I hope Zheng isn't going to get caught in the unfriendly fire of this bidding war. Enid regretted that she had not made the time to catch up with him this morning when he landed in Hong Kong. Sure, Zheng could more than afford even double this amount, but it became a question of worth. This amount could build hospitals and orphanages in Sichuan province. Hopefully, Zheng was wiser and more prudent than this. She wanted the best for her friend, and it was definitely not some ridiculously priced painting. This was not an investment in the future; it was an expensive folly. Bidding had now reached an impasse and Charles was allowing split bids of USD 100,000. Not that hundreds of thousands of dollars made a difference since the bidding price was now USD 49 million. Excluding premium.

What will happen if the Wang brothers buy back the painting? Or the gallery does? It is too ridiculous to fathom. Will they cough up the money? Or is this another scheme à la Royal Oyster Ricci where someone will be left holding the hot potato? Enid's palms slicked up with nervous sweat. They fell under the Shanghai client portfolio. If anyone's neck was on the chopping block, it was hers. With a sinking feeling of dread coupled with elation, Enid saw Zheng shift about in his seat and call out in a ringing tone, "50 million dollars!"

Everyone turned 180 degrees from their seats to stare at Zheng. Whispers emitted from all corners of the room like piped-in background music. Zheng needed no introduction since he had made number one on the prestigious Forbes list of 30 Young Entrepreneurial Disrupters for the past two years running.

The ambush worked. Winston and Li Shen's manager dropped their paddles and shook their heads. *Such good actors, that look of fake disappointment in their faces.* Enid was incensed. She had been a pawn in all this, manipulated by the Wang brothers and Cedric. She hoped to God that Zheng would forgive her and not think that she had taken advantage of their friendship. *I've sucker-punched him and, worst of all, he looks like the cat that got the cream.* Enid stared across the phone bank, trying to catch Ines' eye. She could not bear to stare a minute longer at Zheng. If she felt this terrible, Ines must feel a million times worse. The crescendo of applause for the world record high was as loud as the blood rushing in her ears. She was overwhelmed by guilt and worry.

Strangely enough, she could not say the same for Ines. She watched Ines proudly accept the congratulations of colleagues sitting nearby. The room was in an uproar, and it barely settled down in time for *Cranes*. If Enid did not have to handle telephone bids for the upcoming lot, she would have rushed after Zheng. He stood up and buttoned his suit jacket after the next lot was announced, poised like a GQ cover model. A swarm of reporters trailed after him like bees to honey. The rest of the auction went by in a blur; Enid was too disturbed and distracted to focus.

"Ines! Ines!" Enid rushed after her as she walked to the Bids Office. "What are we going to do? What are we going to do about Zheng?"

Ines gave her a funny look, "What do you mean, a bottle of champagne? He should be treating us, not the other way round!" Then the Gallic shrug, "Yup, lucky him, he got *Along the River* for less than he budgeted."

Ines looked searchingly at Enid's troubled expression and then motioned toward the Bids Office with her folder. Sensing that Enid was about to launch into one of her monologues, she pulled her away to the side.

The rest of the conversation was continued in French, in case any nosy reporters or clients were snooping.

Ines began with a dramatic sigh before launching into a forceful rebuke, "Enid, this Bambi act has had one too many encores. Zheng is my friend too, and I have known him for years longer than you. Did we cheat him? Absolutely not. Do you know why? Because we have now created the artist's value and made his market. This is what we do. Enid, this is the auction business. Li Shen now holds a record high for contemporary ink painting at Rothesay's. We help everyone. Zheng, the art market, the artist, hotel guests eager to see this painting. A world record high means more than dollars and cents. Zheng is more street-smart than anyone at Rothesay's.

He did his homework. Believe me, he is not feeling hoodwinked. That artwork is going to be an asset of his hotel company, and if he sells it at a loss once interest dies down, it will be a tax write-off. Win, win!"

Phrased in such terms, Ines' explanation made perfect sense to Enid. *She is the same age as me, but she must think I am an idiot. She has to continually give me motivational talks, detailed explanations, and advice. I feel completely naïve.* On the plus side, Enid knew that she could count on her friends' seemingly bottomless store of patience. They had a soft spot for her because she was eager to learn and eager to please. Where she came from, she was the wiliest of her friends and family, but in this circle, she was the country bumpkin. Enid smiled at Ines gratefully and let her continue with her work at the Bids Office. Her simplicity embarrassed her, but she did not take it too hard. It was a continuous learning curve after all, on both a professional and personal level. The same mistake would not be made again; she was an avid student.

The Works of Art auction sold 92% by lot and 78% by value. The Summer Palace bronzes spearheaded the auction. After the lot was hammered, half the auction room emptied like a stink bomb had been let off. So much publicity had been generated that the lot eventually hammered at twice the high estimate. To Enid's surprise, the lot was not purchased by the usual VIP collector. It was a fairly new client, a Mr. Yang whom Angela boisterously claimed as her own, despite his residing in Shanghai. She was so territorial that Enid could not get close. She had barely spoken a dozen sentences to him, even though Mr. Yang was well known in the collecting community as a trustee of the China Antiquities Association.

Victoria was still shaking hands in congratulations with her business manager when Sean from Marketing came running. Their pleasure at the excellent results was ridiculously short-lived, barely lasting more than five minutes. "Mr. Yang is standing at the main entrance speaking to reporters. He and his fellow trustees pre-arranged it." Sean bent over and paused to take a much-needed breath. Angela chimed in, "Well, why not? He paid USD 20 million for it, surely he earned himself a little picture in the newspaper," with a smug smile on her face. "No, no, Mr. Yang announced that it's a protest bid. He has zero intention of paying even a single dollar. He claims to be the ultimate patriot and he is doing what any proud Chinese should. He is letting the press know that he deliberately sabotaged our auction, and they are jubilantly lapping it up. We are going to be on the front page of every major newspaper tomorrow for the wrong reasons."

Enid watched the scene unfold as if in slow motion. Angela, with the smile still frozen on her face, backed away as if Sean were a stranger with a highly contagious skin disease. *So much for Mr. Yang being her precious client. Now Angela will get what she deserves. She can't wash her hands off Mr. Yang, she's his Designated Contact in the client system.* Everyone in the department turned the same shade of grey. Without further ado, they rushed off to the bullpen. Enid knew precisely what was going to happen — full crisis mode, just like when Liu-*jie* had sold the Hung Estate's ruby and diamond necklace to the defaulter. It was going to be a long night for them, and Enid was gratified that she did not need to be part of the war cabinet. She was looking forward to room-service congee and a quiet night with Bai. Her stomach was still uneasy after last night's lychee martinis. After today's tumultuous events, last night seemed like it belonged in the distant past.

Back in the room, Enid ran the bubble bath while scrubbing off her make-up. She was about to get into the tub when Bai came in with her phone, "Hey, your phone was ringing so many times that it vibrated off the table." He shook it before setting it down.

"What shall we have for dinner, congee or fried noodles or both or you want *al dente* pasta, since now you know what it is?" he grinned cheekily.

Enid smiled and took a swipe at him with her towel; she was so appreciative of him and his modest ways. She could not imagine sitting down to a fancy steak or sushi dinner after such a long day. At least they could be real with each other. *Argh, eleven missed calls from Jean-Pierre's assistant and four more from Meng.* With a heavy sigh, Enid kissed Bai goodbye, instructed him to go ahead and order first, then ambled slowly back to the HKCC.

Before Enid could even take a seat, Jean-Pierre let forth a volley of questions. She knew it was serious, the French flawless poise had evaporated. His tie was hanging at loose ends around his neck and his suit jacket was off, exposing a sweat-stained shirt. His assistant, Victoria, Meng, and their business manager stared at her. The accusation fired out like a rifle shot, "How could you let this Yang character bid? This is far worse than the Liu-*jie* situation! It is so public. No underbidders will touch that lot for fear of being tarred as disloyal to their heritage!"

Enid looked around and said in a small voice, "He's Angela's client, she is his D.C., you should speak to her about it. And anyway, Victoria and Meng know him well and did not object to him having a paddle."

Jean-Pierre slammed his hand so hard on the table that Enid saw his signet ring mark a groove in the wood. "Are you an idiot? What kind of excuse are you making? Don't pass the parcel. He is from Shanghai. It is your job to know what the Shanghainese clients are up to. I feared that you were too incapable to handle such an important role, and you have proved me right." The accusatory lecture continued but Enid was so incensed that she barely heard his words. The blood boiled in her ears. *So this is how it is going to go down, sacrificing me as the scapegoat. Well, I am not going to be an easy mark.*

Everyone in the room was shocked when Enid loudly retorted back. No one had ever dared to challenge Jean-Pierre in public, especially such a junior-level staff. At that instant, she no longer cared. *All the advice from everyone has not helped me, why should I keep my head down and trudge around like a stoic foot soldier. That way, I am cannon fodder.* "J'accuse! Do you even have the facts before you hang me out to dry? Angela, Victoria, and Meng were the ones cultivating this client. I've barely had a full conversation with him. This house is run by divide-and-conquer, with everyone so territorial, I stayed far away from him. You are pointing the finger at the wrong person, and the blame game politics of this house is detestable."

Stunned silence. Even Jean-Pierre was lost for words, "Ummm aaaah, if this is true then we need to get to the root of this matter."

Enid silently walked over to the computer and logged into the client system. Clear as day, Angela's name was there as the point of contact. Without a word, she printed out the record, handed it to Jean-Pierre, and stormed out of the room without looking back. She shook like a leaf. Back in the room, Bai opened a whisky from the minibar to calm her down before she could utter a word. It burned her throat when she downed it in a single gulp, "I had to do it, I had to stand my ground. If I didn't, I would have lost my job, so either way, I had to open my mouth. Damned if I do and damned if I don't. Well, at least I don't have to wake up early tomorrow. I am done for, dog meat."

When Enid went to bed that night, she did not bother to set her alarm clock. In fact, she switched off her phone. She could not remember the last time she had done that. The shock of her outburst settled in, and it was replaced with euphoria. She felt the weight drop off her shoulders; perhaps she could travel with Bai for a while or become a French teacher. There were many possibilities now that she had so many clients who liked her. With her new circle of friends and acquaintances, she was confident that she would be able to find a new job. Bai shyly hinted that perhaps she did not have to work at all, but Enid graciously refused. "I need to be independent. What would I do all day? Polish your car? Stay home and make *jiaozi*?" Enid had enough savings to feel confident, and she knew that her mother would have saved pocket money for a rainy day like this one.

That night, she slept like a baby. It was the slumber of the innocent and the vindicated. She would have continued to snore past noon if the hotel phone had not shrilled piercingly in her ear. Ines' voice bubbled with merriment, "Sleeping Beauty, aren't you supposed to be at the jewelry auction? Everyone is looking for you now that Angela has been served some much-needed humble pie. Edward, in particular, wants to worship at your feet or at the very least, buy you a kir royale. You have some mighty big kahunas! You go, girl!" Enid yawned and rubbed her eyes, barely taking it in. *They want me back at work?*

Sure enough, when she was awake enough to brush her teeth and turn on her phone, there were dozens of messages from colleagues and one particularly nasty one from Angela. Enid had never received so many smiley emoticons or read such a nasty and mean message. "Don't think that being Bai's whore means that you can get away with throwing me under the bus? You are going back to the pigpen where you belong, you villager!" Enid did not have time to worry about Angela; she slipped on some clothes and ran to the HKCC, applying makeup in the lift and combing her fingers through her bedhead.

Charles was announcing the beginning of the auction when Enid slipped into the room. Edward beckoned and motioned that he had saved the seat for her. The room was full of bidders and gawkers — the former was needed to raise the paddles, and the latter was even more important to keep those paddles raised. Edward was such an old hand at juggling telephone bids, he took two calls on the same lot and kept a third on hold with jokes about what the audience was wearing or should not have been wearing. Enid loved sitting next to him; it was Charm School 101. He may have been busy, but he had ample time to get caught up on last night's incident.

Scrawling on the edges of his catalog, "Tell meeeee, tell meeeee," accompanied by a caricature of Angela and Enid with oversized punching gloves on. Enid had to pop his bubble and let him know that there had been no physical altercation. She had merely served up the antidote after the viper — Angela — had bitten her. It had been the final push to bring her over the edge. "Well, I am no martyr and wasn't going to take this lying down." Edward grinned and pretended to dab his eye, "Awww baby bird has flown from the nest. So, what next? Now they know you have a backbone, you delivered the goods, and you did your job. Maybe you can get that promotion. Word on the street is that Angela may have to start answering to you when the season is over."

It was never Enid's intention to become the lead representative of China. If what Edward said was true, this was a gift that had practically fallen in her lap. She would never have the cunning of Angela, the aggressiveness of Vera, or the guts of Liu-*jie*, but somehow, she had secured all this. It was too early to start celebrating or congratulating herself, but Enid began imagining the interior finishing of her new home, how her parents could finally retire and move to a small place in the countryside. Of course, she needed a status symbol to show that she had arrived, so buying a Hermes handbag ranked at the very top of the list.

There was open as well as grudging respect from the colleagues. It was funny that Enid losing her temper was all that it had taken. Christine and Jade were shocked and warned her, "You came out on top this time, but be careful, please, Enid. If a man does this, he is fighting for his rights but if a woman does this too often, people may say she is throwing a hissy fit or getting hysterical. You may have made yourself indispensable for now, but you need to continue to do so, especially if you make a habit of throwing this kind of temper tantrum." Enid completely understood why they were being so harsh with her. They had always kept their heads down, done their work, and witnessed so many people thrown under the bus for one wrong mistake. Their caution was backed up by years of experience and observation.

Jade and Enid sat napping on the hard plastic chairs by the gate, leaning against each other for support. As usual, the flight was delayed 20 minutes, then three hours, and then finally five hours. They were too tired to even get up to use the free meal vouchers. They should have taken the earliest flight out, but there had been a last-minute meeting with Jean-Pierre and the rest of the China staff. No promotion was announced but Enid had a good feeling that this soon lay around the corner. Hope blossomed in her heart when he pointedly asked her questions about the clients and took barely any notice of Angela. With super-efficient and capable Jade by her side, Enid knew that they were a formidable pair to be reckoned with. She felt so rewarded with recognition that she lied to herself that even a token bonus would suffice.

Chapter 26

HOME BASE

‖   ‖

It was wonderful to be back in Shanghai. She loved the winter atmosphere: the scent of charcoal roasted chestnuts on the streets and the sight of little children bundled up like snowballs. At this point in her life, everything seemed perfect. She was so thankful for the support of her friends and family. If they had never advised or asked her to come home, she would still be floating around lost in Hong Kong or trying to fit in to New York. How comfortable it was to not constantly look over her shoulder now that Angela had dug her own grave.

It was not a complete stroll in the park, even though auction season was over. The specialists could take a break but there was still the very significant matter of payment. Jade and Enid put on their most sugary voices when calling the clients to wish them Happy Holidays and, more importantly, to extract promises of checks in the post or bank transfers on the verge of being transmitted. For the most part, it was like taking candy from a baby. Nearly all the bidders wanted their lots in time to show off at year-end parties, with the notable exceptions of the bronzes and the *Cranes* painting.

Enid and Jade watched the drama unfold from afar, keeping as much distance as they could from the counterfeit *Cranes*. There was always the danger of (un)friendly fire. After all, this had been Cedric's client and strategy, so it should be entirely his risk. Fan Guanzhang scholars, Chinese ink painting experts, scientific authenticity examiners, experts, and counter-experts were flown in to see the artwork. The press were having a field day after the bronzes debacle, they had tasted blood and now they were hungry for the kill.

At this point, Cedric voluntarily plunged headfirst into the abyss, privately because of his ego and publicly because he needed to salvage Rothesay's reputation amongst the Chinese clientele. In normal circumstances, they would have returned the artwork to the seller as a canceled sale. Now, even if they managed to extract the full payment, Enid calculated that the premiums would not even cover half the expense. Like a contested divorce, the only people making money out of this whole debacle were the experts.

The public relations pit that Rothesay's had dug themselves into seemed bottomless. It remained of paramount importance to safeguard their reputation as the authority on all objects lovely and lavish. With Rothesay's over-the-top advertising budget, Mr. Bosewell had expected the media to come to heel. But like ungrateful pets, they resolutely snapped at his manicured hand.

The revenue from full-page advertisements failed to match the increase in readership and interest from other advertisers. Patriotism, lies, foreign manipulation, big business — all the ingredients for day-after-day of sensational news stories. The only aspect missing was sordid sex. The PR team hoped that the press would eventually tire and more onto someone else's drama, but pickings were slow with many people absent on Christmas break. There were no fresh scoops, so Rothesay's old news cold cuts were repeatedly being served up.

The bonus was better than anticipated, six months' salary was double what she had expected and five months more than Jade received. Enid was jubilant; it meant that she could finally get her own place and stop having to outrun Xia in the morning rush for the bathroom. Enid was mindful not to celebrate too much in front of Jade, she felt so guilty that she treated her to a fancy dinner and a Taobao gift voucher worth half a month's salary.

"Enid, I appreciate how thoughtful you are. You really don't have to feel bad that you are paid so much more than me. And of course, I know exactly how much you are paid. Who do you think cuts the checks? Honestly, I feel so touched that you are taking me out for a nice dinner. It means so much to me because all your predecessors never bothered, they treated me like a glorified secretary. Please don't ever change how good-hearted you are." Enid was so touched by Jade's post-dessert speech. They truly were a team. If Jade would consider it, Enid would have shared her bonus without hesitation.

All seemed right in the world. Including the relationship front. This is the way it was supposed to be. All those magazine articles were right, and her endless hours occupied doing those surveys were worth it. *Bai treats me like a princess. I hope he doesn't propose soon, but Ma keeps dropping non-stop hints and irritating questions; if she should invite her third cousin removed to the wedding, if her figure is good enough to fit into a qipao.* All this made Enid nervous; she was far from ready for a lifetime commitment despite her daydreams to the contrary. On one of her regular snoops through Bai's phone, it made her queasy when she spotted her home number in the call log. She really hoped that she could rely on her father to delay matters. Of both her parents, he was the more reasonable and reticent one. He barely made an effort with Bai and had brought him up once, in a negative way. Post-Sunday lunch and pre-afternoon nap, her father had grunted and pointed at a magazine article about Bai's ex-wife's property portfolio.

It was definitely too early! She may have known Bai for a couple of years, but they had dated for less than six months. Having tried to rationalize in her head the various reasons why he would not propose, Enid knew deep down the single reason why Bai would. He was ultra-needy, hence the succession of wives. He could not even fall asleep alone. If she was not with him, he needed his two Chow Chows in the bedroom for company. Bai claimed that the dogs needed a nightlight and companionship, but Enid knew it was for Bai. She did not understand how someone so grown up and worldly could be such a little boy at heart.

At New Year's Eve dinner in Hangzhou, Enid was so touched that Bai flew her parents in by helicopter for the evening. They looked ill at ease sitting in the Four Seasons' restaurant pavilion overlooking the West Lake, but Enid appreciated Bai's effort to make them feel comfortable. *No wonder we are eating Chinese cuisine for New Years', and there is hua diao instead of champagne.* When they ushered in the New Year, Enid inwardly celebrated with more than auld lang syne joy. Pure relief. She downed her toast in a single gulp. *So, the calls were about planning this dinner celebration and, as usual, Ma was building castles in the sky. Now, I know where I get my powers of fantasy from!* For once, Enid was content to live in the moment.

On the 2nd of January, the calls started. Bouquets of flowers, boxes of chocolates and bird's nest, invitations to fancy dinners. Not courtship gifts from potential suitors, this was even better: aggressive headhunters. The numbers they offered sounded ludicrous — double or triple her pay. But Enid did not feel tempted in the least. Despite all her troubles at Rothesay's, she felt loyal to them for giving her the opportunity to prove herself. Naturally, she took Jade into her confidence. Enid recognized that part of her success with the clients and bids was due to Jade. "Aiyah, don't even think about it. This is your first season doing well as a rep, you need years more of experience. Never underestimate the value of working for a two-hundred-year-old international auction house, compared to a three-year-old Mainland upstart. Look how Liu-*jie* is faring. Nowadays you don't hear anything about her right? For good reason, because she was egoistical enough to try setting up her own auction house. It is impossible to compete side-by-side against the might of Rothesay's or Thompson's."

Enid understood the point that Jade was trying to make, but she thought that her point of view was too simplistic. China was where the growth and power were. Perhaps it was the influence of Bai and his family, who drank the Kool-Aid of Chinese superiority and might. But if Alibaba could outgrow Amazon as the biggest e-commerce company in terms of market cap, who was to say that one day one of these small local houses would not contend head-to-head with Rothesay's or Thompson's? The mess with the bronzes and *Cranes* was proof enough that a cultural disconnection between company and client could lead to serious problems.

As a junior-level staff, even though she was client-facing and the press contact on the ground in Shanghai, Enid did not learn of the solution to the bronzes fiasco until after the fact when she received the press release for dissemination. The morning that she received the email, Mr. Bosewell had already landed in Beijing a couple of hours earlier. His flight companions were the precious bronzes that he was humbly presenting as a gesture of respect and friendship to the Chinese government. The sheer genius of Mr. Bosewell and Rothesay's! Their business savvy and acumen were unsurpassed. Overnight, Rothesay's became everyone's favorite auction house. They were pardoned, back in favor, and the telephones started ringing off the hook again. Enid knew that sourcing and bidding in the next season were going to be a breeze. Meanwhile, out of the press' spotlight, Cedric's battle of the experts was quietly wound up and *Cranes* was returned to the consignor.

It seemed like it happened overnight, but Jade and Enid discussed that it must have taken days of persuasion for the laissez-faire loving Mr. Bosewell to kowtow to the Chinese government. Let alone for the powers that be to graciously accept a donation, which they felt was rightfully theirs to start with. The press release, conference, and handover ceremony were carried out with much pomp and fanfare. Mr. Bosewell's smug face was everywhere, in black and white on the front page of the *People's Daily* to the opening news segments on every channel of the China Global Television Network.

Surprisingly, Angela was nowhere to be seen on any of the publicity materials. As the Beijing rep, she should have been part of the ceremony. Enid tried to spot her on stage or even amongst the spectators, but it was a failed Where's Wally search. Bai commented in an underhand fashion that she was fortunate to be in the right place at the right time, but it was a fortnight later before she understood his import. Mr. Bosewell was granted permission for Rothesay's to become the first international auction house to operate in China without a local partner. It was phenomenal news, and it seemed like their little Shanghai outpost had barely digested the good tidings before the directive came from Jean-Pierre to expand office premises into a whole floor at a prestigious building nearby.

Enid was running on adrenalin, coffee, and candy. There was so much to do now that it was decided that the China office would house resident specialists from every department. And best of all, she would be managing them! She vowed not to take advantage of anyone and to always be a fair and considerate boss. More than ever, she felt fortunate to be part of Rothesay's. The market was thriving, and the scene was shifting. There were rumors that there would be less red tape and censorship surrounding the arts, which invigorated everyone from dealers to clients to buying more, more, and more. The promise of a Free Trade Zone where valuables could be stored on duty-free terms galvanized buyers further.

Now they could finally enjoy their purchases instead of secreting them overseas, where they were loved from afar but unseen and untouched.

Rothesay's seemed to pop up everywhere like an ubiquitous Golden Arches franchise — billboard and magazine advertisements leftover from auction announcements, tabloid features from the auction record highs, and a series of prominent newspaper announcements about the expansion of their worldwide offices. New money and more money were needed for technology, online bidding, and investment in infrastructure. Enid could not resist teasing Jade that she had been wrong about Rothesay's, even they knew to play nice with China and not bite the hand that feeds. Enid felt so proud to be Chinese. The announcement that ICO, the Insurance Company of China, was buying a 15% stake in Rothesay's was met with much celebration in the office. Well, in truth it was more from Enid's side than Jade's. As usual, Jade received the developments with cynicism. Enid proclaimed, "It can only be better for us if our own countrymen own a stake in our company. The best of both worlds, Confucius business culture with Western principles." Jade emitted a snort, rolled her eyes, and diligently returned to comparing the cost of cubicle fabrication.

Enid spent a sleepless night tossing and turning. She had been indulging herself with fashion blogs and gossip articles until 2 am. *Groan, and I have to be up in four hours to meet the Feng Shui master at the new office. Is there any point in trying to sleep? I will feel worse after four hours of sleep. Maybe I should go in early so that I can leave after lunch for a massage. It is such a pain that we have to light the joss sticks and chop the suckling pig up at sunrise. It's the 21st century; surely there is some leeway in this day and age? Maybe dimming the lights so it looks like the crack of dawn?*

Fortunately, she was awake to notice the blue light and buzzing from her phone; she picked it up and playfully teased, "Are you spying on me? How do you know that I am still awake? Anyway, all is forgiven if you take me out for late-night supper/early morning breakfast." Bai sounded strangely business-like when he told her that he was waiting downstairs. Enid jumped up eagerly and put on a thick duffle coat over her pajamas. *Who am I going to meet at the market stalls this morning, anyway?* She did not feel in the least bit irritable when she had trouble spotting Bai's fluorescent yellow Maserati GT convertible.

To her discomposure, a white Toyota Corolla belonging to the last decade pulled up, and Bai waved to her from the driver's seat. "Hey, traveling incognito? What's the deal?" Enid thought it was a joke; she did not always get Bai's sense of humor. Which was why they never had double dates with Zheng and Fabien. *Translating and explaining was too much of an effort. Bai was more backstreet than Bond Street.* Bai could tell her mind was not focused on him, so when he pulled to a stop a couple of streets away, he unbuckled his seatbelt and leaned over with a serious look on his face.

Bloody hell. I hope he is not going to propose. I am wearing a polyester down jacket over my woolen pajamas. My pajamas have reindeer and Santa Claus all over them, for God's sake! And Christmas was over a month ago. It was then that Enid noticed with relief that Bai had on a white singlet and tracksuit bottoms. *What kind of proposal story is this?* She firmly made up her mind that she would say no. This was the moment that she had been dreaming about since she was a little girl. And it had been on a bridge over the River Seine, not some tiny alley in West Nanjing. She gave an affronted sniff, hoping that Bai would get the hint.

He took it as the opening cue and to Enid's dismay and surprise, put his head in his hands instead of holding both her hands. "Enid, I have to make this quick. I don't have much time. My father has been arrested for corruption, and the authorities want to bring me in for questioning. All that jewelry that I bought from the auction houses over the years, they couldn't trace that back to me because I bought them under my ex-wives and girlfriends' names. But I got foolish and bought for you the De Beers pink diamond at Rothesay's. It is your engagement ring, and I wanted it to be meaningful, so I bought it under my name."

Enid flushed with pleasure. *The De Beers diamond!* That amazing one-of-a-kind, 8k fancy vivid pink diamond that even she — an employee of Rothesay's — had not been permitted to take out of the case to show to clients because it was so rare and valuable. *It cost USD 26 million!!!* She couldn't believe it. *Pajamas or no pajamas, I am going to say yes sitting in this smelly Toyota Corolla!*

Bai snapped his fingers, "Did you hear what I said? I need to leave! Now, Enid. And I want you to come with me."

Enid halted her dreamy reverie like cold water had been splashed on her face. "Oh my God, what, where? Am I implicated? Are you sure they arrested your father? But everyone takes kickbacks! Why your father? But what will we do with no career and no money?"

"I really don't have the time to answer all your questions in detail. It's a witch-hunt, and my father is being made an example of. We always feared this day would come, so we have emergency plans in place. America has no extradition treaty with China and will grant asylum to political dissidents. We have everything in place. Homes, money, assets. The best lawyers to fight for asylum. You don't have to worry or work another day in your life. We can send for your parents when we are settled."

He reached over to Enid, making physical contact for the first time since she stepped into the car, "Enid, I don't want to beg you but here is our chance to have a life together. I understand your hesitation, but my family would not have been in the limelight if I hadn't bought that engagement ring for you. I really have to go now, there is a private plane waiting on the runway." Bai handed over a thick envelope, "Here is enough money for a plane ticket and whatever you need. I don't need a definite answer now, and I don't want to pressure you. If you decide to join me, get on a plane without leaving a trail. Don't do anything silly like tell your colleagues or friends...The government could decide to come after you too and say that you are an accomplice."

Without a word more, Bai gave her a perfunctory kiss on the cheek and impatiently gestured toward the car door. Enid was completely lost for words. She stood on the pavement in shock, holding the wad of cash. *Is this a marriage proposal? Or a half-hatched getaway plan? This is all so abrupt. I can't marshal my thoughts.* She stared down the road until the red taillights faded into the distance. Her mind was numb with shock, and her face bit from the cold winter air. She trudged back to her flat, shaking her head. Every aspect of her life was so interlaced, and any decision would have rippling incremental effects. *I can't believe it. What am I going to do?*